DEAD IN RED

A JEFF RESNICK MYSTERY

DEAD IN RED

L. L. BARTLETT

FIVE STAR
A part of Gale, Cengage Learning

MYSTERY BARTLETT, L.
Bartlett, L. L.
Dead in red

$25.95
CENTRAL **31994013978264**

GALE
CENGAGE Learning

p2

Detroit • New York • San Francisco • New Haven, Conn • Waterville, Maine • London

GALE
CENGAGE Learning

LIBRARY OF CONGRESS CATALOGING-IN-PUBLICATION DATA

Bartlett, L. L. (Lorraine L.)
    Dead in red : a Jeff Resnick mystery / L. L. Bartlett. — 1st ed.
      p. cm.
    ISBN-13: 978-1-59414-640-4 (alk. paper)
    ISBN-10: 1-59414-640-3 (alk. paper)
    1. Psychics—Fiction. 2. Murder investigations—Fiction.
3. Brothers—Fiction. 4. Buffalo (N.Y.)—Fiction. 5. Psychological fiction. I. Title.
PS3602.A83955D43 2008
813'.6—dc22   2008000699

First Edition. First Printing: June 2008.

Published in 2008 in conjunction with Tekno Books and Ed Gorman.

Printed in the United States of America
1 2 3 4 5 6 7 12 11 10 09 08

For Frank

ACKNOWLEDGMENTS

Every author I know has a group of friends who read and critique her/his work, and I'm no different. My first readers come from my Sisters In Crime Chapter, The Guppies. My thanks to Nan Higginson, Marilyn Levinson, Liz Eng, Elizabeth Becka, Sheila Connolly, and especially to Sharon Wildwind for their comments and suggestions.

Thanks also go to Michelle Martin and Judy Stock for their expertise on running small bakeries; Hank Phillippi Ryan gave me pointers on journalism, and Michele Fowler shared her knowledge about theater and wardrobe. D.P. Lyle, MD, provided his expertise in medical matters. (Likewise, Sharon Wildwind, RN.) Any errors in that respect are definitely of my own making. I can't forget my staunchest cheerleaders and critique partners Liz Eng and Gwen Nelson, nor my agent Jacky Sach and editor Hugh Abramson.

Thank you all!

1

My footsteps echoed on the pavement that cold night in early March. Huddled in my old bomber jacket, I dodged the mini skating rinks that had once been puddles on the cracked pavement. Preoccupied. By the creepy thing I'd experienced only minutes earlier. By thoughts of a new job. Of the fifty bucks I'd just won playing pool at the little watering hole near my apartment. Five months of unemployment had cleaned me out. I was on a roll and determined not to let anything spoil it.

Then two imposing figures stepped out of the darkness, demanded money. I gave them what I had. It wasn't enough. One of them grabbed me, decided to teach me a lesson.

Not if I could help it. I yanked my arm back, kicked one of them in the balls— and paid for it.

Backlit by a streetlamp, I saw the baseball bat come at me, slam into my forearm, delivering a compound fracture that sent skyrockets of pain to obliterate my senses.

Couldn't think, too stunned to move as the bat slammed into my shoulder, knocking me to my knees.

The bat came at me from the left, crashed into my temple, sent me sprawling. My vision doubled as I raised my head and the bat walloped me again.

"My cousin's dead."

The voice brought me out of my reverie, or rather the nightmare memory that claimed me at inopportune moments.

Tom Link's bottom lip quivered and he looked away. Heavy-set, with a barroom bouncer's countenance, I hadn't expected him to reveal any trace of what I was sure he would call weakness.

My fingers tightened around the cold pilsner glass as something flashed through my mind's eyes: The image of a sparkling red, woman's high-heeled shoe.

I tilted the glass to my lips to take a gulp of beer. Bursts of insight—if that's what they are—bring with them a certain creep factor, something I doubted I'd ever get used to.

I concentrated on breathing evenly as I sipped my beer and waited for Tom to continue. It isn't often a bartender confides to a customer. I know. Years before I'd spent time on that side of the counter, listening to the stories of lonely men—and women—who had no other confidants.

Tom wasn't just a bartender at the little neighborhood sports bar that teetered on the verge of going under—he was also the owner of The Whole Nine Yards. I'd been patronizing the unassuming place for the past couple of months, getting the feel of it, a part of me hoping I could one day be a part of it.

I'd heard about but hadn't known the murdered man—Walt Kaplan. He'd opened the bar early in the day, whereas I'd never been there before eight p.m.

"How can I help?" I asked.

Tom's gaze shifted to take in a group of regulars crowded around the large-screen TV bolted to the wall, before turning back to me. "You said you used to be an investigator—"

"Before I got my head caved in," I said, referring to the mugging I'd suffered some three months before. I'd read about Walt's murder in the paper, but Tom probably knew more about it than the news had reported. "What happened?"

Lips pursed, Tom ran a damp linen cloth over the old scarred oak bar. "Walt worked here part-time. He left here on Saturday afternoon and never came back." His worried brown eyes met mine. "Your name's Resnick. We're *landsman*, Jeff. Would you be willing to look into it? I'll pay you."

We weren't *"landsman."* I was a lapsed Catholic, not Jewish, but now wasn't the time to dispute that. Besides, the idea intrigued me. I'd been hanging out at the little neighborhood tavern with the idea of eventually asking Tom for a part-time job, and now he was offering an employment opportunity far different than what I'd anticipated.

"What about the cops? Don't you trust them?"

"I've been robbed four times in the last twelve years. Did they ever catch the guys? No."

Part of me—the smart part—knew if I accepted his offer I'd be sorry. Another part of me wanted to jump at the chance to feel useful again. I tried to keep my eagerness in check. "Tell me more about Walt."

Tom's jowls sagged. "You woulda liked him. He was a lot like you."

My stomach twisted. "How so?"

A small smile twitched Tom's mouth. "Quiet. A loner. He wasn't one to talk about himself. You've been coming here for a couple months now and I know your name and what you used to do before your accident, but that's all."

He had me pegged there. Spilling my guts to strangers wasn't in my program. At one time I'd been a top insurance investigator, but office politics weren't my forte. I screwed myself one time too many and ended up on the unemployment line. On the eve of starting a new job, I'd been mugged by a couple of street thugs. The resulting brain injury had changed my life forever.

"The newspaper said Walt was found by the Old Red Mill. That he was stabbed and had apparently been robbed."

Tom nodded. "His wallet was missing. So was a big diamond ring he always wore. His father gave it to him when he graduated from high school. I went to the mill. Nothin' much to see but some crime tape." His gaze met mine, hardened. "But you'll get more than I did."

Get more? The words made my insides freeze. How did he know? I could count on one hand the people who knew I was— that I could . . .

Cold sweat broke out on the back of my neck. The word "psychic" didn't really apply to me. Since the mugging, I'd been able to sense strong emotions. Not from everyone I met— but sometimes from those who were no longer alive. Sometimes I just knew things—but not always. It was pretty much haphazard and damned disconcerting when it happened. And often these feelings and knowledge brought on migraines that so far drugs hadn't been able to quell.

Tom's gaze bore into mine.

"Get more?" I prompted, afraid to hear his answer.

"Being a trained investigator, I mean."

I heaved a mental sigh of relief. "Yeah."

"When can you start?"

As a teenager I'd ridden my ten-speed all around Snyder and Williamsville, and could still recall some of my old routes. The area behind the Old Red Mill had always been weedy, with a steep embankment that loomed near a rushing stream. No way would I risk my neck to take a look in the dark. "Tomorrow morning."

Tom nodded. "It wouldn't hurt for the regulars to get to know you. Dave"—he indicated the other bartender drawing a beer at the brass taps across the way—"doesn't want Walt's early shift. You up to working here at the bar three or four afternoons a week?"

I looked at my reflection in the mirrored backbar. My hair had grown back from where some ER nurse had shaved it, but the shadows under my eyes and the gaunt look and sickly pallor were taking a lot longer to fade. I'd been living with my physician brother for the past three months. While I was grateful he'd rescued me, allowing me to recover at his home, I was tired of the enforced inactivity he'd insisted upon. The idea of actually having something to do and somewhere to go appealed to me.

"I'd like to try."

"Okay. Show up here about eleven tomorrow and I'll give you a run down on how we operate." He turned, took a cracked ballpoint out of a jar and grabbed a clean paper napkin, on which he scribbled a few lines. "This is what you have to do. I don't need workers' comp or the IRS breathing down my neck."

My hand trembled as I reached for the napkin. Who would have thought that a part-time job in a neighborhood bar would make me so nervous? A warm river of relief flooded through me as I read the short list. "I can do this. Thanks, Tom."

"A bartender?" My half brother, Richard Alpert, looked up from his morning coffee, his expression skeptical. His significant other, Brenda Stanley, lowered a section of newspaper to peer at me. The three of us sat at the maple kitchen table in the home Richard's grandparents had built decades before in Buffalo's tony suburb of Amherst, the egg-stained breakfast dishes still sitting before us.

"I need a job."

"Okay, but why a bartender?" Richard asked.

I'd been rehearsing my answer for an hour. Now to make it sound convincing.

"I've done it before. It's pretty much a no-brainer, which is something I can handle right now."

Richard scowled, studied my face. Being twelve years older than me, he's felt the need to look after me since the day our mother died some twenty-one years earlier. Back then I was an orphaned kid of fourteen and he'd been an intern with generations of old money behind him. "Have you thought about the consequences of this kind of social interaction?" he asked.

I frowned. Consequences?

"Touching peoples' glasses, taking their money. What if you get vibes about them? Stuff you don't want to know."

I knew what he was getting at. Truth was, I hadn't thought about that aspect of the job, although I had been counting on the somewhat erratic empathic ability I'd developed after the mugging to help me look into Walt Kaplan's death. I couldn't read everyone I encountered—Richard was a prime example. We were brothers—okay, only half brothers—but he was a total blank to me, yet I could often read Brenda like an open book.

I met his gaze, didn't back down. "I guess I'll have to deal with it."

He nodded, still scrutinizing my face. "And what's the rest of it?"

"Rest of it?"

"Whole Nine Yards—isn't that where the bartender who was murdered last week worked?"

My half-filled coffee mug called for my attention. "Uh. Yeah. I think so."

"You know so."

"Okay, I'm taking his job."

"And . . . ?"

Talk about relentless. "And the owner asked me to look into things. Nothing official. The guy was his cousin."

Richard's mug thunked onto the table. "Jeff, don't get involved."

"I'm not."

Richard's gaze hardened. "Yes, you are. The question is why?"

Brenda folded the newspaper, all her attention now focused on me, too.

How much of a shit did it make me to admit I wanted the

dead man's job? And that I was willing to endure a certain amount of unpleasantness to get it probably said even more. It's just as well that Richard's MD wasn't in psychiatry, not that I was about to admit any of this to him.

"Okay, as you won't answer that question, then when do you start?"

"Today. Afternoon shift."

He raised an eyebrow.

"You'd better tell me if you'll be late for dinner—not that you eat enough to keep a sparrow alive," Brenda said.

"How long a shift will you work?" Richard asked.

"I didn't ask."

His other eyebrow went up. "How much will you make an hour?"

"I didn't—"

"You didn't ask," he said, glowering.

I got up from the table, cup in hand. "You want a warm-up?"

He shook his head. "I'm worried about you, Jeff. You're not ready for this."

I poured my coffee, my back stiffening in annoyance. "Is that a medical opinion?"

"Yes. You've made tremendous progress, but your recovery is by no means complete."

He was one to talk—Mr. Short-of-Breath. I wasn't about to argue with him though, as I felt responsible for him being that way. He'd been shot trying to protect me not ten weeks before. Walking up stairs or any distance was still a chore for him. I didn't want to cause him undo concern, and yet . . .

"*You're* about to start a new job," I said, more an accusation than a statement.

"It's only a volunteer position. It's not full time, and doesn't start for almost another month. By then I'll be fully recovered. Head injuries like yours don't heal on that kind of timeline."

Somehow I resisted the urge to say, "Oh yeah?" Instead I turned to Brenda. "What do you think?"

"As your friend or a nurse?"

"Take your pick." Why did I have to sound so damned defensive?

She sighed and reached for Richard's hand, her cocoa-brown skin a contrast to his still pasty complexion. "As a nurse, I agree with Richard."

He smirked at her, his mustache twitching.

"As your friend." She turned to face me. "You're driving me nuts—the two of you, because you're both going stir-crazy."

Richard's smile faded. He sat up straighter, removed his hand from hers.

Brenda pushed herself up from the table, and headed out of the kitchen. "You're going to do what you want anyway, so—get on with it."

I avoided Richard's accusing stare, added milk to my coffee and stirred it. Stir-crazy, huh? Too often, Brenda could read me, too. Still . . .

I faced my brother. "You want to come with me?"

Richard blinked. "To work?"

"No, to check out where the guy got stabbed."

"I thought you weren't getting involved in this?"

"I'm not. I'm just curious."

"And curiosity killed the cat."

I sipped my coffee. "I figure I've got at least eight lives left."

"Don't kid yourself, Jeff. You could've died from that mugging."

"And I could get hit by a bus going to the grocery store. Are you coming or not?"

Richard drained his cup, pushed back his chair and rose. "I'll come."

★ ★ ★ ★ ★

The vibrant green grass down the steep grade stood out in chunky tufts, belligerent in the wake of someone's weed whacker. It had probably been cropped a week before, but already looked long and lanky and ready to defy another swipe by a plastic whip cord. A six-foot remnant of yellow crime tape fluttered in the breeze. Twenty or thirty feet below and a hundred yards further on, Ellicott Creek rushed past.

Ignoring the "Danger—No Trespassing" signs, Richard craned his neck to gaze down the hill. "So where was the dead guy found?"

"I'm not sure." I glanced over my shoulder at the scarlet-painted barn of a building that hugged the embankment. As in years before, a huge stone wheel once again milled corn, wheat and rye, but was the end product more for show than commerce? Pallets of ground grains in sacks sealed in plastic were stacked on the mill's back porch. The north end of the building housed a little café and bakery. Could they really use that much flour?

"Tell me about the murdered man," Richard said.

I repeated what Tom had told me the night before.

"You get any impressions yet?"

"Depends on your definition of impressions. So far, not here. But I did flash onto something weird that relates to the dead guy last night at the bar. Probably because he spent so much time there. I don't know what it means." And I wasn't ready to talk about it.

Richard did not look pleased, but he didn't push. He understood what I'd said—that I was already caught up in the guy's death, and that something beyond my usual senses was going to feed me information about it until . . . well, corny as it sounds . . . until justice was done. One way or another.

Goat-footed, I tramped down the rocky slope, over flattened

grass and weeds to where the crime tape flapped. As Tom said, there was nothing much to see. No blood marred the spot. The ground hadn't been dug up for evidence. Had Walt been killed elsewhere and just dumped here?

I closed my eyes and the flash of what I'd seen the night before came back to me. A sparkling—sequins?—woman's stiletto-heeled shoe. I tried to tap into that memory once again, opening myself up, but it was someone else's experience that assaulted me. *Walt's face, chalk white—his body drained of blood. Milky eyes open, staring up at the sky.*

Nausea erupted within me, doubling me over. I grabbed onto a sapling to keep from falling down the hill, retching, choking, until the inevitable. Then Richard was beside me, his hand on my shoulder until my stomach had finished expelling my breakfast.

"What the hell happened?" he demanded.

I coughed, gasping, trying to catch my breath. "Not me. I got caught in someone's reaction to seeing Walt. I dunno. Maybe some rookie cop's first time seeing a body."

"Good Lord," Richard muttered.

I wiped my mouth on the back of my hand. Poor Walt had been dumped here like so much garbage.

"Excuse me, but what are you doing here?"

We both turned. A tall, buxom blonde stood between the sacks of grain stacked on the porch. The morning sun highlighted the fine lines around her eyes, but the overall effect was not detrimental. Dressed in a denim skirt and peasant blouse, she was the epitome of Southwest fashion from her silver-and-turquoise squash-blossom necklace to her tooled leather boots.

"Just looking around," I said lamely, and staggered back up the hillock, with Richard following me.

"This is not public property. I'm the owner, and unless you're a mill customer, I'll have to ask you to leave."

"Cyn Taggert—is that you?" Richard asked.

The blonde squinted at him. "I'm sorry. Do I know you?"

"Richard Alpert. We were friends when you were at Nardin and I was at Canisus High."

The anger dissolved from her features and a mix of astonishment and delight lit her face. "Richard?" She lurched forward, capturing him in an awkward embrace.

I got another flash—so fast it almost didn't register: *Hands. Blood.*

She pulled back, the movement startling me, and examined Richard's face. "How many years has it been?"

He laughed. "Too many."

The two of them stood there, staring at one another, oblivious of what I'd just experienced. Then the woman gave a nervous laugh. "I'm Cynthia Lennox now. I was married for twenty years to Dennis. He passed away last fall."

"I'm so sorry," Richard murmured.

Her smile was wistful. "So am I."

I looked away, realizing my fingers were clenched so tight they'd gone white. Flexing them, I noticed half-moon indentations in my palm. That latest burst of insight had affected me more than the sparkling red shoe or the vision of Walt Kaplan's body.

The woman took Richard's hand. "What happened to you? Last I heard you were in medical school."

"A lot of years ago," Richard admitted, smiling. "I got my MD and moved to California for eighteen years. I'm back now."

I waited for him to say something like, "about to get married to the most marvelous woman in the universe," but he kept looking at this stranger with a vacant, sappy grin. Ex-girlfriend, I mused? So what. Why not tell her about Brenda?

I cleared my throat.

Richard seemed to surface from the past. "Cyn, this is my

brother, Jeff Resnick."

"Brother?" she asked, puzzled.

Richard hadn't even known about me when he was in high school. "It's kind of a long story."

She didn't look interested in learning it. I was too far away to shake hands—not that I wanted to—so I nodded at her. She did likewise. No love lost there.

"Well, come on in," Cyn told Richard, gesturing toward the mill. "We've got the best coffee in Williamsville, and a wonderful apple strudel." She looked at him with eyes half focused on the past. I wondered if I should just slink back to the car and disappear. Then again, it had been someone from the mill who'd found Walt Kaplan, and I wanted to know about it. Uninvited, I trotted along behind them.

We followed Cyn up the stairs and into the mill's side entrance, stepping into the dim interior of what looked to be a storage barn. Crates and more pallets of grain and flour were stacked so that there was only a narrow path between this and a larger room with bright lights to the left: the bakery and storefront.

Cyn stopped dead ahead of us and like two of the Three Stooges, Richard and I bumped into one another. Richard's at least six inches taller than me, so it was difficult to see around him.

"Tigger," Cyn chided. A fat tabby leaped onto the stack of crates, giving a lusty yowl and looking self-satisfied. "Stay there," Cyn told us. "I'll take care of it."

Richard stared down at his shoes—no, just beyond them, at a gray, furry lump. Either a very large mouse or a small rat.

Cyn returned with a worn and stained gardener's glove on her right hand. She picked up the limp creature and inspected it. "Good work, Tigger." Cyn started off again, paused to take aim at a trash barrel with a black plastic bag folded over its rim, and tossed the body in. Two points!

Richard followed, his gaze straight ahead as he passed the barrel. I had a quick look inside and grimaced.

Cyn ditched the glove.

We entered the café, taking in the mingled aromas of fresh-ground coffees, vanilla, and baking that filled the upscale bakery's storefront. Only one of the white-painted bistro tables stood empty. At the rest, customers sat lingering over conversations with cappuccinos, lattes, and decadent pastries. Not a bad mid-morning weekday crowd. Had business been this good before the dead man had been found on the property?

Cyn sailed across the room to a door marked "Private," ushering us in. "Gene, bring us some coffee and strudel, will you?" she called over her shoulder.

"Sure thing, Cyn," said a thin, balding, enthusiastic young man behind the café's main counter.

"That's not necessary," Richard said.

"Nonsense. It's the least I can do for an old friend." Cyn closed the door behind her.

Like the storefront, the brightly lit office was immaculate. No stray papers marred the desktop or hung out of the four-drawer file cabinet in the corner. Unlike the country charm outside this small room, Southwest accents of hanging ristras and a stenciled border of coyotes were cheerful against pale turquoise walls. Behind the desk was a large-framed photograph of a younger, happier Cyn arm-in-arm with a sandy-haired man—the now deceased Dennis?—in front of a low adobe building with the legend "Santa Fe *Café au lait*."

"Sit," Cyn urged and took her own seat.

We complied, taking the two upholstered office chairs before her antique wooden table of a desk.

Cyn folded her hands and leaned forward. "It's wonderful seeing you again, Richard, but what on Earth were you doing behind my café?"

"Curiosity," he said with a touch of embarrassment. "Murder isn't an everyday occurrence in Williamsville."

"Who found the dead man?" I asked.

Cyn turned hard eyes on me, her mouth tightening. "Our miller, Ted Hanson."

"Is he in today? Can I talk to him?"

"No." Her rebuke was adamant.

"Excuse me?" I pushed.

"No, Ted isn't here today. In fact, he's out of town on a buying trip."

"When will he be back?"

"In a few days. Why are you so interested?"

"Morbid curiosity," I said, echoing Richard's words. "Last night I was hired to take Walt Kaplan's job at a bar down the street."

She gaped at me, unprepared for honesty; sudden fear shadowed her eyes.

A sharp knock preceded the door opening. Gene held a loaded tray in one hand and bustled inside. He set cardboard cups before Richard and me, placing frosted rectangles of strudel on baker's tissue next to them. His smile was genuine. "Enjoy." He eased the door closed behind him.

The awkward silence lengthened.

Richard cleared his throat. "Ever see any of the old crowd, Cyn?"

Cyn seemed grateful for a change of subject. "Since I came back to the area nine months ago, I've only caught up with Cathy Makarchuk. She married Barry Garner. They have five children—can you believe it?"

Nothing on Earth is more boring than listening to old school chums reminisce. I reached for my coffee, eager to rid my mouth of the lingering sour taste of vomit, and my hand brushed the edge of the desk. The image of a smiling man burst upon my mind. Heart pounding, I snatched up my cup with a shaking hand and took a sloppy gulp.

At some time before his death, Walt Kaplan had sat on the edge of that desk.

2

"Fill the beer cooler, and later we'll talk," Tom said, and slapped me on the back, nearly knocking me off my feet.

"Sure thing," I said and faked a smile.

He left me standing by the bar's back door, where a Molson truck had just made its weekly delivery. Thirty cases of beer sat stacked against the wall. I found a dolly behind the door, so at least I wouldn't have to kill myself dragging the beer into the cooler. Then again, I wondered how much stress my recently broken arm could take. I'd only been out of the brace about seven weeks.

The first five cases proved easy to lift. By the time I'd hauled the rest of them in I'd worked up a sweat and had rethought my ambition to work as a bartender. I much preferred cutting up fruit garnishes and washing glasses to actual physical labor.

Four construction workers sat at the bar nursing beers, picking at bowls of pretzels while they watched ESPN on the TV bolted to the wall. Since Tom didn't serve food, I wondered if liquid bread—aka beer—constituted their midday meal. Tom had already given me the cut-off lecture. Nobody left drunk from his establishment unless they had a designated driver. In the twenty years he'd owned the tavern, he'd never been sued and wanted to keep it that way.

I hadn't worked behind a bar in at least twelve years, but it all came back within minutes as I waited on my first few customers, rang up the sales, and collected my first paltry tips.

No doubt about it, I wasn't going to get rich working here. Still, it felt good to be among the employed once again. For as long as it would last. Tom hadn't mentioned this being a permanent arrangement.

Luckily I wasn't picking up too many disquieting vibes, either. One of the guys was behind in his truck payments, sweating the repo man. Another hadn't been laid in three weeks and wondered if his old lady was boffing someone else. Just the usual errant signals I picked up on shopping carts, door handles and money. Inconvenient at times, but I'd learned to ignore most of it. I knew when to pay attention, too.

The lunchtime crowd had emptied out when Richard ambled through the side entrance. He'd never been to The Whole Nine Yards before, and I guess he wanted to see for himself what I'd gotten myself into.

He paused at the end of the bar, taking in the dark bead board that went halfway up the walls, the chair rail, and stucco above it decorated with sports posters and memorabilia. He took the first stool, rested his forearms on the bar. Dressed in a golf shirt and freshly ironed Dockers, he looked out of place in this working-class establishment.

I strolled down and halted before him. "What can I get you, sir?"

He looked up at me with no show of recognition. "Got any Canadian on tap?"

"Labatts."

He nodded.

I drew him a beer and set a fresh bowl of pretzels down in front of him. "What about those Bisons," he said, setting a ten spot on the bar.

I didn't follow minor-league baseball, but I guessed I'd have to while working in a sports bar. Bummer. "Uh, yeah. What about 'em?"

Richard's mustache quirked as he reached for his glass.

I rang up the sale and gave him his change. Tom was stooped over the other end of the bar, watching TV. I wandered over to him. "I've got some questions I wanted to ask about Walt."

Tom tore his gaze away from the tube. "Sure thing."

"You said he was a loner. No best friends?"

Tom shook his head, then looked thoughtful. "Well, maybe me. But we didn't talk all that much. I gave him the job because he'd been hurt working construction and couldn't go back to it. He got some kind of disability payments, which is why he only had to work here part-time."

"What kind of disability?"

"Bad hip. Had a limp. Sometimes he used a cane."

"What did he do with his free time?"

Tom shrugged. "He never really spoke about it."

I glanced over my shoulder. Richard was looking down the bar beyond us, gazing intently at the TV. He'd never shown a burning desire to watch waterskiing before and was no doubt eavesdropping.

I turned back to Tom. "Did Walt ever mention women or describe his ideal girl?"

"Not that I recall."

"He wasn't gay, was he?"

Tom straightened, his eyes widening. "No!"

"Just asking." Where did the red stiletto heel fit in? "He go to strip joints?"

"Not that I know of."

"Did he buy his sex?"

Tom squirmed. "I don't know. I don't think so. Walt was private. He didn't talk about stuff like that. But he listened when the other guys would talk. Why'd you ask such a personal question?"

26

"I didn't know Walt. Maybe nobody—even his family—really did."

Tom's brow wrinkled. Maybe he hadn't wanted to know.

"It would help if I could see where Walt lived. See *how* he lived."

"I got his keys from the cops. I'll give them to you later." Tom cleared his throat and glanced over his shoulder at the back room. "I've got some paperwork to take care of. Will you be okay out here alone for a while?"

I gazed at our only customer, Richard, and nodded.

Tom took off and I grabbed the damp rag by the sink. The bar didn't need wiping down, but I did it anyway, ending up back in front of Richard.

"How's the job going?" he asked.

"So far so good."

He nodded, but seemed to expect more of an answer. I didn't have one.

"I'm gonna check out Walt's apartment later. Wanna come?"

Richard drained the last of his beer. "Why not?" The words sounded bland, but the crinkle in his eyes and the set of his mouth betrayed his interest. Brenda was right. He'd been bored silly during his convalescence, but looking into Walt's murder wasn't a lark. Odds were we wouldn't be in danger this early in the game. I had no desire to put myself or anyone else in harm's way. But the last time I'd gotten caught up in the web of emotion surrounding a murder, it was Richard who'd nearly paid the ultimate price. Truth was, I wanted him to accompany me, and yet anxiety gnawed at my nerves. For all the insight I'd experienced while pursuing a murderer three months earlier, I'd never had a clue that Richard might be in danger. That he'd be so grievously injured.

I didn't like to revisit that guilt.

Pawing through Walt's possessions was another matter. We

might not find anything that would give me answers. And if I did, well, I didn't have to share it with Richard.

"Want another?" I asked Richard, indicating his glass.

He stood. "I'm all set. Give me a call later and I'll meet you."

"Sure."

He headed for the door. Under his empty glass was a five-dollar tip.

The south side of Main Street near Eggert Road was already in shadow as Richard and I stood on the sidewalk looking up at the apartment windows over a dress boutique. The drapes were drawn. Good. I wasn't interested in attracting the attention of the neighbors. Not that it mattered. I had permission to be there. Still, poking around a dead man's possessions cranked up the creepiness factor a notch.

Steep, narrow stairs led up to the second floor.

"Did I hear your boss say the guy was disabled? Why didn't he find first-floor digs?"

I shrugged and pulled out the keys Tom had given me. Richard stooped to pick up newspapers that had accumulated. The shelf under a two-receptacle apartment mailbox overflowed with Walt's junk mail. He grabbed that, too, and we trooped up the stairs.

I picked out the key Tom said would open the door. It did. I stepped into the apartment's dark interior, groping for the light switch just inside the door. I flicked it and wan yellow light illuminated the entryway. Walt had been dead only five days, but already the place smelled of disuse. Still, the air felt heavy with Walt's presence. Not that I could take in the essence of his soul, but I could feel some residual part of what and who he was, and also the first tendrils of migraine stirring behind my eyes.

Richard thrust the mail at me and shoved his hands into his pants pockets, gazing around the cramped place. The cops hadn't made too big a mess, leading me to believe Walt kept his home meticulously clean. I sorted through the circulars, dumping them into the empty kitchen waste basket, then backtracked to open the entry's closet door and found winter coats and boots. Nothing very interesting.

Back in the tidy galley kitchen, the cabinets housed plain white Corelle dishes and Coke glasses from fast-food restaurant giveaways. In the closet pantry, cans were stacked in descending sizes, heavy on store-brand tomato soup and mac and cheese. I'm no gourmet, but when it came to dinner prep even I could do better than Walt.

I wasn't eager to touch everything, but already I understood a lot about Walt Kaplan, a man who listened and rarely gave much of himself to others. There was no sense of joy in his home. Nothing that mirrored the smile he had given someone in Cyn Lennox's office.

The spotless bathroom brandished much-washed, frayed brown towels on the racks by the sink and bathtub. I poked through the medicine cabinet and found mint mouthwash, toothpaste, dental floss and a prescription bottle of anisindione. "Rich?" He poked his head around the door and I handed it to him.

He read the label, frowned. "It's an anticoagulant. You might be more familiar with the commercial name, Coumadin."

"What do you think was wrong with Walt?"

Richard shrugged. "Blood thinners treat deep vein thrombosis, pulmonary embolus, arterial fibrillation—any number of things."

"So what's that mean?"

"Prevents strokes."

He might've said so. Richard scrutinized the label again. "Being stabbed while on this dose would've greatly speeded up his death."

The thought made me shudder.

Richard went back to the living room.

The bedroom door was ajar; the place most people stored their secrets. Not a wrinkle marred the fiberfill burgundy quilt that lay across the full-sized bed. Like the living room, no reading material littered the flat surfaces of the dresser or nightstand. No dust, either.

A dresser stowed underwear, socks, and golf shirts folded with expert precision, although the contents had been disturbed—probably by the cops. Suits, shirts and slacks hung in color-coordinated order stuffed the pokey little closet. A plastic shoe rack attached to the back of the door contained six pairs of Walt's shoes, polished to a glow. A stack of nine identical, nondescript shoeboxes sat huddled on the closet floor. No manufacturer's name graced the generic boxes. A couple of year's worth of Victoria's Secret catalogs sat beside them in a tidy pile. Pretty tame stuff. My gaze kept wandering to the stack of shoeboxes. I knelt and ran my right palm over the front of the boxes. It gravitated toward one in particular on the top left of the pile. I pulled it out to examine it.

The wide box was standard gray cardboard, nothing out of the ordinary, and no different than the others. I held it in my hands and the red sequined shoe flashed before my mind's eye once again, bringing a stab of pain with it. I ground my teeth and concentrated. This time, the view was from the back; pear shaped, cupped to accept a soft-skinned foot upon its tapered heel, the ankle strap looping to look like an overgrown, sparkling halo. No saint wore shoes like those. And why associate Walt's death with the shoe? It was gaudy, flashy—not at all Walt's style. I hadn't come across any sex toys—not even a box of condoms. I doubted he'd ever brought any of his playmates home.

And come to think of it, in my vision I only ever saw one shoe.

I lifted the lid. Empty, except for a couple of papers: A brochure of Holiday Valley, the ski resort south of Buffalo, and a scrap with four hand-written numbers: 4537. Pin number? Combination lock? Last four digits of a phone number? And I got the feeling that the collection was incomplete. Walt had hoped to add more things to it. His time had simply run out.

I replaced the cover and set the box behind me, grabbing the one that had been right next to it. The collection of items in this box was much more varied. Piece by piece, I withdrew an ordinary blue Bic pen, a plain white, soiled cocktail napkin with no embossed name of a bar printed on it or other clue as to its origin, an unsigned birthday card with a lipstick kiss. The last item was a small black velvet pillow with the name Veronica embroidered on it in DayGlo pink thread. I picked it up by its pink-ribboned hanger, and was assaulted with the same image I'd seen when we met Cyn Lennox: *Hands. Bloodied.*

Startled, I dropped the pillow so fast, it went flying. Nerves jangled, I sat there for a few seconds waiting to recover. God, I hated that flashes of insight could catch me off guard like that—sour my stomach and make my muscles quiver. And I was glad Richard hadn't witnessed it.

I took a couple more breaths to calm down before retrieving the pillow, lifting it by its hanger with the pen and replacing both items in the box before setting it aside, too.

The idea of checking all the shoeboxes was not pleasant, but it had to be done. Methodically, I went through every one of them, making sure I handled each item. No insight, no creepy feelings. Each box held just as curious collections of oddball items that could have meaning only for Walt—and none of them with the emotional investment the first two had had. Had the shoes been gifts to his lady friends? Why had Walt kept the boxes? If the sparkly shoe I kept seeing was representative of the rest, they were not cheap.

I replaced the boring boxes, closed the closet door and picked up the two interesting ones, tucked them under my arm, and returned to the living room.

Richard sat at the desk, Walt's receipts and papers spread out before him on the blotter. He looked up, zeroing in on the boxes. "What's so special about those?"

"I'm not sure," I lied. "But I think I'll take them home with me. Find anything worthwhile?"

Richard scooped up the papers, replacing them in the manila folder. "All his bills and receipts are segregated into envelopes by year. You want the latest?"

"Sure. I'm most interested in credit card and phone bills."

"Looking for anything in particular?"

"Yeah, a clue to his sex life. I think his death may have hinged on that."

"Wouldn't be the first time." Richard selected a couple of envelopes from the lower left-hand drawer, pushed it shut and handed them to me. "This ought to hold you for a while. You about ready?"

"Yeah, let's go."

Richard followed me to the door. "Brenda's making shrimp scampi tonight."

"With garlic bread?"

"You got it."

I closed and locked the door behind us. Richard trundled down the stairs without a backward glance, but something tugged at my soul. I turned back to stare at the featureless steel door. *Find the truth,* something whispered inside my head.

Walt or my conscience?

I'd have to figure that out.

3

Richard's after-dinner Drambuie sat on a Venetian tile coaster. He'd parked behind his grandfather's big mahogany desk, pouring over yet another book. But this wasn't some dry, medical tome. Fuzzy black-and-white photographs checkerboarded the pages, with short paragraphs of text annotating each one. Brenda brushed past me in the doorway, clutching the latest Tess Gerritsen hardback. "Run for your life," she hissed. "He's parked back on Memory Lane again."

Amused, I watched her make a beeline for the stairs.

I cleared my throat and stepped forward. "That your high school yearbook?" I asked Richard.

He didn't bother to look up. "One of them."

I entered the room and rounded the desk to stand behind him. He tapped a faded color photo that had been used as a bookmark. "Here's Cyn Taggert—er, Lennox."

The now-buxom blonde had been a skinny brunette with timid eyes some thirty years previous. Hard to believe the little waif had grown into the hardened businesswoman I'd met earlier that day.

I hadn't told Richard about the flash of insight I'd experienced in Cyn Lennox's office. On its own, it meant nothing. Maybe Walt had once applied for a job at the Old Red Mill. Perhaps he was an old or a new friend—someone Cyn had known Richard hadn't trucked with. The fact that Walt had been in the place, only yards from where his body had been

found, wasn't proof of anything. Yet it did give me a starting point. Something I was pretty sure the Amherst Police didn't know.

I hadn't asked Cyn if she'd known Walt. The timing wasn't right. I needed to know more about the dead man before I went that route. And I was pretty sure I wouldn't hear the truth from Ms. Lennox anyway.

Once again Richard had a sappy look on his face, still studying Cyn's picture.

"I thought you went to an all-boys Catholic high school."

"Yeah, Canisus guys always hung out with the girls from Nardin."

"You enjoyed those years, didn't you?" My words came out like an accusation.

Richard didn't seem to notice. "Yes, I did."

Why shouldn't he sound satisfied? He hadn't been wrenched out of his freshman year at the three-quarter point from an inner city school and dumped across town with a bunch of snotty rich kids. He had fit in from day one. He hadn't been beaten to a pulp on his first day, either.

I moved around the front of the desk and sat in one of the leather wing chairs, surprised at the depth of my bitterness. I tried to let it go. "What if your friend Cyn knows more than she's telling about this murder?"

Richard looked up from the decades-old pages. "Cyn's a good person. I'm sure she's told the police everything she knows."

"You knew this woman over thirty years ago. You don't know who she is today."

"Yeah, but people don't change that much. Look at you."

"Me?"

"In some ways, you haven't changed at all from when you were fourteen."

Anger flared within me. I'd come a long way from that cowed boy who'd been forced to go live with strangers. I changed the subject. "Once I wire up the light over the dining room table, the apartment is finished. I guess we ought to think about calling movers to come and I'll be out of your hair on a daily basis."

He closed the yearbook, a smile raising the edges of his mustache. "You ready to leave the nest?"

"Moving sixteen feet across the driveway is hardly leaving the nest."

He shrugged.

The loft apartment over the three-car garage had been empty for at least twenty years before I got the brilliant idea to make the place my own. I'd intended to give it a good clean and move right in, but Richard wouldn't hear of it. The next thing you know he'd hired a contractor, put in a new heating and cooling system, all new wiring, had the hardwood floors sanded and sealed and the walls painted. All the planning had kept him occupied for a few hours a day while he recovered.

Brenda had entrusted her friend Maggie Brennan to help her decorate the place. I'd introduced the two women. At the time I thought I might have a shot at a relationship with the lovely Ms. B. That hadn't worked out, but I also hadn't given up on the idea, either. Gut feeling told me we'd be more than just acquaintances one day. I listened to my gut.

"Go ahead and arrange for movers whenever you want. It's on me," Richard said.

Yeah, like everything else these last few months.

He'd reopened the book, his attention back on the picture of young Cyn Taggert. Was it the memory of puppy love that made his smile so wistful? The present-day woman gave me bad vibes. I'd have to pursue that avenue of investigation.

And if Richard found out his long lost love had some deadly secret—how much would he blame me?

I punched the rheostat switch and bright white light flooded the apartment's empty dining area. I cranked it back to a tolerable level, grateful the pills I'd taken earlier had quelled the headache that had threatened.

My gaze traveled around the pleasant room. There was no reason not to call a bunch of movers for estimates first thing in the morning. And yet, I wasn't quite ready to move in and I wasn't sure why. The most painless route was to do the deed while Richard and Brenda were on their honeymoon.

Painless. What did bloody hands have to do with Walt's death? Okay, he'd bled to death. But I was pretty sure the image of the hands had nothing to do with his death. I'd had flashes of clairvoyance and they were different than seeing things from the past. The shoe was the past. The bloody hands were something yet to come. So who was Veronica and why was she in danger? Perhaps the next victim?

The phone rang, making me jump. Once, twice. I never pick up until at least the fourth ring, just to thwart telemarketers, who usually hang up after three. Besides, only Richard, Brenda, and the employment form I filled out for Tom at the bar had my new telephone number. I had only one sort-of friend in Buffalo, Sam Nielsen, now a reporter for the *Buffalo News*—and I hadn't even given him the two-week-old number.

I picked up the phone. "Hello?"

"Where do you get off involving Richard in another one of your dumb psychic schemes? Haven't you done enough to the poor man?"

I should've just hung up, but the voice was vaguely familiar. "Excuse me?"

"I said—"

36

"I heard what you said. Who is this?"

"Maggie. Maggie Brennan."

Ah, the lovely Ms. B. Only now I was on the fiery end of her Irish temper. Brenda must've given her the number.

"Did Brenda ask you to say something?"

"Well . . . no. She wouldn't. But I thought—"

"Yeah, well you thought wrong. Just butt out of my family business, will you?"

"No, I won't. Brenda and Richard are my friends. And in case it escaped your attention, you nearly got Richard killed at Easter."

"Hey, I was the target. Richard pushed me out of the way."

"Yeah, well it's still your fault."

A lump rose in my throat. I didn't need *her* to tell me that.

"If that's all you called for—I think it's time we ended this conversation."

Silence.

I counted to ten. "Was there something else you wanted to say?"

"I guess not." Did I detect reluctance in her voice?

When we first met, we'd connected almost immediately. That is, until we found a body in her ex-lover's condo. That had definitely put a damper on what seemed like the beginning of a meaningful relationship.

I decided to take a chance. "You want to go out with me sometime?"

More silence.

I counted to ten again.

"Maybe," Maggie answered at last, and again her tone was soft. "What did you have in mind?"

I remembered the Holiday Valley brochure in Walt's shoebox. "Just a ride in the country. A day trip."

"A magical mystery tour?" Aha! Intrigued.

"Something like that."

Again silence.

This was like a replay from my high school days. My sweaty hand tightened around the receiver as I counted to ten one more time.

"Okay. When?"

I let out the breath I hadn't realized I'd been holding. "Saturday."

I never drove to the bakery up on Main Street. I'd walked there in snow, rain, and on starless nights to find Sophie Levin standing behind the plate glass door in her faded cotton house dress, maroon cardigan sweater, and silver hair tucked into a wispy bun at the base of her neck, ready to usher me into her backroom inner sanctum. That night was no different.

"In, in already," the elderly woman said, locking the door behind me. I followed her to the small card table she had set up beside a pallet of collapsed bakery boxes. She pointed to my usual seat, a metal folding chair, and settled her bulk on the one adjacent. The coffee was hot and my favorite macaroons, still warm from the oven, sat piled on a chipped white plate.

I set the plastic grocery bag with the shoeboxes on the table.

"Show and tell?" she asked, her brown eyes riveted on it.

I took the boxes out, shoved one of them closer to her. "I'll show and you tell me what you think."

She leaned on the wobbly table, clasping her hands before her and studied the box. "Hmm. Fancy shoes once lived in this box." Her voice, with its slight Polish accent, held reproach. She rested her fingers on the top of the other box. "Hmm. This one, too."

I sipped my coffee and nodded. I thought of Sophie as a kind of psychic mentor, although her inner radar was much different than mine. She saw auras—colors, she called them—and then she knew things. And it made me feel less of a freak to have a kindred spirit to confide in.

Sophie traced a finger along the first box top. "Not the kind of shoes a *nice* woman wears."

I tried not to smile. "Depends upon your definition of nice. But in this case, I think you're right."

She raised the lid, setting it aside. Her gaze fell on the contents and she frowned. "Hmm. Not too interesting." She selected the Holiday Valley brochure. She stared at it for a few moments, then ran her fingers along the long edge. "A good time was had."

"That was my impression, too. But that was all I got. Take a look at that little scrap and tell me what you think."

Sophie replaced the brochure. Her weary, red-rimmed eyes widened when she picked up the paper fragment. "Now this is more interesting."

Intrigued, I leaned forward.

She closed her eyes, concentrating. "Hmmm."

"What is it? What do you see?"

Sophie opened her eyes and frowned at me. "You aren't usually this impatient."

I backed off. "Sorry."

She rubbed the scrap between her forefinger and thumb, her head bobbing. "Yes. That's it."

"What?"

She reached over, grabbed my hand, pressing the fragment into my palm with her thumb. A negative image burst upon my mind; trees, a rural mailbox with the numbers 4537 glowing upon it. Then the pressure was gone and I found myself sitting there, open-mouthed, staring at Sophie's self-satisfied expression.

"Wow. How'd you do that?"

She flicked the paper from her thumb and it drifted back into the box. "It's a gift." Her smile faded. "But knowing it's a house number doesn't tell you where to find the house."

"It's obvious. It's in Holiday Valley."

She picked up a macaroon and inspected it. "Oh sure. If you know what street it's on."

I thought back to the image she'd shared with me. The fact that it had been a negative made it harder to discern details. A mailbox, glowing numbers. Maples and pines in the background, but nothing else to help me identify the location. And she had a point. "Can you tell me anything about this place?"

"More about the paper the numbers were written on."

I was all ears.

"The man who wrote it is dead." She shuddered. "Died violently."

I nodded.

Sophie concentrated. "He wasn't well."

I nodded again.

Her gaze strayed to the other box, then to me. "This one frightens you."

"I wouldn't say 'frightened.' More—" Okay, she was right. But it wasn't the box; just the damn little pillow inside it.

"Yes?" she prompted.

"Concerned."

"Mmm." She lifted the lid, peered inside and frowned. "Oh. Yeah. Not nice."

We could fence around it all night. "How so?"

Her chin rose defiantly. "You tell me."

"That would taint your perception. Come on—give."

Her brow again furrowed with concentration. When she spoke, her voice was pensive—subdued. "Blood. Like a slaughterhouse."

Damn, I hadn't wanted to hear that. "Yeah. Walt Kaplan bled to death."

She shook her head. "What we see is not his blood."

My heart sank. She'd used the present tense. "I got that, too."

"What will you do about it?"

"What can I do?"

"Try to stop it from happening."

"Can I?"

She shrugged. "All you can do is try."

"What about fate? If it's supposed to happen—"

"If I had my life to live over, I would always try harder to do what was right. Always. It's too easy to turn away, to give up. I would be very disappointed in you if you took the easy way out."

Sophie had a knack for inducing guilt. I found I couldn't meet her gaze.

She tapped the other shoebox. I looked up to see her frown, her brow furrowing. "What about this fancy shoe?"

"I saw it, too," I said, grateful for the change of subject. "But I don't know what it means."

Sophie nibbled on her cookie, her expression thoughtful. "Foot."

"Huh?"

"The man who died had one of those feet things."

"Feet things?"

"You know—he was fascinated by toes."

Understanding dawned. "A foot fetish?"

"Yes!" She popped the rest of the cookie in her mouth, chewed, and swallowed, quite pleased with herself; then her expression soured. "Why would anyone want to suck on another person's smelly toes?"

"Ya got me."

Sophie shrugged, selected another macaroon and winked. "These are better."

4

He was dead. Chest, clothes saturated with blood. A lifeless body stretched out on the cold, stone floor. No hope of revival. No hope at all.

Dead.

Forever gone.

Like everyone else I'd ever loved.

My father. I don't even really remember him. Not his face. Nothing.

My mother. The haggard-faced Madonna with a whiskey glass clutched in one hand, pleading for release from this life.

My wife—Shelley, her eyes glazed and vacant, lips smiling after a line of blow.

And now . . .

The image of the dead dissolved, replaced by a pair of masculine hands covered in blood. Palms away from me, rivulets of blood dripping down the wrists, snagged by a forest of dark forearm hairs— someone's life blood gone, as though in a slaughterhouse. Just like—

I jerked awake, sweating, muscles quivering—my heart pounding like the rhythm of a rap tune.

I rolled over onto my stomach, hugged my pillow. The scarlet numerals on my bedside clock read 4:09. I closed my eyes and tried to get my ragged breathing under control.

I didn't need a shrink to tell me the significance of the nightmare. It came to me a couple of times a week, only now it had a new ending. But the dream lied. Unlike my parents and ex-wife, Richard *hadn't* died.

Another reality was that Richard *could've* died because of me. He'd been willing to sacrifice himself to save me, and I wasn't sure if I was worthy of that. Worse, if I'd find the courage to do the same for him.

Those circuitous thoughts were unproductive. I had a new problem: the vision of the bloodied hands. What did it mean and how was I going to prevent seeing them in reality?

Warm, incandescent light washed over the kitchen table where I'd scattered the envelopes of financial information Richard had appropriated at Walt's apartment. The contents—heavy on receipts—indicated Walt had fallen into the trap of credit card debt. He'd maxed out four major cards, with finance charges far exceeding the monthly minimum, which he dutifully paid. Top creditors were Erie Professional Laundry, Sunoco Gas, a smattering of family restaurants, and Macy's. He also had a car loan with Bison Bank. His disability payments were direct-deposited to a checking account regularly drained by ATM withdrawals, and had an ending balance of forty-seven cents for the previous month.

I sipped my second cup of coffee. Disability payments would've saved me from my current deadbeat existence. Richard had consulted an attorney about my filing a Social Security claim, but taking a job at the bar had probably killed my chances at ever seeing a check.

I pushed the thought aside as I shuffled through Walt's monthly credit card statements. Pay-per-view was a favorite with Walt, and I could guess the content of the movies he chose—not that they were listed. Was that the total extent of his sex life? Had his disability prevented him from performing with women, or was he shy about a scar or other infirmity? Revealing a colostomy bag or stoma would not be the highlight of a sexual encounter.

No shoe company was listed amongst his creditors. Walt didn't have a computer, so did he buy the footwear over the phone or via mail order? I glanced over the miniature checks printed at the bottom of his statement, but most of them were either for his regular bills or the local grocery chain.

Richard hadn't snagged a savings account statement or anything from a brokerage firm. How long had it been since Walt's settlement? If he'd been a union man it could've been hefty—minus the attorney's fee, of course. Even so, where had the money gone?

It was almost seven-thirty and I was about to pour my third cup when I heard footsteps in the hallway. Seconds later Brenda entered the kitchen, heading straight for the fridge. "Someone's got a date," she teased in a singsong cadence. She took out a pound of bacon and the egg carton, setting them on the counter.

"News travels fast." I doctored my cup and sat back down at the table, collected the papers and returned them to their Kraft envelopes.

Brenda retrieved a skillet from a cupboard, set it on the stove and lay the bacon strips across its bottom. She always made too much food, expecting me to tuck in when I just didn't have the appetite. When I moved across the driveway, it was possible cold cereal or coffee alone would fill the bill of fare twenty-four/seven.

I pulled out the coffeemaker's basket, dumping the grounds in the wastebasket before starting a new batch. "You and Maggie tracking each other's hourly movements these days?"

"She is my best friend here in Buffalo. Naturally she keeps me informed on what's going on in her life."

A little too well informed.

Richard entered the kitchen from the hallway. "So, you're

taking a trip to Holiday Valley tomorrow."

Once upon a time nobody knew or cared when I came and went or what I did. Next I expected a headline in the *Buffalo News*.

Richard sat down at the table, his expression wistful. "I had some good times skiing there, back in the day."

I remembered those days, too. Not for skiing. I'd been stuck here in the house with the elder Alperts, one of who despised me, while Richard would escape on his all-too-rare days off from the hospital.

Brenda turned the bacon. "Get the bread and the toaster out, will you, Jeffy."

"So, you're taking Maggie Brennan," Richard said.

I busied myself at the counter. "Uh, yeah." I glanced back at Richard, whose eyes had widened, though his face remained immobile.

"What's on tap for today? You working at the bar or on your case?"

Brenda cringed. "Don't call it a case."

I took out plates from the cupboard. "She's right. But maybe a little of both."

"Uh-huh."

"What are you guys doing? Making more wedding plans?"

"It's two weeks away, and as far as I know all I have to do is show up at City Hall in a suit."

"You'd better be prepared for more than just that," Brenda said.

Richard ignored her. It wasn't like they were planning a splashy affair. Just the two of them with me and Maggie as witnesses, then lunch at a swank restaurant before they caught a plane for Paris.

"Got enough money for your date?" Richard asked me.

My stomach tightened. "It's not a date. And yeah, I've got

money." Of course I did. He'd peeled off a couple of twenties for me a few days before. I'd be taking the day trip with his gas in the car he bought me. I didn't feel good about any of that, but being practically destitute engenders humility. I intended to pay him back for everything now that I was working, but as the days passed, and the debt I owed him increased, I found it harder and harder to look him in the eye.

"I'm sure Richard would love to hang out with you today, Jeffy, but we've already planned our day." Hands on hips, Brenda aimed her pointed stare at Richard. "Or are you trying to get out of marrying me?"

Richard leaned back in his chair and frowned. "Did I miss something?"

"We're going to get the license."

"We have plenty of time."

Brenda stood rigid, her steely gaze arctic cold.

"It's good for sixty days," Richard continued, then cleared his throat and looked away. "Isn't anybody going to offer me a cup of coffee?"

Brenda shook her head in disgust and turned her attention back to the skillet. I took two more mugs from the cupboard, pouring coffee for both of them.

Truth was, I wished the four of us *were* going to Holiday Valley. Safety in numbers and all that crap. I had a feeling I was going to learn something that Richard either wouldn't want to know or wasn't likely to believe.

I had an hour to kill before reporting to the bar and figured I may as well work on the apartment. It didn't look or feel like home and the only way that was going to change was to unpack some of my stuff; the furniture would come later. None of the boxes had been labeled by the moving company Richard had employed to move my possessions from Manhattan to Buffalo, but I didn't need an itemized list. There are some perks to having acquired a sixth sense.

The kitchen seemed the best place to start, and I found the boxes of silverware and dishes with no problem. They'd sat in the garage for months, and who knew how clean the hands were that had packed them, so into the dishwasher they went.

As I sorted the knives, forks and spoons, putting them into separate sections of the silverware rack, I considered all I knew about Walt Kaplan and the circumstances of his death. Not much. There were shortcuts I could take to obtain more information, and the easiest was to contact my ex-schoolmate Sam Nielsen. The problem was, he'd want to deal and I didn't yet have anything to offer him.

What the hell, I figured, and dumped in the dishwashing powder, shutting the door with my foot. I hit the start button then picked up the phone. It was answered on the first ring.

"Newsroom. Sam Nielsen."

"Hey, Sam, it's Jeff Resnick."

A long pause, then, cautiously, "Long time no hear from. Got any hot tips for me?"

"Don't play the slots at Batavia Downs."

His tone changed. "Okay, what do you need?"

"Have I ever called you for a favor?"

"No, but there's always a first time and this is it, right?"

The silence between us lengthened. I could hear other phones ringing in the newsroom, the chatter of a busy office.

"Is there a story for me in this?" Sam asked finally.

"Maybe. Eventually. Tell me what you know about Walt Kaplan's death. He was the bartender in Williamsville who—"

"I know, I know." Sam exhaled a long breath. "Look, I didn't write the piece."

"I know that. What's the office scuttlebutt? The articles only said stabbed multiple times and other wounds. How many is multiple?"

"Forty-six."

"Jeez. He must've really pissed somebody off. Any defense wounds on the hands or arms?"

"No."

"A stiletto, wasn't it?"

"Yeah. That wasn't reported in the media. The fact you know means you're looking into this, huh?" Sam knew about my . . . gift. So far he hadn't tried to exploit it—or me—much.

"Kind of. I took his job."

"And what does your intuition tell you about his death?"

"I'm not ready to talk about it yet."

"But you will some time in the future."

"Possibly. What about those other wounds mentioned in the articles."

"Burns."

"What kind?"

"Hey, I told you this wasn't my story. But I'll tell you what, I'll keep my eyes open. If anything develops, I'll let you know. By the same token—if you find out anything, I'd better be the one you call."

"Guaranteed."

Like at most other bars, the Friday crowd at the Whole Nine Yards was larger and more exuberant than the regular weekday group. And they wanted to talk—about Walt.

I could tell Tom was uncomfortable recounting what he knew about the murder—several times during the day—but who could blame the customers for their curiosity. None of them had ever known a murder victim. I didn't contribute to the conversation, listening carefully in case Tom mentioned something I hadn't

yet heard, but it seemed I knew more about Walt's death than even he did.

"To a great guy," said one T-shirted man in jeans and geeky-looking safety glasses. He raised his glass and a host of others raised theirs as well.

"I didn't know Walt," I said. "Tell me about him."

"Natty dresser. Always had a crease in his slacks."

"Great listener," another one of the guys piped up.

"Yeah, but he was also a walking encyclopedia of golf. Knew all the players for the last fifty years—and their stats. Could even tell you who won all the major tourneys and their scores."

"Did he play?" I asked Tom.

"Not that I know of."

I could see the appeal of the game to a man like Walt. Quiet, and for the most part, solitary. A player's greatest competition was himself.

I thought about the shoeboxes. I'd already determined I wasn't going to mention the red shoe to Tom, but the other one was fair game. "Did Walt ever have a girlfriend named Veronica?"

Discomfort flashed across Tom's features. He shook his head. "I don't think so." He looked around at the crowd. "Anybody need a refill?"

Okay, so he wasn't being straight with me. Eventually he'd have to. For the moment, I decided to let it slide.

The testimonials continued throughout the afternoon. Walt was a helluva guy. He didn't deserve what he got. Why hadn't the cops arrested someone? But in all the talk there was something missing: the essence of who Walt really was. He'd been part of the scenery around the bar. Didn't talk much, didn't make waves, and yet someone had been angry enough to stab him over and over again. Why hadn't he fought back, why hadn't he tried to protect himself?

And all he'd left behind for me to try to find his killer was the image of the damned red shoe.

5

Maggie's little blue Hyundai pulled into Richard's driveway at precisely eight fifty-nine the next morning. "Right on time," she said as she got out of the car. She looked terrific in a sleeveless white blouse over light blue slacks with her red-polished toes poking out of a pair of white sandals. The outfit looked a bit cool for the mountains—or should I say tall hills—of Holiday Valley, but she grabbed a white sweater along with her purse before slamming the car door.

I opened the passenger door of my car and ushered her in, wondering if my next gig should be valet parking. Within moments, we were on our way.

The Thruway traffic was heavy, and I forced myself to concentrate on driving, not easy when Maggie, an emotional powder keg, sat a mere foot from me. The tension continued to build with each passing mile.

"Why Holiday Valley?" she blurted at last, looking at me askance.

I kept my eyes on the road, grateful the traffic had begun to thin. I kept my voice calm. "Just a hunch."

"I asked Brenda about this." She paused. I risked a look to see her lip had curled. "This psychic thing you think you have. She believes it."

"What about you?"

"I want to see it in action."

"Well don't count on it." I hoped she caught the annoyance

in my voice. "It shows up when it wants to and comes with some pretty dreadful aftereffects." I glanced back at her. Her expression was still skeptical. That I could accept. If it hadn't happened to me, I'd've been skeptical, too.

"It's been years since I visited Ellicottville," she said. "As I recall, it's quite charming. Lots of cute little boutiques, restaurants, and bed and breakfasts."

"I've never been there."

"Then we're both in for a treat." Her lips turned up—a very pretty smile, and for the first time in three months, I felt the chill she'd been directing toward me warm. I smiled, too.

The rest of the journey passed with Maggie humming along with the songs on the radio. She seemed glad for a day out of harness. My internal pressure intensified as I considered my mission. I'd be looking for a mailbox among the thousands lining the roads of this winter vacationland. Of course, without snow they'd be a lot more visible. But I wasn't sure I'd recognize the right one even if I saw it.

I slowed the car as we entered the village. Maggie's eyes widened in delight as she took in the quaint little shops. I kept up with the rest of the traffic—a crawl. "Ooooh. Pretty," Maggie cooed, craning her neck. "Did you see that gorgeous landscape in that little gallery's window?"

I braked. "No, I'm driving."

"We keep passing parking spots. Aren't we going to stop?"

"I hadn't planned on it. At least not right away." I glanced at her.

Maggie's brows had narrowed. "Why not?"

"I came here to find something."

"What?"

"A mailbox."

"What's the big deal? Just go to the address."

"I don't know the address."

She turned her head to stare straight ahead. The big chill was back.

"Don't worry. I'll find it."

No reaction from Maggie. I was going to look like a real jerk if I didn't find the damn thing.

The charming storefronts diminished and I accelerated as we left the village behind us.

For the next hour we drove slowly up and down the hillsides, trying to peer through the trees and foliage to see the expensive homes. Mostly we saw mailboxes and long narrow drives posted with "No Trespassing" signs. But that was okay; I was looking for a specific address. I just didn't know what street it would be on.

Maggie kept sighing restlessly, but I was too preoccupied to give her much notice. Probably not the way to win her heart.

We drove up yet another steep road. The sequence of numbers on the mailboxes fell into line: 4517, 4527, 4537. "That's it!"

I jammed on the brakes. Maggie's seatbelt locked as she lurched forward. "Hey!"

Slamming the car into park, I yanked off my seatbelt and jumped out.

Another car slowed, its driver staring at me as I ran my fingers over the freshly painted numbers on the rather battered old mailbox. Less visible were the faded letters of a name, probably painted decades before: T-GG-RT.

Cynthia Lennox's maiden name was Taggert.

Being a Saturday, of course the town hall was closed. I wondered if Ellicottville listed their tax information online. If not, then I'd have to return to the area. Still, the return trip would be worth it if it gave me the answers I wanted.

Maggie's stomach gurgled, and not for the first time.

"How about lunch?" I asked.

"Finally," she muttered.

One slice of Quiche Lorraine and a side salad later and Maggie was a charming human being once again. I made a note to self: Never let the woman go hungry and I might just stay in her good graces.

We were the last of the quaint little bistro's midday crowd. Maggie sipped her tea, studying me over the cup's rim. "How did you know?"

I gave her a blank stare. "Know what?"

"Finding that mailbox made you very happy. But it means more to you than just some silly treasure hunt. Why? What's its significance?"

I shrugged, folding my napkin over the half liverwurst sandwich I hadn't been able to finish. "I'm not sure. Yet. I have some suspicions, but I don't have enough information to put it all together. I—"

The heat from her gaze was enough to scorch. Apart from my initial reaction upon finding the mailbox, I thought I'd done a pretty good job at hiding what finding it meant to me. "How did you know finding it made me happy?"

Maggie leaned back in her chair, her expression guarded.

The air between us seemed to shimmer.

My mouth went dry.

She knew.

She'd sensed what I'd felt.

"Have you ever had a psychic experience before?" I asked her.

Maggie looked even more uncomfortable. "No. *I* have not. But when I'm near you . . . I don't know how to explain it. You do something weird to me. It's awful and nice at the same time. I don't think I like you very much, but . . . maybe I'm attracted to you because of it."

"Thanks. I think."

Her cheeks colored. "I'm sorry. That didn't come out right. I'm afraid of you, and yet . . . oh, I don't know."

"Why did you agree to come out with me today? To test it?"

Her gaze wouldn't meet mine. "Maybe."

I reached over, took her hand. Her head jerked up and she gasped, her mouth dropping open. Her fingers felt fever hot against mine. She was afraid and yet fascinated. "What do you feel, Maggie?"

Her breaths were more like pants. "You."

I let go of her hand, remembering how my first experiences with this . . . whatever it was, had freaked me out. We'd briefly shared something similar once before—but I hadn't given it much thought. Obviously she had. I wasn't sure I liked it any better than she did. Then again, it was kind of a kick to know I connected with someone on more than just a physical level.

"What do we do about . . . this?" she asked, her voice sounding small.

"I don't know. What do you want to do?"

"I don't think I can answer that. At least not today." She gathered her purse and sweater. "Can we go home now?"

"Yeah." I signaled the waitress, who brought the check. I paid the bill and followed Maggie to the door.

Maggie didn't look at me during the long, quiet ride back to Buffalo. When I pulled up Richard's driveway, she mumbled a "thanks for the lunch" and got out of my car. I watched as her car pulled away.

She never looked back.

6

My weekend didn't improve on Sunday. I awoke with the grumbling inside my head that always foretold a migraine. I took my medication and stayed in my darkened, quiet room until I absolutely had to get up to go to the bar for my shift.

Tom was on the phone when I got there—ten minutes late—and waved me to take over out front. Several customers were already perched on stools, watching the golf pre-match commentary on the bar's big-screen TV. I leaned against the back-bar, massaging my temples, wondering if I could get away with wearing sunglasses in the darkened bar, and praying it would be a slow day.

No such luck. Six leather- and denim-clad bikers barreled through the side entrance, grabbing a table near the big front window. Boisterous and full of energy, their voices clawed at my already ragged nerves. I had to force myself to approach the screaming white glare of the window. "What can I get you guys?"

"A couple of pitchers of Coors," said the one closest to me, a grizzled, bearded guy with a faded blue bandana tied around his head. Even seated he looked twice my size. His tattoos and leathers were Harley Davidson all the way and he was celebrating, pure joy bombarding my senses like a tsunami. Birth of a grandson? I wasn't sure. But even pleasant emotions can overwhelm when they're directed with battering force. I turned abruptly to get away from the mental assault.

Filling the pitchers took an eternity, the smell of hops seemed overly strong for such a mainstream lager. I balanced them and six glasses on a tray and started for the table when my sneaker toe caught on the rubber mat behind the bar. Time shifted into slow motion and I watched, horror-struck, as the tray flew from my hands, the beer rising out of the pitchers like geysers. The glasses tumbled end over end and seemed to take a lot longer than me to hit the floor. The spectacular, shattering crash threatened to split my already aching skull. Thank God I shut my eyes as beer drenched me and glass shards peppered my face.

Except for the drone of the TV commentators, the bar had gone silent. I lay on the floor, dripping with blood or beer—I wasn't sure which—for what seemed like eons. Then the strongest arms in the world pulled me to my feet.

"Hey, man, you okay?" The big biker leaned me against the bar, found a cloth and was gently mopping at my face. "Did you get glass in your eyes?"

I shook my head—a definite mistake. "I'm okay."

"What the hell?" Suddenly Tom stood behind the biker. "What happened?"

"I tripped."

"Good grief! It sounded like the end of the world. You okay?"

"Yeah, yeah." The biker pressed the cloth into my hand, and I mopped at my dripping arms and neck. "Sorry, Tom, I—"

"Don't worry about it. I'll take care of the customers. Go in back and grab a T-shirt, then get the mop and broom out, willya?"

"Sure thing." I gave the biker a grateful smile. "Thanks."

"No problem," he said and picked his way through the beer and glass to head back to his seat.

Avoiding the gazes of the other patrons, I slunk off in back and peeled off my shirt to hose myself off in the slop sink. I returned a few minutes later in one of the bar's give-away shirts, mop and broom in hand. My hands were shaking as I cleaned up the mess. Tom had the bikers laughing once again. He, too, was in a celebratory mood that even the mess behind the bar hadn't doused.

Sheepishly, I took my place by the taps, feeling the eyes of several customers upon me. My smile was forced—probably a grimace. Tom was still engaged in conversation with the bikers, who had resumed their rowdy revelry. I turned my back to the customers and closed my eyes as waves and waves of emotions engulfed me. Joy from the bikers; misery—a gambling debt?— and worry; someone's wife was dangerously ill.

The pounding in my head intensified, leaving me nauseous and shaky. Someone nudged my elbow. I turned. Tom.

"Good news, Jeff. Your services are no longer required."

The pounding paused for half a second, then shifted into overdrive. Shit. I'd smashed some glassware and now he was firing me. My shock and disappointment must've registered: Tom laughed.

"I mean looking into Walt's death. The cops arrested someone last night. But you're welcome to stay on at the bar, if you want."

I swallowed with relief. Then the red shoe image slammed my mind's eye with the force of a jackhammer. "Tell me more about the arrest."

"Some homeless geek. Been hanging around Williamsville for the past couple of months. The dumb shit still had the murder weapon on him."

"A stiletto?"

Tom nodded, smug.

It didn't feel right. Not only was I still getting flashes of insight, they'd led me to the mailbox in Ellicottville and possibly property owned by Cyn Lennox. While I couldn't be sure without more information, my gut told me they had the wrong person. I pondered that thought for a second. Not man, not woman. Person. Yeah. I definitely needed more information.

Tom frowned. "You don't look so good."

I swallowed down the bile threatening to erupt. "Sorry, Tom. I want to keep the job here, but I don't think I can put in my hours today."

The eyes that met mine were not judgmental. "I knew when I hired you that you had health problems. I won't be a prick and make you stay when obviously you're not up to it. Can you get home by yourself? Want me to call your family?"

I shook my head and winced. "I can make it home."

"Don't be stupid." Tom placed a hand on my elbow, steered me to the back room and plunked me into a chair. It was all I could do not to throw up on his carpet. I heard his voice, couldn't understand the words, then he was gone.

I covered my eyes and bent over, concentrated on breathing. In out, in out. I was not going to puke. An eternity later, a tap on my shoulder alerted me to buff-colored Dockers at my side. Richard. "Let's go home."

Too sick to be angry or even embarrassed—that would come later—I let him lead me out the bar's back door. All too soon I felt the sensation of acceleration. I was in the passenger seat of my car with Richard at the wheel, and no memory of how I got there.

"How'd—?"

"Brenda's driving my car back. What happened to your face?"

I rolled down the window, hot air blasting my eyes. "Long story." But I didn't offer it, too busy trying to quell the urge to purge my stomach. I leaned back against the upholstery, concentrated on breathing only. A million years later, Richard braked and I saw the shimmering outline of his house out the driver's side window beyond me. Richard got out, slammed the door with a deafening bang and seconds later hauled me out and was leading me up the steps and through the door. Half a minute later I was on my bed, head hanging over the edge. Richard grabbed my left hand, placed the wastebasket in it.

"Just in case," he said.

I closed my eyes and his footsteps faded away. Time stopped for a couple of decades. I wasn't truly asleep, but I wasn't awake, either. Caught in a limbo that threatened but refused to deliver blessed oblivion, my mind kept recycling thoughts and images of the sparkling red shoe, glistening, scarlet-drenched hands, and a blood-drained Walt, his vacant eyes forever focused on an empty eternity.

The sun had been up at least three hours when I cracked my eyes open the next morning. I wasn't sure how bad I felt—but I knew it was better than I'd been the day before. Before the thought of food or even coffee entered my mind, I needed to find out about the arrest Tom had told me about the day before.

I sat on the edge of my bed, phone in hand, and punched in a number I'd memorized months before.

"Newsroom. Sam Nielsen."

"The cops made an arrest?"

"Jeff? I was going to call you. You need a cell phone."

I closed my eyes against the onslaught of light leaking around the back window. "You can always reach me here. Besides, cell phones take money and I've only had a job for four days."

"Your brother's sitting on millions. He can't buy you one?"

Sam and I weren't close enough for me to get into that situation. "Just tell me what you know."

"Schizophrenic homeless guy. Name's Craig Buchanan. He had the murder weapon on him."

"A stiletto."

"You got it. But he didn't do it, right?"

"I don't think so."

"You got a line on who did?"

"Not yet. What else can you tell me?"

"Just the guy's next of kin. A sister in Cheektowaga—not far from you." Paper rustled, as he must've consulted his notes. "Cara Scott. I'll save you some time." He gave me her address. "The story's in today's edition. You can check it online now."

"I'll do that." He was being too helpful. What would he want in return?

I pushed some more. "The cops gave Kaplan's cousin his house keys. Did they say anything about his wallet or the missing ring?"

"Nothing on the wallet. The ring hasn't been hocked—at least not yet. I guess the keys were on the body, along with pocket change. You know, Jeff, we should work together on this."

The memory of Richard's blood-soaked trench coat was still too fresh for me to want to take up anyone's offer of help. As it was, had I put Maggie in danger by allowing her to come with me to Holiday Valley?

"I thought you said this wasn't your story."

"It wasn't. The guy who had it went on a cruise. The Caribbean in June, can you believe it? So what've you got?"

"Nothing I can talk about yet. Just some impressions that don't add up."

"Yet."

"Yeah. Yet."

"The two of us would make a helluva team," he tried again. "I don't have to name my sources, you know."

"I know. But I don't have anything concrete to give you yet."

"Yeah, well keep me in mind. I'll be talking to you, Jeff." The receiver clicked in my ear.

I wasn't ready to talk to Craig Buchanan's next of kin. Instead,

I called Tom to apologize, but he blew me off and told me not to bother to come in that day as he'd already asked Dave the other bartender to step in, but I'd better show up the next day. Fair enough. I was just grateful I still had a job.

After showering, I inspected the small cuts on my face—no worse than razor nicks. But the patches of redness were not attractive. So what. It's not like I'd be going on a date with Maggie—or anyone else—any time soon.

The thought of food didn't turn my stomach, so I downed my medication with a chaser of Cheerios and two cups of coffee, then appropriated Richard's computer to read Sam's article. It didn't tell me much more than I already knew. Next up I tried to find a Web site with information on the Cattaraugus County tax base to track down the owner of the house at 4537 Alpine Road. If it was there, I couldn't find it.

Sophie was convinced Walt had a foot fetish and Google gave me an assortment of URLs to try. Each was set up like any standard porn site. Lots of shots of hot lesbians licking toes, naked bi chicks sucking toes, contorted women sucking their own toes. Walt didn't have a computer. Did he buy the magazines with skinny, scantily clad or naked chicks on the cover, tongues hanging out seductively and masturbate to his heart's delight? And if he did, where did he hide them?

Footsteps approached from the hall and Richard wandered into his study. "You must be feeling better this morning." I turned to see him do a classic double take as he focused in on the image on his nineteen-inch monitor. "What are you doing with my computer?"

I leaned back in his big leather chair and swung around to face him, struggling not to grin. "Checking out foot fetish Web sites. Wanna look?"

"No, thank you. Is there a reason for this sudden interest in feet?"

"Walt Kaplan. Seems like it might've been his Achilles heel, if you'll pardon the pun."

Richard shoved his hands into the pockets of his slacks. "Oh-kay. I suppose you know they've made an arrest."

"Yeah, but they've got the wrong guy."

Richard scowled. "And you're going to keep pursuing this."

"They've got the wrong guy," I repeated, enunciating clearly.

"That really isn't your concern. Did your boss ask you to keep looking into it?"

I let out a sigh and got up from his chair. "He wants to believe the cops have solved the crime. I haven't told him everything I've found out yet. When I do—"

"He may still tell you to give it up. Will you?"

I didn't answer.

"Jeff."

"I don't know."

Richard frowned. "What do you get out of it? You've already got the man's job. Does it give you a vicarious thrill to play investigator?"

I exhaled a breath and chose my words carefully. "It used to be my job."

"And it isn't anymore. Maybe it's time you accepted the fact you have limitations. If nothing else, yesterday should've proved that to you."

Anger and shame burned through me as I pushed past him. "Thanks for the use of the computer."

"You're welcome."

I tramped through the house with a single thought: escape. Next thing I knew, I was in my car and driving north toward Main Street with no clue as to where I was going. I pulled over and switched off the ignition. Since the mugging, I was prone to anger outbursts. The quack back in New York had warned me about it. But had it really been necessary for Richard to rub my nose in the fact that I wasn't yet capable of holding a full-time job?

Memories of decades-old hurts surfaced. Our first Christmas together, when Richard canceled plans we'd made to spend the day together just so he could suck up to a surgeon he never ended up working with. The times his family's chauffeur showed up at school to cheer me on when he was too busy working to make it himself.

I thought I'd let it all go, but there it was rubbing my ego raw once again.

Playing investigator, huh?

Well screw him! If nothing else, I'd find Walt Kaplan's murderer and bring the bastard to justice just to shove it up Richard's ass once and for all. And I had a place to start, too. Sam's story had mentioned a witness. I started the car and headed for Main Street.

The Sweet Tooth Chocolate Shoppe was devoid of customers, but the silver-haired, well-rounded proprietress greeted me with enthusiasm even before the bell over the door had stopped jangling.

"Welcome! I'm Sue. Let me know if I can be of any help," she offered from behind the glass counter.

The rich, fudgy scent of chocolate was heavy in the air. The day before it would've sent me to the curb to purge my gut. I could handle it now. I'm not a candy freak, but the aroma took me back to something good from my childhood, though the exact memory had been lost thanks to a baseball bat slamming into my skull three months earlier.

I gazed into the multi-shelf display case at the mountains of bonbons and truffles, milk, dark and white chocolate, creams and caramels—the presentation alone was worth the exorbitant price per pound. I took a deep breath, exhaling loudly. "It smells so good in here, I'm not sure what I should get."

"Are you looking for a gift?"

"For a special lady." Brenda wasn't likely to turn down chocolate. It would cost me at least a pound's worth to get the information I wanted—but in the long run, a cheap price to pay. "I'll take a pound—your choice."

"You can't go wrong with our ultimate selection."

"Let's go for it."

I watched as she brought out a flattened box with embossed gold script proclaiming the shop's name. She twisted it into shape and slipped in a piece of baker's tissue before selecting a number of chocolate covered morsels from the mounded glass plates until she'd filled the box.

"I take it this is your first visit," she said, securing the lid.

"I read about you in the *Buffalo News*. That story about the homeless man they arrested for murder."

She shook her head, her welcoming smile fading. "I didn't think they'd quote me."

"It sounded like you knew the guy."

"He Dumpster-dived in all the area merchants' trash. I suppose that's the only food he got. I felt a little sorry for him." Her expression soured further. "But the smell."

"Smell?"

"A combination of body odor, pee and—" She shuddered.

"He never changed clothes?"

"Not in the four or five months he hung around the neighborhood."

"Was he arrested in those clothes?"

"Of course."

And I'd bet there wasn't a drop of Walt Kaplan's blood on any of them. "Do you remember what they looked like?"

"I saw him nearly every day," she said, taking my purchase over to the cash register. "Grubby jeans, a stained tan sweater, and one of those long, black duster coats. Even when the weather warmed up, he still wore it." She lowered her voice. "It probably came in handy for shoplifting."

Sue rang up the sale and I extracted all the tip money from my wallet. "You've got a great shop here. I'm sure I'll be back again."

"Thanks. Have a nice day now."

Back in my car, I wrote down Sue's description of the suspect's clothing. Maybe Sam and I could work together on this. He had a pipeline to the cops, and I wanted to keep a low profile. I reset my trip odometer and headed back to the Old Red Mill. It clocked in at six-tenths of a mile when I parked by a motorcycle in the lane off the main drag. Buchanan had probably tramped up and down Main Street in search of food and a dry place to sleep.

I got out and walked around to the side of the mill. The fresh red paint and white trim lent the place a cheerful atmosphere. That Walt Kaplan's body had been found on the property didn't detract from its ambiance.

The grass still hadn't been cut, but the crime scene tape was missing. Probably Cyn Lennox had wanted to remove any evidence of Walt's death. Already the parking spaces in front of the mill weren't as full as they'd been when Richard and I had visited four days earlier.

I made my way down the incline to the spot where I believed Walt's body had lain, closed my eyes, breathing deeply, and tried to soak up something, anything. Something niggled at the edges of my mind. I crouched down and laid a hand on the grass. An image of the red shoe exploded in my mind. Shit! Other than finding the box it had been purchased in, the shoe didn't mean anything to me. But it had to Walt. It must've been pretty damned important to him for the memory of it to linger even after he'd died.

"Are you back again?"

I straightened and turned to find an irritated Cyn Lennox standing, hands on hips, on the mill's back porch. "Good morning."

"What are you doing here?"

I feigned innocence. "Nothing."

"Then why are you here?"

"I told you. Morbid curiosity."

"Which should have been satisfied on your last visit. Look, Richard's my friend; you're not. And I'd appreciate it if you'd stop hanging around my property."

"I was hoping to speak to your miller. Has he returned from his trip?"

"Yes," she grudgingly admitted. "But why should I let you talk to him?"

"Because we live in a free country, and presumably he and you have nothing to hide."

Her eyes widened, her cheeks going red. Either a hot flash or I'd just made an enemy.

"Get out of here."

Yup, she'd definitely never be my friend now.

"I'm sure you heard they made an arrest."

"Yeah. Which means you should give up your Sherlock Holmes routine and just go home."

"I don't think they arrested the right man. Or should I say woman?"

Fury boiled beneath her seemingly in-control facade. "You keep talking and I'll have one helluva fine lawsuit against you."

"Wishful thinking," I bluffed. "We both know you haven't told the police everything you know about Walt Kaplan's murder."

"What I did or didn't tell them is none of your damn business. Get off my property—NOW—or I'm calling the cops."

I waved a hand in submission. "Sure, but we'll talk again. I guarantee it."

"Not if I can help it."

There was no point in annoying her further. I walked back to my car, feeling the heat of her stare on my back with every step. Confronting her hadn't given me any new information, but it had confirmed what my gut kept telling me: however convoluted, Cyn Lennox had some involvement in Walt Kaplan's death—as either a participant or a witness. Only time would tell which.

In the meantime, I'd made an enemy. Not a smart move if she'd had a hand in Walt's death. But I didn't feel threatened. Not yet at least.

Since I didn't have to be anywhere else that day, I figured I'd look up Craig Buchanan's sister. Cara Scott's white colonial stood in stark contrast from every other house on the street in Buffalo's Cheektowaga suburb. Forest green paint on the trim was its only decoration. No trees, shrubs, or flowers adorned the yard, but the grass was freshly cut and there wasn't a stray blade on the driveway. The woman who answered my knock looked just as severe, with her dark brown hair scraped back into a ponytail and no makeup. Her navy slacks and sleeveless white shirt were crisp with a just-ironed look to them.

"Cara Scott? My name's Jeff Resnick. Can I ask you a few questions?"

"I don't have any more comments for the press," she said, about to slam the door in my face.

"I'm not from the press. I'm a friend of the murdered man." Okay, not a friend. But I had his interests at heart.

She avoided my eyes. "I'm sorry. I—"

"Can we talk for a few moments?"

Cara sighed, her weary face seeming to age five years in five seconds. She stepped out onto the concrete porch. "I'm sorry," she repeated, her lips going thin. "I've spent most of my life apologizing for Craig, but that's all I can offer you."

"I'm not so sure. You see, I don't think Craig killed Walt Kaplan."

Her head snapped up and she gazed at me with suspicion. "The police wouldn't have arrested him if they weren't sure. What makes you think he didn't do it?"

I had nothing concrete. "Just a hunch."

"This'll sound cruel, but getting caught for this murder is probably the best thing that could've happened to Craig. He'll be in a place where he can be cared for—he'll be off the streets."

"And he won't be your problem anymore," I guessed.

She crossed her arms across her chest. "I'd be lying if I didn't agree. You have no idea of the hell Craig has put my family through. My father left us when Craig was seven. My mother bailed him out of one mess after another. He drove her to bankruptcy and finally suicide because she couldn't take it any longer. He disrupts my life—my kids' lives. It would be easier on us and society in general if the cops locked him up and threw away the key."

"But what if he's innocent?"

"Don't be absurd. They found the knife on him."

"He might've come across it picking through Dumpsters."

Her level glare was as cold and uninviting as her sterile house and yard.

"He's your brother," I tried again, thinking about Richard and what, in a short time, he'd come to mean to me.

"Excuse me, Mr. Resnick, but I really don't have time for this."

She slammed the door in my face.

"Enjoy your freedom, Mrs. Scott."

As I climbed back behind the wheel of my car, I couldn't help but think that arresting Craig Buchanan solved everyone's problem. Tom was satisfied someone, anyone, had been arrested for Walt Kaplan's murder; the police were happy to close the books; and Cara Scott was finally free of her space cadet brother.

The problem remained—he didn't do it. And there was still a murderer hanging around lovely, picturesque Williamsville.

7

Evening shadows filled the backyard as I worked at emptying my third bag of mulch, carefully nestling a blanket of fragrant cedar fragments around my begonias. The smell of damp earth reminded me that Walt Kaplan had been committed to the ground less than a week before, and that maybe I was the only one who cared if his killer was caught. I left a message on Sam's voice mail, asking him to find out about bloodstains on Buchanan's clothes; now to wait and see if he followed up on it.

Brenda approached me from the house. I hadn't seen her all day, but had left the box of candy on the kitchen counter with a note. She paused about five feet away and gazed down the east border, which had taken me more than an hour to weed, then focused on the clump of flowers in front of me. She'd wanted a garden and Richard had given me *carte blanche* to make it happen. I'd staggered the pink and white begonias with darker vincas. After years of neglect, the perennials were in sad shape. In the back of my mind I had a plan for how I wanted to bring the garden back to its former grandeur over the next couple of years, but it would take careful planning.

"Such industry. I can't believe what you've accomplished in this yard in such a short time. Wherever did you garden in Manhattan?"

I looked over my shoulder at her. "I didn't."

"Then how do you know so much about it?"

I scattered a handful of mulch around a pink-veined coleus.

"For years I saved for a house in Jersey. Shelley and me and a picket fence, and maybe a pack of kids. I read up on gardening. Figured it might make a good hobby."

"Has it?"

"It's only been three weeks, but . . . yeah. I like it—it's calming. Plants don't give off weird vibes like people do."

"And they don't say things to upset people, either."

Brenda hated it when Richard and I had disagreements, and this was her chance to play peacemaker. She watched as I dumped the rest of the bag, trailing its contents over a six-foot area. "Why didn't you come in for supper?"

"I wasn't hungry."

"There's leftovers if you want something later."

I didn't meet her gaze. "Thanks."

"Richard doesn't understand," she said. "He thinks you should just ignore those funny feelings and the insight you get. I know you can't."

I leaned back on my heels and looked up at her, saw the depth of concern in her dark eyes.

"He's worried about leaving you alone for two weeks when we go on our honeymoon," she continued. "After yesterday—"

"Oh come on. It's only the second time in three months it happened. I'll get a handle on it eventually. But I don't need him holding my hand for the rest of my life, either."

"I know. I trust you to make the decisions you need to. When we're here, we're your backup. I just hope you'll take care of yourself while we're gone. Promise me."

I exhaled. It wasn't exactly admitting defeat to say what she wanted to hear, but it felt like it. "Okay. I promise."

She patted my shoulder, her genuine concern and caring washing over me like a warm, pleasant breeze. "Thank you. And thanks for the chocolates. They're really decadent."

"You're welcome."

A cardinal scolded us from the silver maple next door. Brenda had something else on her mind. I can always pick up on her anxiety.

"You want to ask about Maggie, right?"

"I think she'd like to talk to you," she said.

"And you're playing go-between?"

"Sort of."

Brenda waited while I finished spreading the mulch, then offered a hand to pull me to my feet. "Ugh. How can you stand dirt under your fingernails?"

I shrugged. "I don't like gardening gloves. They get in the way."

"Then I hope your tetanus shot is up-to-date."

She was stalling.

I grabbed the empty plastic bags and headed for the garage. Brenda trotted along behind me. "Are you going to call her?"

"I don't know." I shoved the bags into the garbage tote and glanced at my watch: Seven-thirty. Maybe I'd call her. Maybe I wouldn't. "I'm going up to the apartment to empty more boxes. Want to help?"

Brenda frowned. "If I do, you won't call her."

She was probably right.

"Okay, I'll think about it."

She nodded. "Then I won't nag you anymore tonight."

"That mean tomorrow's fair game?"

She smiled. "Always."

I was beginning to really like what would be my new digs. It was actually double the size of my Manhattan apartment, and every time I entered the space I felt at peace. I knew I could live here and be happy, and yet . . . it wasn't quite home. The elusive piece of the puzzle was still missing. Maybe once I had all the furniture in place it would feel complete. Still, I wasn't in a hurry to move in.

The only things to sit on were the new stools at the breakfast bar. So far I hadn't needed any more. I plunked down and found my gaze traveling to the telephone. I'd been waiting months for the opportunity to call Maggie, but I hesitated. Timing could be everything, and I didn't want to rush into anything. Then again, if I made her wait too long, would she lose interest?

The trip to Ellicottville had piqued her curiosity about me. Maybe she thought experiencing someone else's emotions could be kinky.

Hmm. I hadn't considered that aspect of my so-called *gift*.

I shook the thought away. I'd begun moving some of the stuff from my room in the big house over; among them were Walt's shoeboxes and the envelope of his financial papers. I'd examined the box with the Holiday Valley brochure from every angle and done everything but wear the damn thing. The absurdity of that thought made me laugh. Then I figured what the hell, dropped the box on the floor and kicked off my grass-stained right sneaker. I stuck my foot in the empty box with no expectations. Instantly, the vision slammed into my consciousness with the greatest clarity yet. *Bare, red-painted toenails slipped into the sparkling shoe, guided by a man's rough hands. With exaggerated care he buckled the thin red strap around the ankle. The toes wiggled in what seemed like delight while the man's hands traveled up to caress the shapely calf.*

When I kicked the box off my foot, the vision winked out. I exhaled a breath and flexed my own toes. Would these dreamscapes eventually escalate into soft- or hard-core porn? That could be interesting, but I didn't really want to experience that aspect of Walt's personality.

And how did Walt's foot fetish relate to his death?

My hands were still shaking as I resumed my seat and put on

my shoe. The creep factor was back in full force. A beer would be just the thing to eradicate it. Too bad I hadn't put anything, let alone a six-pack, into the new fridge.

To distract myself, I spread Walt's financial papers across the breakfast bar, sorting through them to find the checking account statement. I'd glanced at the miniature replica checks before and hadn't noticed anything out of the ordinary. This time I studied them more carefully, wishing I knew in which of my unpacked boxes I'd find a magnifying glass. I went through all the checks and this time one did stand out: Amherst Self Storage.

Well, well, well. And just what could Walt be storing? Tom hadn't asked me to return Walt's keys, and I hadn't surrendered them. The problem was, how many storage units did this place have, and how would I find Walt's? Could I trust my insight to lead me to the right one?

There was only one way to find out.

The night air was cool for late June, and I shivered as I crossed the driveway for my car. I got in, started the engine and was backing out when I saw Richard silhouetted by the lamplight shining down on his side steps.

He jogged over as I braked, tapped on my window. "Where are you going?"

I rolled down the window. "Out."

"Where?"

Anger flared through me. "Why don't you jump in and find out."

Incredibly, he walked around to the passenger side and got in. I watched in awe as he fastened his seatbelt. "Go," he said and gestured with his hand.

I backed out of the driveway. "What's Brenda going to say when she finds you've gone?"

"Oh. Yeah." He maneuvered around the seatbelt, took out his cell phone and called her. "I'm going out with Jeff. Be back in an hour—" He looked at me.

I nodded.

"Yeah, an hour. Bye." He pocketed the phone and glared at me. "Where are we going?"

"Amherst Self Storage on Transit Road. Walt Kaplan rented a unit there."

"How do you know?"

"From the check statement you copped the other day. I looked the place up in the phone book."

"And what do you hope to find in there?"

"I'm just hoping to find it."

Richard rolled his eyes. "I should've told Brenda two hours."

I concentrated on my driving. "Oh ye of little faith." It would've been nice if I'd felt as confident as I sounded.

After that, the conversation ceased. I risked a couple of glances at Richard and he was just as studiously ignoring me. My earlier conversation with Brenda kept recycling through my mind. Finally, I couldn't stand the quiet. "Ya know, I was quite capable of taking care of myself before I came back to Buffalo. I still am."

"Yeah," Richard agreed, his voice full of scorn, "and Santa comes down my chimney on Christmas Eve. Want to sell me a bridge in Brooklyn, too?"

My hands tightened on the wheel. Choking the life out of him would only land me in jail for way too many years.

The gates of Amherst Self Storage were still open when I pulled in and parked. As we got out of the car, a string bean of a kid, no older than twenty, opened the door on what looked like a concrete pseudo guard tower. "We're closing in half an hour."

I waved him off and turned away. Richard followed.

The place was divided with inside and outside accommodations. The outside units had roll-up doors, but I got the feeling Walt had opted for something inside, with better climate control. I yanked open the plate glass commercial door and headed up the well-lit corridor.

"So?" Richard taunted, his voice echoing as he struggled to keep up with me.

"Okay—so I don't know where we're going. Just keep walking."

"Why I let myself get involved— " he grumbled.

I shot him a look over my shoulder. "Hey, I didn't ask you to come."

His glare intensified. "Do the words 'why don't you jump in' ring a bell?"

I kept walking, clasping Walt's keys in my hand, hoping they'd act as a divining rod to lead me to his storage unit. Funny thing is, they kind of did. The farther I walked along the corridor, the warmer they seemed to grow in my hand.

I slowed my pace and started paying attention to the unit numbers. I stopped before the one marked 4537; the same number on the mailbox in Holiday Valley. A coincidence? The mailbox had said—well, almost—Taggert. It had to have some connection with Cyn Lennox. Only now I wasn't sure if I trusted that piece of insight.

A brass padlock secured the aluminum hasp. I held the key ring in my left hand, sorting them until I came to the smallest one. I slipped it into the lock and it turned.

"Jesus, you amaze me," Richard murmured behind me.

I removed the lock, pulling the hasp open, then clasped the door handle, trying to pull it open. Something was jammed behind it. I yanked harder, but it still wouldn't give. "Dammit."

"Let me do it," Richard said, stepping forward, his condescending tone grating on my nerves.

I held him back. "You're just along for the ride, remember."

He looked like he wanted to haul off and hit me, but he did back off.

Grabbing the handle, I yanked it with all my might and the door jerked forward. A cascade of cardboard cartons came tumbling out. The next thing I knew, I'd hit the floor—pinned, the wind knocked out of me.

"Jeff!" Richard hollered, scrambling to extricate me.

I couldn't answer—there was no air in my lungs. I couldn't move at all.

Gasping and puffing, Richard pushed the heavy boxes off me and I rolled onto my side, knees drawn up to my chest, struggling just to breathe.

Richard was panting as hard as I was. "You okay?"

I nodded, but the truth was I didn't know. It felt like I'd broken a couple of ribs. Richard must've had the same thought. Next thing I knew, he had my shirt up and was palpating my chest, sending me into new spasms of agony.

"Doesn't feel like anything's out of place—but I'll bet it hurts."

"Eleven years of medical training and that's what you come up with?"

He yanked my shirt back down before collapsing next to me on the concrete floor, leaning against the opposite storage lockers. "Talk about the walking wounded. What a pair we make."

"Speak for yourself," I managed. "I don't think I'll ever get up again."

I caught sight of a security camera protruding from the ceiling nearby, but if the kid up front was monitoring the corridor, he hadn't raised an alarm or ventured out to help us. We sat there for a couple of minutes, trying to catch our breath before Richard helped me into a sitting position.

"You gonna be all right?" he asked.

78

"Yeah. Let's see what nearly killed me." I crawled over to the closest box. Walt had securely taped it. Using his keys, I worked at the tape until I'd slit it, and pulled open the carton.

Richard peered inside. "Porn?" he moaned.

Scores of copies of magazines with covers similar to the ones listed on the foot fetish Web sites were stacked in the box, none of them newer than five years old. Had he moved on from magazines to . . . something else? "That's why his apartment was so clean," I said. "He kept his collection here. I wonder if he had other storage units?"

"There's got to be more than just magazines. Open another box."

I did. More out-of-date magazines. I pushed it aside. A lighter box contained foot-fetish videos. Another box held old financial records. Nothing very interesting. I tried one last carton. "Hey, look at this." I pulled out a heavy, metal professional shoe sizer. Also inside the box were more of the generic shoeboxes like I'd found in Walt's apartment. Each also had an odd collection of paper and souvenirs. I checked them all but their contents weren't as remarkable as the one with the Veronica pillow. One had a hand-written receipt: Received: $237.54 for custom shoes, dated three years before. "Whoa, this is what I've been looking for."

Richard looked over the faded slip of paper. "How can it help? It doesn't tell you where he bought them."

But it was as though the paper was vibrating against the skin of my fingers. "I hope I get an inkling when I get home and pull out the phone book."

"Closing in five minutes," came a voice from a speaker embedded in the ceiling. I put the receipt in my wallet.

"How are we going to get all this crap back in the storage space in only five minutes?" Richard groused.

"We could take some of it with us."

"I don't want this stuff at my house."

"Just until I can dump it."

"You're not dumping it in my garbage."

If looks could kill and all that shit . . .

Between the two of us, we managed to wedge all but the carton of shoeboxes back inside the unit and slam the door just as the lights winked out. I replaced the padlock and struggled to lift the bulky box. Not that it was heavy, but every part of me hurt.

Out of breath again, we sounded like a couple of asthmatics as we started back down the corridor. Yellow safety lights kept us from groping our way to the exit.

String bean was waiting for us outside the door, keys in hand to lock up. "I warned you we were closing." He turned his back on us and we headed for the car.

Richard watched as I maneuvered the box into the back seat and slammed the door. He was pale, his skin looking eerily white under the lot's mercury vapor lamps, and we were both sweating in the cool night air. Richard groaned as he settled himself into the passenger seat. Gingerly, I climbed behind the steering wheel and chanced a look at myself in the rearview mirror; my own face was chalky. Walking wounded sounded about right.

"Wanna go somewhere for a drink or something?" I asked Richard, wincing as I buckled the seatbelt around me.

"Just take me home."

I started the engine. "You didn't *have* to come."

"If I hadn't, you'd've been suffocated by those boxes."

He was right about that, not that I'd give him satisfaction by agreeing.

"This is the second time in two days I've had to pull your ass out of the fire. What the hell are you going to do for two weeks when I'm gone?"

"Give me a break. I got along fine for eighteen years without you. You think I can't make it for fourteen days?"

"No, I don't."

The light ahead turned yellow and I jammed on the brakes. Only Richard's seatbelt kept him from sailing through the windshield.

He glared at me. "It doesn't make sense."

"It's called inertia. I put my foot on the brake—you keep going."

"No, that Walt had all this stuff in storage, but there wasn't a trace of it in his place."

"What do you mean?"

"Well, from what I remember from abnormal psych, people with fetishes like their trigger objects near them. That kind of personality just can't turn it off, either."

"You think someone cleaned out the apartment before we got there?"

"I'm betting it was your boss. You sure he really wants this thing solved?"

No. I wasn't.

The light changed and I pressed the accelerator. I hadn't thought to look in the Dumpster behind Walt's place when we'd been there days before.

The rest of the drive back to the house was a replay of the drive out—silent. But despite a little lingering animosity, we were at least speaking to one another again.

I parked in front of the garage. Richard got out and shuffled toward the house. "You coming?" he called over his shoulder.

"I'm going upstairs. Be over in a while."

I left the carton in the back seat, too pooped to deal with it, and trudged up the stairs to the apartment. Easing myself onto a stool, I stretched to grab my brand new telephone book. Big mistake, as it set off more twinges of misery along my ribs. I squeezed my eyes shut and counted to ten. This was already getting old.

There were six listings under SHOES—CUSTOM MADE. All but one of them were generic and boring; only Broadway Theatrics sounded flashy enough to have made the sparkling high-heeled beauty in my visions.

I punched in the phone number. It rang three times before a recorded male voice spoke: "You've reached Broadway Theatrics. We're open by appointment only. Leave a message at the sound of the tone and we'll get back to you." Beep!

No point in leaving one now. I hung up, noting the address before closing the phone book. Maybe I'd just drive over there tomorrow after my stint at the bar. The more I thought about it, the more I warmed to the idea.

The clock on the microwave read nine twenty-five and I wondered if it was too late to call Maggie.

Probably. And what was I going to say to her anyway? "Hi, you're hot and I want you as much as you want me."

Yeah, that would go over well.

Then I figured what the hell—I'd already risked death once tonight; nothing else could faze me—and grabbed the phone, punching in the number I'd memorized three months before.

It rang twice before Maggie picked up. "Hello?"

"It's Jeff."

"Oh." She sounded startled—or maybe disappointed.

"I can call back another time."

"No, now is fine. Uh, hi."

"Hi." Now what? *I'd* called *her.* Say something you idiot!

"Are you okay? You sound funny."

"I tangled with some boxes."

"Oh yeah. Brenda said you'd be unpacking tonight. Listen, did you find out who owned that property outside of Ellicott-ville?"

"I haven't had a chance to go back yet."

"Well, I have a cousin whose husband works for the Cattaraugus County Highway Department, and his sister works for the Ellicottville Town Clerk, and he—"

"Whoa—slow down. I can't keep track of all those people."

She laughed. "You don't have to. Bottom line—I found out who owns the house and where the tax bill is sent."

For a moment I was speechless. "Cynthia Lennox?"

"How did you know? Oh yeah," she said and laughed again, "I forgot. You're psychic."

"Never use the 'p' word in front of me," I chided her.

"Want the address?"

"Definitely." I jotted it down. Cyn lived somewhere in the northern part of Amherst. "How can I ever repay you for this?"

"That's not necessary. Although . . . maybe we could go out again sometime. Maybe another magical mystery tour."

My heart rate picked up. "I'd like that. A lot."

"Yeah, me too."

So ask her out already, ya dumb ass!

"Well, thanks for calling. Bye."

"Maggie, wait—" But the connection was already broken.

I hung up the phone.

That didn't exactly go as planned, but at least she wasn't pissed at me anymore. I glanced at the address I'd just written down. At least now I knew for certain that Cyn Lennox had a connection to Walt Kaplan.

Now to prove it.

8

It had taken twenty minutes under a hot shower to ease the aches that twisted my poor bruised body the next morning. It was after ten by the time I staggered into the kitchen, with no Richard or Brenda in sight. She'd left a note, however: "We're off to look at wedding corsages. See you for supper." Then she'd drawn a little heart and signed it with a B.

Corsages? Poor Richard. He wasn't even married and already he was pussy whipped.

I knocked back a couple of aspirins and hoped they'd take out the rest of the soreness. Primed with that and a couple of cups of coffee, I headed off to work.

Off to work. I liked the sound of that—especially after being unemployed for more than eight months. The Whole Nine Yards was beginning to feel as much like home as my new apartment. And after only six days I even knew a couple of the regulars by name. But I wasn't feeling optimistic as I entered the bar. It was time for Tom and me to discuss what I'd discovered about Walt's murder.

The place was empty except for Tom at the bar cutting fruit garnishes. He'd end up tossing more than half of it at the end of the day since beer was his biggest seller, but he liked to have it ready—just in case.

He looked up from the cutting board. "Hey, Jeff. What's new?"

I came around to the back side of the bar and tied an apron

around my waist. "Depends on the subject. For me, nothing. But I wanted to tell you what I've learned about Walt."

Tom straightened, ever so slightly, his jaw tightening. "So talk."

I took a fortifying breath before starting. "Tom, I don't think the cops arrested the right person."

Tom snorted a laugh and put the knife aside. "Come on, they found the murder weapon on him."

"That doesn't mean he used it. Where'd he get it? Witnesses say Buchanan was a Dumpster-diver. He might've found it anywhere. And what's his motivation for killing Walt?"

"Maybe it was a mugging."

"Walt was stabbed forty-six times. That says big-time anger. He had no defensive wounds. He might've been unconscious when it happened. It's also possible Walt knew his killer. Where would he have encountered Craig Buchanan?"

"Jeez, I don't know. Anywhere around town. Walt lived in the area."

"From what I gather, Buchanan never made it up as far as Eggert Road, and Walt didn't hang around Williamsville."

Tom frowned, his conviction faltering.

"What happened to Walt's settlement?"

He grunted. "Long gone. The lawyers got the biggest chunk and Walt blew the rest on a big red Caddy and a year of high living. After it was gone, he moved into that dump of an apartment. It was only monthly disability payments and the money he made here that kept him going."

"What happened to the Caddy?"

"He traded up every few years, although I don't know how he managed to pay for it."

"Do you have the car?"

Tom hesitated. "Uh, no."

"I didn't see it at his apartment. You might want to report it as missing."

"Aw, shit." He slapped the bar with his open palm. "Tell me Walt didn't keep the title in the glove box."

Tom's shoulders slumped. "I don't know, but I wouldn't be surprised."

I leaned back against the bar. "I doubt Walt's killer would be driving it—too conspicuous. It could've been dumped or maybe even sold, if only for junk value. That would make it harder to find, but not impossible. The cops can trace it with the VIN number."

"If we can find that."

"The DMV will have it. It's tied to the registration and title." I wondered how much more Tom could take. But I needed answers. The question was, would he give them.

"I found some stuff in Walt's apartment that led me to check out a vacation home in Ellicottville. Did he ever mention going there?"

Tom shook his head.

"It looks like the owner of that house also owns the property where Walt was found. Do you know a Cynthia Lennox?"

He shook his head, his expression hardening. "Did you tell the cops any of this?"

"I don't have enough evidence yet."

"What do you need to get it—and get this over with?"

"Time. And maybe a little luck."

"You will keep looking into this, won't you?" The words were right, but the conviction was missing. I couldn't dismiss my gut feeling that he knew much more than he'd shared with me.

"Of course," I answered. As Brenda said, I really didn't have a choice. I knew the flashes of insight would continue until I got to the bottom of this—case, situation—whatever it was.

"You didn't by any chance go through Walt's apartment before I got there, did you?"

His eyes flashed, his cheeks going pink. "What do you mean?"

"Just that it seemed awfully neat, considering the cops had already been there and all."

Tom shook his head, looked ten years older when he picked up the knife and finished his dissection of a lime. He didn't ask me any more questions and he obviously wasn't ready to hear what my next lines of inquiry would be.

At least not yet.

It was almost four-twenty when I pulled up to the little cinder-block building on Colvin Boulevard. Broadway Theatrics was a flashy name for such a dumpy locale. I almost didn't find the place because it was tucked behind a derelict gas station. A forlorn and battered blue Lumina sat near the entrance. No windows graced the front of the building, and its unattractive and peeling brown paint made it look like it had survived a war.

I got out of my car and wondered if I really wanted to venture inside. I pressed the grimy button of a doorbell and waited for thirty seconds before trying again. And again. I was about to give up when the door was wrenched open by a stooped man with long white hair, captured in a ponytail at the back of his neck. He couldn't have been more than fifty, but looked older because of his posture. His face hadn't seen a razor in at least a week. "You want something?" he growled.

"Women's shoes. Red stiletto heels. Lots of sparkles."

His eyes lit up, his spine straightening. He looked me over, shrugged, and held open the door. "Come on in."

Broadway Theatrics was a good name for what I found inside the shabby little building. Theatre props—a golden-haired angel in white with a ten-foot wingspan was suspended from the ceiling. Hand-carved marionettes, the expressions on their painted faces macabre and menacing, glared at me from pegs on the wall. Shelving units stood in parallel rows, neatly stacked with shoe and other boxes. Bolts of metallic purple and red fabrics rested on a makeshift service counter, its old-fashioned register painted a DayGlo shade of pink.

"The workroom's back here. Follow me," the proprietor said. I did.

The back room was even more magical than the first. Original drawings and paintings decorated the walls. Flashy costumes on hangers hung on racks, while shoes-in-progress littered a work-table.

The owner pulled an oblong box off a shelf and set it on the table. Lifting the lid, he pawed through the hundreds of photographs inside before selecting one. He tossed it to me. "Those the shoes you mean?"

I glanced down at the picture in my hand. The shoes were exactly the same as the one in my visions. "Yeah. How'd you know?"

He shrugged, a smile tugging his lips. "I have a sixth sense when it comes to shoes."

A shiver ran up my spine, and it wasn't from the air conditioning. "Do you remember who you made them for?"

"It's on the back."

I turned the photo over. A typed sticker listed the date, two years before, the price, and the customer: Andrea Foxworth. Damn. I'd been hoping it would say Cynthia Lennox. "You know this woman?" I asked.

"Sure, she's the wardrobe mistress for the Backstreet Players—a theatre group here in town. I made them for some show they were doing. Integral to the plot or something. I've actually made two pairs of them. Another customer came in a few months back and requested something similar. I showed him that picture and he asked me to make another pair."

"Do you have a photo of them?"

"I didn't bother, since I already had this one."

"You remember the other customer's name?"

"Sure. Walt Kaplan. He's a regular customer. Likes to give his lady friends mementos of their friendship. I must've made a couple pairs of shoes for him every year for almost a decade."

"Did you know he was murdered?"

"Walt? God, no. What happened?"

I explained.

The older guy looked genuinely upset. "I get so wrapped up here, sometimes I don't read the paper or watch TV for weeks at a time. Poor Walt."

"Did you know him well?"

"Just as a customer. He loved women's shoes—was very knowledgeable on the subject. Sometimes he'd bring me in a picture he'd seen in a magazine and want me to copy it. I told him he'd be better off buying knock-offs on the Internet, but he wanted original, hand-crafted shoes—and he was willing to pay for them."

I indicated the photo. "Were these the last shoes you made for Walt?"

He nodded. "He picked them up a couple of weeks ago."

"Do you remember exactly when?"

He thought about it, exhaled a breath. "First of the month maybe. He usually paid me after he got his disability checks."

I studied the picture. As an amateur photographer myself, I recognized a damned fine shot. This was professional quality work. "Can I borrow this?"

He shook his head. "It's my only record."

"Can I get a copy?"

"I wouldn't know where the negative is. I take digital shots nowadays."

I held the photo out. "You did this? It's great."

"Thanks."

"You got a scanner? I'll give you a five to copy it."

He laughed. "That I can do. I think I even have some photo paper around here somewhere."

Ten minutes later I left the shop with my copy of the picture and the address for where I'd find Andrea Foxworth. She might be another dead end, but there was no way to find out until I spoke to her.

Bottom line: I was making progress.

But I had another stop to make and would've risked a speeding ticket to get back to Williamsville if it weren't for all the damned red lights and stop signs at every friggin' intersection. Still, I pulled up to a vacant parking space near the mill at 5:04 p.m.

The mill officially closed at five, and I wondered how long it would take for the employees to leave. I kept watch on the building's front entrance as the minutes dragged by. So far I'd only seen Cyn and the counter guy, Gene. By process of elimination—and if there weren't any other employees—the only other employee should be Ted Hanson, the miller. And I hoped he wouldn't be accompanied by Cyn when he left—otherwise I'd have to try again on another day. That or follow him home. I didn't want to do that and be accused of stalking the guy, which I was sure Cyn would do.

The minutes ticked by and my car began to feel like a sauna. I couldn't decide what was worse, stake out duty in the winter or the summer. One constant—it was always a bore.

The counter man was the first to leave at 5:22. He paused just outside the main door, checking out the street, caught sight of me and charged ahead. Cyn must've warned him I might lay in wait for the miller.

He stopped only feet from my car. "What're you doing here?"

"Sitting in my car. What's it to you?"

"Cyn told me to watch out for a runty guy who'd try and harass us."

Runty? I was at least two inches taller than this jerk.

"You've been warned to stay away from the mill," he continued.

"I was warned not to trespass. I'm not on mill property."

"Yeah, well—well—"

Articulate, he wasn't.

"We'll just see about this." He did an about-face and headed back for the mill. Less than a minute later, Cyn Lennox came flying out of the building and down the stairs, reminding me of a charging rhino as she made a beeline for my car. I got out, ready to face her.

"What're you doing here?" she demanded, fists clenched, face pink with anger.

"I want to talk to Ted Hanson."

"This is harassment."

"For whom? I'm not on your property. You came to speak to me— I didn't seek you out."

She pursed her lips, looking ready to implode.

"But as long as you're here, I wouldn't mind asking you a few more questions. Like do you have a pair of red, sparkling stiletto high heels?"

Anger turned to shock as her mouth dropped open, and it could've been fear that shadowed her eyes. "Get out of here."

She turned and stalked back to the mill. Another man had joined Gene on the little front porch. I leaned against the driver's door of my car and watched as the three of them conferred for a couple of minutes. Cyn kept gesturing, her arms waving in anger while the newcomer tried to reason with her. Eventually she threw her hands up in the air and reentered the mill. The man descended the stairs and started toward me.

"You Ted Hanson?" I asked when he got within earshot.

"Yeah."

"Name's Jeff Resnick." I offered my hand. He ignored it,

which was just as well. I sensed a bubble of animosity sur-rounding him and wasn't eager to embrace it.

"Cyn says you want to talk to me."

"You found Walt Kaplan's body."

"Yeah, and I've already told the police everything I know."

"They didn't share it with me."

"What's your interest?"

"I work for Walt's cousin. He asked me to look into it."

"What are you, some kind of investigator?"

Not anymore, I could've told him. I lied. "Yeah."

Hanson looked skeptical. "You have a license?"

"I'm not a private investigator. Insurance."

"Oh." His hostility instantly backed off. As a businessman, he understood liability. "What do you want to know?"

"Just what you saw."

He shrugged. "I had an order of rye flour that was supposed to go out the next day and I came out to the porch to check how many sacks I had. At first I thought it was a bag of trash on the hillside. I looked again and saw it was a person."

"Did you think he was dead?"

"No. I figured he was a drunk or something. The Hawk's Nest," he jerked a thumb over his shoulder to the restaurant across the way, "has a bar. A couple of years ago someone fell down the hill beside the mill and broke his neck."

I glanced at the pile of rubble at the side of the road. "Why doesn't somebody put a fence around it?"

"They demolished an old building earlier this year. There was a construction fence. I don't know what happened to it. Kids probably tore it down."

"So you found Walt," I prompted.

He shuddered. "Yeah."

"The body was on its back, looking up at the sky," I said, describing what I'd already seen in a vision.

"Yeah. No blood that I could see, but he was this awful blue-white color."

"No blood on the clothes?"

Hanson shook his head. "Not that I saw."

"That's strange. The medical examiner said he was stabbed forty-six times."

"Really?" The news seemed to trouble Hanson. "He was wearing a dark red shirt, dark pants, and shoes. I suppose there might've been stains, but . . . not for that many wounds, and there was no blood around him on the ground. That would mean someone had to clean him up and dress him after they killed him."

"Yeah," I agreed. "Then somebody dumped him here. There had to be a reason they chose this place. Had you ever seen Walt around here?"

Hanson shook his head. "I'm not a part of the retail operation. Cyn and Gene deal with the customers on a one-to-one basis. They have a baker, Dana Watkins, but she's usually gone before I get here in the morning."

"You have a phone number for her?"

"No, and Cyn would just be pissed if I gave it to you anyway."

"I hear you, man." I relaxed against my car once again. "Cyn called you a miller, but I noticed most of the stuff in the warehouse has already been ground."

"That's my product. They use what I mill and I sell the rest to boutique bakeries throughout the northeast. The coffee shop is just the icing on the cake. The real money is and always has been the mill."

"That wasn't the impression I got from Cyn."

"She doesn't own the mill. It's been in my family for over a hundred years. If she tells people she owns the business—well, it's kind of true. The coffee shop is her baby—but she just leases space from me. Cyn's very good at what she does. She's only been in business here about six months and is already turning a profit. And she's helped me find new markets for my flour. She's hoping to sweet talk me into selling her the place, but that'll never happen."

"She's got money, then?"

"She and her late husband owned a chain of coffee shops in the Southwest. She sold them when he died and came back to Buffalo. I guess she's got family here, which is why she returned."

With a home in Amherst and a vacation home in Holiday Valley, yeah, that sounded like money. I'd have to check out the address Maggie had given me to get an idea of how much Cyn was worth.

And why would someone with that kind of dough be caught dead wearing a pair of sparkling red hooker shoes?

Hanson shot a look back at the mill. "She's probably having a fit because we've talked so long. Please don't come around anymore. There's nothing to see. The guy's dead and the cops have already made an arrest. It's over."

"Thanks for your time."

"No problem."

I offered him my hand, and this time he took it, and I tuned into him. He'd been straight with me. Now all he wanted was a beer, his recliner, and the Mets game on the tube.

Hanson headed back for the mill and I got in my car and turned the key in the ignition. The steering wheel was hot to the touch as I maneuvered onto the street and turned the corner for Main Street. Talking to Hanson had definitely been worth it. And I now had the name of the mill's baker. If she left before he got there, she had to start work before dawn. She probably opened the place, which meant I'd have to be out here first thing in the morning if I wanted to catch her.

The red light at the corner took forever. I glanced down at

the photo on my passenger seat. Was there any point in trying to chase down Andrea Foxworth this evening? Brenda was expecting me for supper, and I had the feeling I had better show up. But I also wasn't sure of the reception I was likely to receive.

Still, I steered for home. With every mile, uncertainty tightened my gut.

9

I arrived back home just after six to find Maggie's little car parked in my usual spot in the driveway. Curious. I pulled along beside it. The feeling of unease intensified as I entered the house through the back door and headed for the kitchen, where I found Richard, Brenda, and Maggie sitting at the table having a drink; wine for the ladies and Richard's usual scotch sat on a coaster in front of him.

"There you are," Brenda said with a decided maternal lilt. "I was beginning to think you'd fallen into a black hole."

"Hi," Maggie said and blinked, her eyelashes looking longer than I remembered. She looked pretty in a pink sleeveless sweater and matching slacks. Business casual never looked so good.

"I invited Maggie to stay for supper," Brenda said.

I chanced a glance at Richard, who raised his eyebrows and his glass in salute.

Set up!

I flashed a smile, wondering if it looked forced. "Boy, I could use a beer." I stepped across the kitchen to the fridge, pulled out a bottle of Labatts, cracked the cap and took a fortifying swig.

"Tough day?" Maggie asked.

"Long." I leaned against the counter, suddenly feeling very tired. "It's been a while since I worked, and I had some extracurricular stuff tacked on at the end."

"Oh?" Brenda asked.

"Yeah." I wasn't about to go into detail about where I'd been or who I'd talked to. Instead, I took another long pull on my beer.

Brenda and Maggie were on different frequencies, but the feelings they transmitted were pretty much the same: smothering.

I took a couple of deep breaths, which made my ribs scream in protest, worsening the tightness in my chest. Brenda wanted Maggie to take care of me—presumably while she and Richard were on their honeymoon—while Maggie's hunger for sexual release loomed like a dark gray cloud.

"Is it hot in here?" I asked and took another gulp of beer.

Richard swirled the ice in his glass. "Not that I noticed."

My breaths were coming short and fast, and the throbbing had already started behind my eyes. I had to get away from Brenda and Maggie before I went through a painful repeat of two days before.

"You grilling tonight?" I asked Richard.

"Yeah."

"Maybe we should get it going?" I hoped Maggie wouldn't detect the desperation in my voice.

Richard shot a look at Brenda. "Sure," she said, resigned, and rose from the table.

Maggie's lips pursed, but she said nothing as Brenda retrieved a plastic-wrapped plate of steaks from the fridge. She grabbed a long-handled fork from the counter and passed them to Richard. "Don't burn mine," she said, but her humor sounded strained.

"They'll be perfect." Richard retrieved his glass and made for the door. I gave Maggie a smile and a wave, but I was so close on Richard's heel I nearly stepped on him.

The screen door slammed on my back and Richard turned

on me. "What the hell is wrong with you?"

I was nearly hyperventilating and collapsed in a sit on the back steps with a jolt that reawakened all my other aches and pains. Hunched over, I set my beer down and covered my eyes, not sure if I was about to puke in the geraniums. "I thought I was gonna die in there."

Richard's pique instantly turned to concern. "What's wrong?"

I hauled in a few good breaths, my head still muddled, my stomach still threatening to erupt. "That kitchen was like a tornado of emotion. Between the two of them I felt like I was about to be squashed."

Richard studied me with his physician eyes—and yet there was puzzlement behind them as well. "I don't get it. I thought you liked Maggie."

"I do. But she wants . . ." Christ, she was practically vibrating with desire, not that I was going to tell him. "I'm not sure what she wants. And Brenda, she's definitely in matchmaker mode."

"Tell me about it."

I rubbed my eyes, grateful the anxiety was starting to ebb.

Richard juggled his glass and the plate of steaks, grasped my left arm under the bicep and pulled me to my feet. "Come on. Get past it."

Easy for him to say.

I shuffled after him back to the deck and the gas grill. He lit it and shifted the steaks onto the rack. He seemed preoccupied. I dropped down on the top step and held my beer between my hands, trying to absorb the chill into myself, accepting it as a balm for my ragged psyche.

"When are you going to tell me what's going on with you?" Richard said at last.

I squinted up at him. "What?"

"You're chasing around, talking to all sorts of people. Kaplan's death is connected to custom-made shoes, but you haven't told me even half of it. Why?"

I took another couple of breaths, stalling for time. Should I level with him—tell him how I was scared to death that the next time he helped me out I might get him killed—or lie with some cock-and-bull story, especially since I suspected his former girlfriend of murder?

"I haven't put enough of it together yet."

"Maybe I could help."

Yeah, and this time would someone come after him with a knife or a claw hammer or a 2001 Buick, and again I wouldn't see it coming or be able to protect him?

"I need to think about it some more."

Richard poked at the steaks with the fork. "I'm praying you wrap this up before we head for Europe, or that I can talk you out of pursuing it. Brenda will be heartbroken if we have to cancel our flight."

"What are you talking about?"

"I can't leave you here to figure this out alone. If I hadn't pushed you out of the way back in March—" He stopped himself.

He was talking about the gunshot that nearly killed him. "Don't go there, Rich. It was my fault you got hurt. If I hadn't gotten you involved—"

"So this time you want to go it alone—no backup—and get killed."

Pain seared through my head as I flashed again on the dripping, bloody hands. "That isn't going to happen."

"You dig too deep and whoever killed Walt Kaplan is going to come after you."

"It won't go that far. I won't let it."

"Yeah, like you have any control over other people and how they react." He snatched up his glass, slopped scotch on the deck. "Why don't you just let the police handle it?"

"Because they arrested the wrong person."

"Just because you have some kind of insight doesn't mean you have all the answers."

"I never claimed to. Look, why are you so angry?"

"Because, goddamnit, I don't want to lose you." He forked a steak with unnecessary force and flipped it. It sizzled as it hit the grill. "The thing is, you like all this intrigue. You revel in it."

"I do not. Tom asked me to look into Walt's death. The insight kicked in and now I'm trapped. It'll keep happening—"

"Until it stops," he finished.

"Yeah."

He turned the steaks again. They weren't ever going to cook at this rate. "Will you be able to eat dinner?" It sounded like an accusation.

"No. I can't be around those women with what they're feeling."

"Maggie will be disappointed."

"For months she wouldn't give me the time of day. Now suddenly I'm a hot commodity."

Richard eyed me, his anger dissolving as his mustache quirked upward. "In more ways than one, apparently."

I glared at him, but that jibe was what was needed to soothe his ire.

"Please ask Brenda to back off. I can't take being double-teamed. If anything's going to happen between Maggie and me, it has to develop naturally."

He nodded, poking at the steaks once more. "Sure you can't make an effort to sit through dinner?"

I closed my eyes to assess how I felt: marginal. "No. Will you make my apologies?"

"Yeah. You going up to the apartment for a while?"

"No. Think I'll hit the rack." I had somewhere to be in the

middle of the night, and I wanted to feel, if not rested, at least better than marginal.

I wrapped my arms tighter around my chest and winced. Thirty-two hours down and my ribs still hurt, and though I was cold, at way-too-much a gallon I didn't want to waste gas by running the engine for the heater. Besides, cold I stayed awake; warm, I'd probably fall asleep. I hadn't wanted to miss Dana Watkins, so I'd been parked a short distance from the mill since three a.m., cursing myself for not stopping for coffee first. And why hadn't I worn a heavier jacket?

Headlights broke the darkness and a car pulled up in front of the mill's front door. Seconds later, a figure exited the car. I yanked open my car door and made to follow. "Dana Watkins?"

The person at the door turned. A flashlight's beam caught me straight in the eyes. "Hey." I held an arm up to block the light.

"I've got a gun," the woman warned, "and I'm not afraid to use it."

I tried to peek around my fingers. "I hope you've got a permit."

"A permit?"

"Yeah. I wouldn't want to be shot illegally."

The light dipped. "Are you that Resnick guy?" She sounded annoyed.

"Would you rather I be a robber?"

No answer.

"Look, I only want to ask you a few questions."

"Cyn told me not to talk to you."

"It's a free country—you can talk to anybody you want." I still couldn't see behind the ice white light.

"Let's see some ID, buddy."

I reached behind me.

"Ah-ah-ah!" she warned.

"It's in my pocket." I turned my back to her and slowly retrieved my wallet, took out my driver's license, and handed it to her.

She scrutinized the photo and winced. "Oh! Bad hair day."

"I wasn't at my best," I admitted. My head had been partially shaved at the hospital after I was mugged. The picture was taken three weeks later.

She kept looking at the photo and back at me. "Well, I guess it looks a little like you." She handed it back and I put it away.

"Come on in," she said and turned for the door.

I had to blink until I could make out her silhouette on the little porch. I stumbled up the stairs. She had keys, not a gun, in her other hand, and used the flashlight to find the keyhole. "Cyn said you'd probably ambush me when I left work. I wasn't expecting anyone to be here now."

"I didn't want to run into Cyn. She doesn't seem to like me."

Dana reached inside and flipped a light switch. "And why should I?"

"I'm a nice person." She stepped inside, and rounded on me. "Once you get to know me."

"Uh-huh."

I shrugged. She did an about face and crossed the overly bright café and made for the espresso machine. Maybe I'd get offered a cup. "Gotta get this thing going first thing," she said. "That way it builds a good head of steam so I can have one before I leave."

That would be hours away. Scratch one free espresso.

She breezed through white swinging doors and flicked on the lights. I followed her into the kitchen where she tossed her purse on a counter to the left. Her next stop was the professional coffeemaker on the back wall. "Want some?"

"You bet. This is a bit earlier than I usually get up."

She dumped beans into a grinder before retrieving water from the triple sink's faucet, and filled the reservoir. With the coffee brewing, she fired up the ovens before heading for the industrial sized fridge, where she extracted trays of what looked like bread dough, croissants, and cinnamon rolls. Next she scrubbed her hands like a surgeon before donning gloves to work with the food. She worked with such efficiency that I was mesmerized.

"You've been here almost five minutes and haven't asked one question. You a bakery spy or something, trying to steal my pastry secrets?"

I laughed. "Sorry. I don't even like the stuff, but it's fascinating to watch." I cleared my throat. "I assume you never saw the dead guy."

She shook her head. "Only after Ted called the police. I suppose he was there when I came in early that morning." She shuddered. "But like I told the cops, I didn't see anything or anybody. No familiar cars—no strange ones either. Coffee's ready. Pour me a large black and get whatever you want out of the fridge. Sugar's on the counter if you need it."

"Would Cyn approve?"

"Course not. Why do you think I invited you in?"

A smile creased my lips. I might just get some good gossip out of Dana.

I poured the steaming coffee and doctored mine before setting hers on the counter beside her. She grabbed it with flour-dusted fingers and took a huge gulp. I wondered about the state of her esophagus as I sipped mine more carefully.

"I take it you and Cyn don't get along all that well."

"That's not true," she said, spreading apple filling over the bottom of a dough-filled pan. "We just don't see eye to eye on certain aspects of the business. Like her staying out of my kitchen. She hired me to bake, but she thinks she's got to have her sticky fingers in everything."

"So delegation isn't her specialty?"

"Control freak might be a more accurate term. My first day here I churned out half a dozen strudels, three dozen scones, two dozen cinnamon buns, and a couple dozen doughnuts. Since then she's expected that on a daily basis—and then some. Don't get me started about the biscotti fiasco back in March."

I smiled as she obviously wanted me to. "Ted Hanson said Cyn's already making a profit on the café."

Dana shook her head. "Nah, it's the outside orders that put us in the black. But people first try our pastries as customers in the café, then make special orders. We're a little too successful for a three-person operation. I've been trying to get Cyn to hire me help, but she's resisting. Gene helps out now in the afternoons. He's the one who got all this dough ready for me. He comes in around eight and gets the café set up, too. Restocking bags, taking phone orders, and polishing the display cases. We should be paying someone for that, too."

"How does Cyn get so much work out of Gene?"

"He's her nephew. I think she promised him a percentage of the profits. He works too hard for just a straight salary."

So, nepotism was alive and well at the Old Red Mill. "His name Taggert?"

"No, Higgins. I think he's her younger sister's kid."

"You and Cyn aren't related, are you?"

Dana looked up from her work, her eyes ablaze. "Hell no!"

"The two of you ever socialize?"

"Cyn rub elbows with the hired help? Please." She gulped more coffee.

"So you wouldn't know if she ever lets her hair down."

"Cyn? I can't imagine. Then again, I sometimes think she's a frustrated actress."

"How so?"

Dana folded the dough over the filling, sealed the ends and cut steam holes, then went to work on another. "Those costumes she wears. She's been a cowgirl for weeks now. I guess she wore that stuff out West, but it looks kind of silly here in Williamsville, don't you think?"

"Oh, I dunno. They do call this the Niagara Frontier."

Dana laughed, from deep down in her belly. "No wonder Cyn hates you. You've got a sense of humor."

I'd rarely been accused of that. "What other kinds of costumes does she wear?"

"Accessories mostly. Shawls, lots of rhinestones, big earrings. And she usually manages to carry it off."

"Think she'd ever stoop to red-sequined stiletto heels?"

Dana looked thoughtful. "Maybe." Then she giggled.

"What?"

"I'm trying to imagine her in heels, pasties and a G-string. *That* would be too funny."

Dana finished with the strudel, popped them in the oven, and began working on the cinnamon buns.

"Tell me more about Gene," I said.

"I get the feeling he's the son Cyn never had. He worked for her in Santa Fe, too."

"Did he want to come back east?"

She shrugged. "I guess. He's here. I really don't know much about him. Our conversations usually revolve around orders and supplies. He seems nice enough. Very protective of Cyn."

I remembered him scoping out the street the afternoon before. "So I noticed. What do you know about Cyn's place up in Holiday Valley?"

Dana frowned. "I didn't know she had one. She never talks to me about personal stuff—like, 'How was your weekend, Dana?' It's more, 'Can you come in early tomorrow to fill the Henderson order?'" This last she whined.

"Why do you stay?"

Dana laughed. "Because I love it. I love the work; I love the place—and I don't mind working with Gene. I only have to put up with Cyn for half an hour every day before I'm outta here. If I get some help, I could be happy working here for years." She smiled at me and I hoped I gave her one of equal wattage. But as I looked around the spotless kitchen, the racks of product and the shining equipment, I knew the place would soon be closed and Dana would be baking elsewhere.

That at least cheered me. Dana would go on, find work somewhere else and be happy doing it.

The future didn't look so bright for Cyn and Gene. I only wished my insight gave me more hints as to what that would be.

I made it home before six a.m. Brenda and Richard were still in bed and I figured there was no reason to even let them know I'd been out. I crashed for a few more hours sleep and found my way back to the kitchen and the aroma of fresh-brewed coffee at a little after ten.

No one was in sight, but a flower arrangement bright with pink carnations and white daisies sat on the kitchen table. I stopped cold. Had I missed Brenda's birthday? No—that was in the fall. A glance at the wall calendar told me nothing had been penciled in on this day. So was there an occasion I wasn't aware of, or had the flowers arrived from one of Brenda's cross-country friends in advance of the wedding? Maybe the corsage florist they'd visited days before was desperate for business and . . .

I abandoned the thought, grabbed a mug from the cabinet and poured myself some coffee. Footsteps echoed in the hall—too heavy for Brenda—and Richard entered the kitchen.

"Finally up, I see."

I blew on my coffee to cool it. "I gotta be at the bar by eleven."

He nodded and parked his ass against the counter. "Your car got moved since last evening."

Gee, and I thought he wouldn't notice. "Uh, yeah."

Richard crossed his arms over his chest, waiting.

"I got up way too early. Figured I'd go out for a cup of coffee."

"We didn't run out."

"Uh, yeah. But I guess I felt kind of restless."

"Uh-huh."

"Yeah." I sipped my coffee and then changed the subject, hoisting my cup toward the flowers on the table. "Pretty. They make Brenda happy?"

"Well, they might've—if they'd been for her. It's your name on the card."

I almost spewed my coffee. "My name?"

Richard nodded toward the vase. "Check it out."

I crossed the kitchen in four steps, set my mug down on the table with a thunk, and tore open the envelope.

Sorry to overwhelm you last night. Let's try again . . . this time on your timetable. Maggie.

I blew out a long breath.

"From anyone we know?" Richard asked with mock innocence.

"Yeah." I handed him the card. He scrutinized it before passing it back.

"No one's ever sent *me* flowers."

"It's a first for me, too."

"What're you going to do about it?"

"I don't know. Say 'thank you' like my Mama done taught me. Then, I don't know."

"You do like her."

I thought about Maggie's all-too-elusive smile. "Yeah, I do."

"Then what's the problem?"

107

Should I tell him that in thirty-five years no one had ever pursued me? That "overwhelmed" was more than an apt description of how I now felt? Sure, I'd been married. I'd had sex with a bunch of women. But sharing what I felt had never entered the equation before. That Maggie could read me, too, was more than a little terrifying. I wasn't sure I could deal with it.

Richard still waited for an answer.

"Fear of failure," I bluffed.

He nodded, then shook his head in what seemed like amusement. "You and Brenda are so much alike."

"What?"

"You're so afraid to just trust what's offered to you."

Man, he just didn't know—couldn't understand—what it was Maggie was after, what I was afraid to give.

I grabbed my coffee mug, walked over to the sink and dumped the contents, then put the mug into the dishwasher. "I gotta go to work." I looked over at my brother, found his expression smug. "See ya."

"See ya," he echoed, and I scuttled out the door.

10

I was getting used to the routine at the bar, picking up the ins and outs of Tom's business and even enjoying being around people again. The regulars weren't used to a bartender with loads of personality, so I filled Walt's absence with surprising ease. And I was learning to better shield myself from the onslaught of others' emotions.

Almost. It was still a drain being bombarded with sensations, but I found distance was a good buffer. If someone at one end of the bar was depressed, I took to hanging around the other. Mundane tasks like washing glasses also helped keep me from absorbing others' emotional baggage.

It was after two when I looked up from polishing the brass taps to see a familiar face studying me from the last stool on the end: my ex-schoolmate, Sam Nielsen. I hadn't changed much over the years, but Sam's head of once-thick dark hair was long gone, and I didn't think I'd ever get used to seeing his chrome dome.

I walked down to the end of the bar. "What can I get you?"

"Beer."

"Any preference?"

"Canadian."

"Draft or bottle?"

"Bottle."

I grabbed him a Molson and a clean glass, set it in front of him.

"You got time to talk?" he asked.

A couple of guys were nursing beers at a table in front, watching the tube. Tom held court at the other end of the bar with one of his cronies. Nobody seemed in dire need of my services. "Sure. How'd you find me?"

"Hey, I *am* an investigative reporter." He poured half the beer into his glass. "I called your brother. You got anything to tell me about Kaplan's murder?"

"Shut up," I whispered, and jerked a thumb toward Tom. "The owner was his cousin."

Sam glanced down at Tom, then shrugged. "Sorry. You got anything?"

"Questions. I understand the body was cleaned up and redressed after death."

"Yeah. Sloppy job, too. I saw the police photos. Shirt buttons were mismatched, no underwear—no socks, and the pants were zipped, but not buttoned."

"And no bloodstains on anything."

"Surprisingly little, plus the usual bodily secretions. Contrary to what you see on TV, it's way too soon for a lab report."

That, I knew. "You got my message about Buchanan's clothes. Any blood on them?"

"No. I asked my contact at the Amherst PD about it and he wasn't interested in pursuing it, either. He figures Buchanan and Kaplan weren't clothed when the murder happened. Either that or Buchanan ditched the clothes he'd been wearing at the time of the murder."

"He only had one set."

"You can't prove it."

"Why'd he re-dress Kaplan?"

"Maybe some kind of ritual?"

"That's bullshit."

"That's politics. They've arrested someone. They don't want

to see their case go down the tubes." Sam sipped his beer. He accepted the situation. I couldn't.

He eyed me. "I gave you everything I had. Time to return the favor."

My spine stiffened. "I'm still putting the pieces together."

"That's what you said two days ago. Come on, give."

I looked down the bar at Tom. I hadn't even confided to him all that I knew—or suspected. But I'd have to toss Sam a bone, if only to keep him feeding me what he knew. I leaned closer, lowered my voice. "I keep seeing a custom-made woman's shoe."

Sam waited for more. When I said nothing, he frowned. "That's it?"

"I've tracked down the maker. He made two pairs, one for Kaplan, another for someone else. Got a line on who ordered the originals. I'm going to look into that later today."

His frown turned to disgust. "Talk about bullshit. What the hell's that got to do with his murder?"

A quick glance down the bar showed me Tom had heard Sam. "Pipe down, willya?"

Sam poured the rest of his beer, took a gulp. "You think whoever wore those shoes killed Kaplan?"

"Maybe. But those two pairs of shoes are tied in somehow."

Sam's gaze bore into mine. A grin slowly curled his lips. "You've got a suspect."

I straightened, looked away.

"Come on, spill it, Jeff."

I shook my head. "Not until I have more than a suspicion."

"Who is she?"

I folded my arms across my chest and leaned against the backbar.

Sam picked up his glass and drank, never taking his eyes off me.

"Jeff?" Tom pointed to the two guys at the table out front.

I headed back for the taps, poured another two beers and delivered them to the customers. By the time I got back to the bar, Sam had finished his drink. "Am I going to have to hunt you down again for my next update?"

"I'll call you when I know something."

His expression said, "Yeah, right," and he stood, reaching for his wallet.

I put out a hand to stop him. "It's on me."

He nodded and headed for the exit. At the door he turned, pointing a finger at me. "Call me."

I'd call. But not until I was certain. And right then I still had a lot more questions than answers.

I hate to admit when I'm wrong, but Richard may have been right about my not being ready to return to work. I was dead on my feet by the time my shift ended at four p.m. And yet, Sam's visit had reignited my curiosity about what had happened to the first pair of red-sequined heels.

I found the home of the Backstreet Players, an old grocery store reconfigured with a stage, near the edge of Buffalo's theatre district, but had to park a block away at a ramp garage. The elevator was broken, so I had to hoof it down three flights of stairs. The humidity was high with ninety-degree temps. I wasn't looking forward to duplicating my footsteps on the way back.

Though I'd called Andrea Foxworth beforehand, she hadn't warned me I'd find the box office dark and all the entrances around the building locked. Someone finally heard me banging on one of the doors at the back of the building, and opened it. "I'm looking for Andrea Foxworth."

A burly guy in jeans and a grubby white T-shirt looked me over. "She expecting you?"

"Yeah."

He shrugged. "Okay." And let me in.

So much for security.

The dim backstage area, plastered with "No Smoking" signs, was full of people. In contrast with outside, the air felt dry and chilled. Voices yelled across one another as stocky men wheeled scenery around the stage and banks of lighting were adjusted overhead. Grubby pointed toward a set of stairs going down. "She should be down there—in wardrobe."

"Thanks."

The temperature dropped another couple of degrees as I descended the stairs into the bowels of the building. A double door marked "Wardrobe" stood ajar and I sidled inside to find several women poised over commercial sewing machines. Dressmakers' dummies stood in full regalia—uniforms and period dresses. The marquee had said "HMS Pinafore." An older, harried-looking woman with gray-streaked brown hair, shouted into a cell phone. A baggy, full-front apron, not unlike what Sophie always wore, covered her street clothes, while an unlit cigarette dangled from her lips.

"You were supposed to deliver them by five o'clock today. It is now," she glanced at a wall clock, "four-thirty-seven and I expect to see those wigs here within the next twenty-three minutes or I will haunt you in this life and into the next!" She pulled the phone from her ear, stabbed a finger on the off button, then looked up to glare at me. "Who are you and what are you doing down here? Security!" she bellowed toward the door.

"Andrea Foxworth? I'm Jeff Resnick. I called a couple of hours ago."

She exhaled a couple of exasperated breaths, yanked the full-size cigarette from her lips and tucked it behind her ear. "Sorry. I forgot you were coming." She turned her back on me and marched over to one of the women sewing. "Those alterations going to be finished any time soon?"

"Chill out, Andrea," the woman said without looking up from her work. "We'll get everything done."

Andrea whirled, and for a moment I thought she might explode—at me. "I don't have a lot of time. We're doing a dress rehearsal tonight and I have a million things to accomplish before then."

"Just five minutes. Please."

She reached up, rubbed the cigarette with her thumb and forefinger, then sniffed them. "I just quit and I'm a little strung out. We'll have to talk while I work."

Second time in one day.

I followed her to a lumpy-looking, faded upholstered chair where she plunked down, snatched up a dress from a table beside it, and started ripping the seams apart.

I figured I'd better talk fast. "I understand you ordered a pair of custom shoes from Broadway Theatrics about two years ago."

"Dear boy, I order lots of custom shoes from Broadway Theatrics."

"I have a picture." I pulled the photo from my shirt's breast pocket, noting the goose bumps dotting my arm as I handed her the picture.

She gazed at it for a second and the smile that appeared took five years off her face. "Ah, the tramp shoes."

"The what?"

"That's what the actress who wore them called them. Said she felt like a fifty-dollar hooker in them."

"Do you know what happened to them?"

"Sure. They were auctioned off with a lot of other costumes and props at our big fundraiser back in the winter. It was in all the papers."

"Damn. That probably means you have no idea who bought them."

"You got that, although the auction company gave me a list

of the buyers and the final lots. That way next year I can pair up the items that sold best and inform our target market. I can't let you look at it, though. It lists addresses and I'm not giving out that kind of information to just anyone who walks in off the street."

"I don't blame you. But if I gave you a name could you confirm this person participated in the auction?"

She thought about it for a few moments. "Mmm . . . I don't think so. It just wouldn't be right."

I looked around to make sure none of the other ladies was paying attention to me. "Are you sure I can't change your mind?" I showed her the edge of a twenty-dollar bill I'd put in my pocket—just in case.

Andrea hesitated, leaned to her left to look around me. "Well, I guess that would be okay. I mean, if you already know the person. But what if the name isn't on the list?"

"I'd still expect to compensate you for your trouble," I whispered.

With a lot more poise than she'd shown just moments before, Andrea set aside the garment, got up from her chair and crossed the room to a file cabinet. She pulled out a ledger, thumbing through it until she came to a particular page. "Who are you looking for?"

"Cynthia Lennox, of Amherst."

Andrea flipped ahead and ran her finger down the list. "Lot ninety-six: red tramp shoes, vampy dress, feather boa, and jaunty hat. Paid two hundred and thirty-five bucks for it." She closed the book and held out her hand. "Very nice meeting you, Mr. Resnick."

Palming the bill, I shook her hand. "Likewise."

I escorted myself back up to the stage area, which felt positively balmy after the icebox below, and aimed for the first door with an exit sign above it. The bright sunshine nearly seared my retinas after the backstage gloom, but this time I welcomed the heat as I squinted my way back to the garage.

So, Cyn Lennox had purchased the original pair of shoes. But what did that have to do with the pair Walt ordered? How had he seen them? Perhaps in the closet of her vacation home in Holiday Valley? Or had he replaced shoes that she'd ruined? I hadn't thought to ask the shoemaker if the shoes had been the same size. Would he even remember, as he hadn't bothered to document the second pair of shoes?

And how did all this relate to Walt Kaplan's murder?

I needed something more—some other piece of the puzzle before I'd be able to put everything together. I needed to grill Sam for additional information, and I needed a picture of Cyn to show around the bar. Maybe one of The Whole Nine Yards' customers would recognize her. It didn't seem likely, and yet I had a feeling a picture was exactly what I needed to move forward in my investigation.

"Don't call it an investigation," I could almost hear Richard rant.

Yeah, and I also needed his camera, computer and printer to do the deed. And I had to take a halfway decent picture of Cyn without her knowledge.

Oh yeah—this was going to be so easy.

Not!

First things first, I told myself. Get the camera; worry about the rest later.

Already sweating, I reached the ramp garage, following a man and woman in office attire, briefcases in hand, their suit jackets draped over their arms. Good looking and cheerful after a hard day's work, they looked like they just stepped out of a Lord and Taylor ad. The three of us entered the stairwell.

Damn broken elevators. Damn stinking muggy weather. A vein in my temple throbbed by the time I made it to the second level, where the woman peeled off with a wave to her colleague. The guy picked up his pace, leaving me shaking with fatigue by the time I trudged up the last few steps.

My car was at the end of the aisle, a million miles away. The guy had already unlocked his car, had ditched the briefcase and was setting his folded jacket over top of the passenger seat as I plodded past.

The roar of an engine reverberated off the concrete and a motorcycle rounded the corner, going far too fast. I froze, like a deer in headlights, as the bike rushed toward me.

"Look out!" the office worker shouted.

The rider's black faceplate reflected the dull glow of the overhead fluorescent lamps.

A jerk at my neck pulled me off balance. I landed on my ass, rolling into the wheel well of a car, my nose scraping rubber.

"Are you okay? What an asshole!"

I'm not the asshole, I felt like shouting, then realized he'd meant the biker, not me.

He helped me to my feet, steadied me. "You okay?" he asked again.

"Yeah." I dusted off my jeans, realized he must've grabbed me by the back of the shirt—pulled me to safety. "Thanks, man."

He studied my face, was probably about my age, and looked as shook up as I felt. "You need help getting to your car or something?"

It was adrenaline that had me shaking now. "I'm fine. Thanks again."

I felt his gaze on my back as I headed for my car. Okay, was the biker just some idiot having fun, or had I pissed someone off?

I preferred to think the former, but I suspected the latter.

★ ★ ★ ★ ★

Brenda was setting the table as I entered the kitchen. She turned to give me an ambivalent stare. "Are you actually going to grace us with your presence tonight?"

I glanced at the table. "Well, there are three plates, so I sort of thought I might. And I might even eat something, too." I crossed to the fridge and took out a beer and cracked the cap.

Driving for twenty minutes in my air-conditioned car had had a calming effect on me. I had no intention of mentioning my little adventure.

I took a tentative sniff of the aroma permeating the kitchen. "Roast chicken—on a Wednesday?"

"Is there a better day?"

"When I was a kid, roast chicken was reserved for Thanksgiving and Christmas."

Brenda straightened the tablecloth. "My mother made it every Sunday—winter, spring, summer and fall. But this came from the Deli Department at Wegmans."

I leaned against the counter and took a long pull of my beer.

Brenda scrutinized my face. "You look tired. You're not pushing yourself too hard, are you?"

If she only knew. "Isn't that what I need to do to find my limits?"

She seemed preoccupied as she turned away to fold the paper napkins into miniature bishop's miters, setting them on the plates; a nice touch. Then again, Brenda always managed to add simple joys to everyday life.

"You okay?" I asked.

"Sure. It's Richard who's bummed. He's making himself crazy over you."

"Me?"

"He's bored. Right now, you're his only diversion. If something's going on with you, couldn't you share it with him?"

Her voice was nonchalant and she didn't bother to look at me. Meanwhile, all my muscles tightened.

I'd been over my little adventure again and again in the last half hour. What had I actually seen in the seconds from the time the bike turned the corner to me landing on the concrete floor? A black motorcycle—manufacturer unknown; a biker clad in black leather and a black helmet. I hadn't even thought to report it. I couldn't give a better description and I'd bet the guy who also witnessed it couldn't either. I might just be paranoid.

I might.

I tilted my bottle back for another swallow. "Nothing's going on with me."

Brenda eyed me for a long moment. "If you say so."

She knew how to challenge me, but I wasn't going to bite— not this time. And yet I felt an unreasonable anger toward my closest of kin. Okay, I was a member of Richard's household, but I still deserved my privacy. I'd lost a lot since the mugging; my health, at least half my possessions, and a hell of a lot of my dignity. I didn't feel the need to consult with him on everything I did or experienced. Especially with what I'd recently experienced.

I didn't need to hear "I told you so."

Footsteps foretold Richard's arrival. He paused at the doorway. It didn't take a psychic to feel the tension in that kitchen. "Supper almost ready?" he asked Brenda, like I'd turned into the invisible man.

"Almost."

He crossed to the cabinet next to me, withdrew the Famous Grouse bottle, then grabbed a whiskey glass. "Ice."

"It's in the freezer," I said.

"Yes." He half-filled the glass with ice, then poured his scotch. He leaned against the counter, his elbow brushing mine, and sipped his drink. "Tough day at the salt mine?"

"Just peachy."

He nodded.

I knew what he was up to, invading my personal space, but I wasn't going to be the first to move. I fixed my gaze on nothing, tipped my beer back and took another swig.

Brenda shook her head and charged forward, pushing us away from the sink. "I need to get the vegetables going—so outta my way."

We retreated to our regular seats facing one another at the table.

Richard stared at me.

I stared back.

"I need to borrow your camera."

"What for?"

"To take a picture."

"Of what?"

"Possibly a suspect."

"Who?"

"I don't want to talk about that right now."

"Why not? Think Brenda or I will go blabbing about it to someone?"

"No, I don't. I just . . . don't want to talk about it. Can I borrow your camera or not?"

Richard took another sip of his drink and shrugged. "I guess. When?"

"Tomorrow."

"Fine."

"Thanks."

Brenda whirled. "Will you two just stop it! I'm sick of it. You're behaving like a couple of spoiled brats."

Richard turned his gaze to me, all wide-eyed innocence. "You know what she's talking about?"

I shook my head. "Nope."

"Neither do I."

Fists clenched at her side, Brenda exhaled a breath, her irritation palpable. "Men!"

11

There are distinct pleasures to being filthy rich—which Richard most certainly was. His top-of-the-line Nikon could probably be found at any newspaper around the country, and it was just what I needed to get candids of Cyn on her way into work. The problem was finding an inconspicuous place to take them from.

I spent an enjoyable evening reading the entire manual and playing with the camera. Not that I hadn't fooled with it before. Photography had long been a hobby of mine, and I still planned to set up a black-and-white darkroom in my new apartment. I loved digital, but there was something about good old-fashioned silver halide that kept me hankering for my old single lens reflex.

By the time I turned out the light, I felt comfortable using the camera. Richard and I hadn't sniped at one another while we went over the downloading procedure on his computer, either. Even Brenda's ire had cooled when I presented her with a minutes-old shot of her most-charming smile.

Dana, the mill's baker, had said Cyn usually strolled in around nine. I wasn't going to take a chance of missing her, so at eight-thirty I'd already parked my car two blocks away on Main Street and hoofed it down the side street to case out a hiding place.

The sun was already blazing and I was grateful to duck into the shadow of a Dumpster near the Hawk's Nest restaurant. Sweat beaded along my temples as I considered Cyn's reasons for legal action should she see me: harassment, stalking. If she was friendly with the restaurant's owner she might even get me picked up for trespassing. And who was I going to show the photo to anyway? The whole idea was beginning to seem absurd when Cyn's black Mercedes with New Mexico plates parked across the way.

I really was out of practice doing this kind of work. My hands were shaking and I had to steady the camera against the Dumpster to take the shots. Bing, bing, bing. She never suspected a thing. I waited for her to get inside the mill before I dared move out of the shadows. Still, I couldn't wait to see the pictures and punched them up. They looked pretty good on the camera's tiny screen. Only an enlargement would tell me how good.

"Hey!" A skinny, T-shirt-and-jeans-clad kid stood on the deck at the back of the restaurant, unlit cigarette in his hand, staring down at me. "What the fuck you doin' down there?"

Shielding the camera, I took off, jogging west, away from the mill and the guy's heated shouts. Cold sweat poured off me as I circled round to the front of the building, easing into a brisk walk—not looking left or right—until I got to my car. I jumped in and burned rubber hightailing it out of there.

The bar didn't open for another two hours, so I had plenty of time to go home and download the shots, but reconsidered. I wasn't yet ready to let Richard know my suspicions about his former friend and instead made for a professional photo shop.

Two of the shots weren't up to my usual standard, but then Cyn wasn't nearly as photogenic as Brenda—or maybe it was just because I didn't like her that the thought occurred to me. The third picture was good enough to show around.

I could've gone home, returned Richard's camera and still had plenty of time to get back to the bar before opening. Instead, I purged the camera of the morning's pictures, packed it in the trunk, and headed straight for work.

I wasn't ready to face Richard's inevitable questions.

Tom was already at the bar when I got there, nearly forty-five minutes early. "Don't you ever sleep?" I asked as I tied an apron around my waist.

"Ya never sleep when you run a business like this," he said, looking over his reading glasses from behind the desk in his office.

I withdrew Cyn's photo from the envelope I'd brought in with me. "You ever see this woman before?"

Tom studied the picture, shook his head.

"She didn't show up at Walt's funeral?"

Tom looked annoyed. "There were five of us there. I think I would've noticed."

I took the picture back. "It's the woman I told you about—Cynthia Lennox."

He studied my face. "You think she had something to do with Walt's death?"

"I don't know. I know he was in her place of business sometime before he died. I just don't know why."

Tom's eyes narrowed. "Where'd you learn that?"

I turned away, unwilling to look him in the eye. "Around."

The Molson truck had made its weekly stop and another thirty cases of beer awaited me. Loading the cooler had to be the worst part of the job. I hauled out the dolly and loaded it with beer. Before I had a chance to move it, though, Tom emerged from his office and headed into the men's room with a squirt bottle of Lysol and a roll of paper towels. It was then I decided I'd rather load the cooler.

Our first customer showed up at 11:02. Construction hadn't been kind to the orange-shirted worker with a heavily lined face, a halo of salt-and-pepper hair and a five o'clock shadow, who took the stool closest to the taps. He rested his arms on the bar, looking up at the blank TV.

"It's too damned quiet in here," he bellowed across the dead-silent room. I found the remote, switched on the set and cranked up the sound two clicks.

"What'll you have?"

The older guy stared up at me. "Who the hell are you?"

I turned from the beer taps to face him. He had to be on the high end of fifty. His voice sounded like gravel—the cigarette pack folded into the upturned sleeve of his T-shirt gave away the reason for that. He didn't seem angry, more . . . depressed. I cut him some slack.

"Name's Jeff. Tom hired me last week. What can I get you?"

He hunkered down on the barstool. "A Molson and a shot."

I poured him the beer and gave him a shot of well whiskey. He lifted the shot glass in salute. "To poor Walt. He didn't deserve to go like that."

I watched him down it in a single gulp, then slam the glass onto the bar top. I reached under the bar to grab a bowl of pretzels, plunked them in front of the old guy to grease the wheels of conversation. "I never met Walt. What was he like?"

"A good guy." He nodded, staring off into space, sadness making his mouth droop.

I forced myself to be patient.

The man took a nip of his beer, set it down and stared into its foamy head. "We worked together for over twenty years with Belfry Construction before he got hurt." He shook his head. "Damn shame."

I waited for him to continue.

"Cable snapped on one of the cranes. Crushed him under a slab of concrete." The old guy shuddered and took another gulp of beer. "Never really was the same after that. Hell, who would be?"

"Yeah," I agreed lamely, and thought of the mugging that had forever changed me.

"Walt didn't have a lotta friends, ya know. Not real ones.

Maybe just me." Then he laughed. "And a course his fancy women." He laughed again, a greasy, smarmy kind of giggle.

"Sorry?"

The old guy leaned closer, lowered his voice. "He liked to buy 'em pretty things. God knows why. They didn't do anything for him, if you know what I mean."

"No, I—"

"Can I get some service?" came a voice from the other end of the bar. I looked away from the old geezer. An overweight man whose sour expression conveyed his outlook on life sat at the far barstool. He punched the bar with a clenched fist. "Gimme a Bud light."

"Excuse me," I told the geezer and poured sourpuss his beer. He gave me a five and I rang up the sale, handing him the change, which he promptly pocketed. By the time I turned back, the old geezer had gone. A five and two ones sat under his glass.

Damn. I hadn't even had a chance to show him Cyn's picture, let alone ask him about Veronica.

Fancy women. That accounted for the sequined shoe. And that Walt got nothing in return from these women bore out my theory that he might've visited strip clubs. Still, it didn't feel right.

I picked up the geezer's glass, hoping he'd left behind some of his aura. No such luck. Like Richard, he didn't leave a trace I could tap into, and I had a feeling he wouldn't return to the bar now that his friend was gone.

But where the hell would I find Walt's fancy women? There was only one person I could ask.

Sourpuss was on his second beer and a couple of the regulars had arrived by the time Tom emerged from his office. Neither of us had done the fruit garnishes and he took a lemon and a lime from the little fridge under the bar and started cutting.

Time to risk it all. I sidled closer. "Tom, what do you know about Walt's fancy women?"

Tom's head snapped up, his mouth dropped open, his eyes wide. He grabbed me by the arm, dragged me out of sourpuss's earshot. "Who the hell told you about that?" He licked his lips nervously and glanced over my shoulder, giving the regulars a once-over.

"Tom, you had to know once you asked me to look into Walt's death that I'd discover his secrets."

"Nobody knew about that stuff. *Nobody.*"

"An old work buddy of his did—he was in a little while ago and mentioned it. So who were these women? Strippers?"

"Not exactly. He only told me about it once. I didn't want to hear, so he never mentioned it again."

"Hear what?"

Tom ducked his head, whispered: "Drag queens."

This time it was my mouth that dropped open. How had my insight missed that little nugget?

"After his accident, Walt couldn't—he wasn't able to . . ." Tom sighed, groping for an explanation. "He couldn't do 'it' anymore. And I'm not sure he really missed it. He was never what you'd call a ladies' man. I think he was afraid of them. But he liked sexy stuff. And he told me he thought the drag queens were more . . . I dunno, more feminine than the kinds of women he was used to meeting. On the weekends he'd go to some place downtown—around Pearl Street. Just to watch, he said. But that can't have anything to do with his death."

"Tom, it could have *everything* to do with his death," I said, thinking about the damned red-sequined high heel and the evil little pillow emblazoned "Veronica."

Tom shook his head, definitely in denial.

"There's more," I said. "Walt rented a storage unit on Transit Road. I checked it out the other night and it's full of porn— specifically, foot-fetish stuff."

Tom's head sagged. He looked like he wanted to puke. "I don't want you digging into this anymore, Jeff. Please, just drop it."

"I can't. The cops arrested the wrong person for his murder."

"So? What's that to you?"

"It means an innocent man will probably go to jail for the rest of his life."

"The guy's crazy. He's a career criminal. He's—"

"That still leaves the person who killed Walt running around loose, and free to kill again. Do you want that on your conscience? Because I sure don't."

Tom sighed, guilt and despair twisting his features. "No, I guess I don't either. But if this stuff about Walt becomes public, it'll kill my aunt. Damn it, Jeff, she's eighty-seven. I don't want her to know how low her son sank."

"It's bound to come out. But she doesn't have to know you were ever involved."

He held out his hands. "I'm not. I'm out of this as of right now."

Exactly what I'd expected. Now to voice my bigger fear. "You want me out of here, too?"

Tom let out a shuddering breath. "If I thought it would keep you from poking around in this whole mess, I'd shitcan you right now." He wiped a trembling hand over his mouth. "You're a damn good bartender, much better than Walt was, and the guys seem to like you. But don't talk about Walt to the customers. Not now—not ever. In this bar, Walt's memory is respected. You got that?"

"Got it."

Tom nailed me with a glare. "Okay. But let's not talk about this anymore. No matter what you find out."

I didn't answer because I couldn't promise I wouldn't need more information from him later.

"You girls about done with your chitchat?" I looked over my shoulder at sourpuss who held up his almost-empty glass.

Tom turned away. I straightened, hardened my features, and faced the jerk. "That was a Bud light, right?"

"Damn straight."

Sourpuss picked up the glass, raised it in salute, tipped it back and took a big gulp.

And may you never lose someone you care about to murder, I wished him. Because whatever else I'd find out about Walt Kaplan, I had a feeling the worst was yet to come. Tom didn't hate me now; how would he feel when whatever else there was to discover came to light?

12

Upon my return to Buffalo, I hadn't been in any shape to investigate the local nightlife, so I knew nothing about it and even less about its drag clubs. The phone book was the first stop in my quest for knowledge. Nothing under bars. Taverns took up an entire page, and nightclubs a mere five inches of type. None of them had display ads. So much for the phone book. Next stop, the Internet.

Since arriving home, I'd successfully avoided Richard, and even found his computer unoccupied. I slipped into the big leather chair in his study and powered up the machine. I needed my own PC, but that wouldn't happen until I got my finances back under control. My palms were damp as I logged onto the Internet, fighting the urge to keep looking over my shoulder for Big Brother.

A Google search later, I had a list of URLs for Buffalo gay bars and drag shows. I clicked on the first one: Club Monticello. White type on a black background gave way to color pictures of the featured acts. Queen Camilla, Libby Lips, Tammy Ten Toes—that sounded like a possibility for Walt—and a trio billed as the Divine Divas. No Veronica.

I clicked on one of the pictures and a bio and several other professional photographs appeared. Tammy Ten Toes, a buxom pseudo-wench, wore a silver lamé cat suit, one hip thrust forward toward the camera, with her best foot forward—encased in a glittering silver platform heel, her silver-painted toenails sparkling.

Walt had been titillated by this kind of stuff; I wasn't. Instead, my thoughts wandered back to Maggie, and the fact that it had been a long time since I got laid.

"Now what are you up to?"

I jerked in the chair—my heart racing. Richard appeared behind me, looking surly.

"Do I have to ask your permission every time I want to look something up online?"

"No," he said, but his expression said otherwise.

It was taking all my self-control to hold onto my temper. "Thank you." I turned back to the monitor and clicked on the "Home" button, then on "Show Times." The image changed, the club's schedule filling the screen. Club Monticello was billed as the "Biggest, Best Gay Bar in Buffalo," but the drag shows were listed only for Friday, Saturday and Sunday evenings.

Richard leaned in close enough that I could feel his breath on the back of my neck. "First foot fetishes, now drag shows? What's next, kiddy porn?"

Slowly, I swiveled the chair around to face him. "I'm going to pretend you didn't say that."

He backed off a step. "You know what I mean."

I kept my mouth shut, afraid of saying something I might always regret. I turned back to the monitor, shut down the connection and turned off the computer. Pushing back the chair, I got up and headed for the door. Richard moved to block me.

"I got a call from Cyn Lennox this afternoon. A worker at the Hawk's Nest saw you taking photos of her. What the hell is going on? Don't tell me *she's* your suspect."

"Fine. I won't." I moved to push past him but he blocked me again.

"You can't be serious. She didn't even know Walt Kaplan."

"She tell you that?"

He had no answer.

"Walt was in her office just days before he died."

"How do you know?"

"How do you think?"

Richard gritted his teeth in annoyance. "You got that the day we visited her?"

I nodded.

"Why didn't you say something then?"

"What for, and get you angry—like you are now? No one wants to hear an old friend might be a murderer."

" 'Might be,' " he repeated. "Does that mean you're not sure?"

"You're damn right I'm not sure. And I don't like going around telling my suspicions to people when I don't have the facts to back them up."

That mollified him, but only for a moment. "She said she'd file charges if you show up again."

"I don't need to go back there anymore. I have what I need to keep going."

"Her picture?"

I nodded.

He shook his head. "I'm asking you, Jeff, please drop this."

"Why, because your friend's got something to hide and doesn't want the truth to come out? Even if she didn't do it, she knows something about Walt's death and isn't telling."

"Then what is it you think you know besides Kaplan was in her office?"

I clamped my lips together and looked away.

"Could it be you haven't got anything *but* a hunch?"

"I've got more. Lots more."

"Then why don't you share it with the cops?"

"I told you, I'm not ready yet."

"Then why don't you tell me?" He waited for an answer. "No, you don't want to talk to me, either. You've hardly said a word to me in days. What's going on?"

The frustration in his voice only cranked up my feelings of guilt. Yet I refused to meet his gaze.

"I thought you counted me as not only your brother, but your friend. Lately you're cutting me out. Why? It can't be just because of Cyn."

The fatigue I'd been denying for days finally caught up with me, and I knew I wasn't in any shape for a battle. "I don't mean to, it's just that—" I shut my eyes and exhaled, wishing I could be somewhere—anywhere—else. When I opened them again, Richard was still staring at me, disappointment shadowing his eyes.

"Look, Rich, you don't approve of what I do, be it getting a job or looking into Walt Kaplan's death, or even how I'm handling this situation with Maggie Brennan. I can't do a damn thing right in your eyes."

"Don't give me that shit. If you can't be honest with me, at least be honest with yourself."

His words stung, but he was right. I wasn't telling the truth. I wasn't capable of telling him what I really felt. I trusted Richard more than anyone else on this Earth and still I couldn't level with him.

Richard was the first to look away. He crossed the room to the dry bar across the way and poured himself a neat scotch. I stood in the doorway, unable to move.

He took a sip and didn't look back. "Go on, take off. It's what you do best."

My memory flashed back to the day, eighteen years before, when he'd driven me to the airport. Without his knowledge, I'd enlisted in the Army. When, bags packed and needing a ride, I finally told him, two hours before my flight, he'd been hurt and angry. Really, really angry. By the time we stood together in the airport's departure lounge, he'd come to reluctant acceptance.

"Thanks for . . ." After nearly four unhappy years in the Alpert residence, I wasn't sure what. "Everything," I'd mumbled.

I'd been shocked when he'd grabbed me in a fierce hug. "I love you, kid," he'd managed to croak in my ear.

I didn't hug him back. I'd been embarrassed beyond words.

When he let go, I'd clutched my carry-on and bolted for the Jetway. Yet at the last second, I'd turned back to see tears in his eyes. Guilt made me give him a perfunctory wave before I charged ahead to escape what had become for me a very painful exit.

I didn't see Richard again for six years, and even then hadn't been able to let go of the bitterness.

Richard's back was still to me. He raised his glass to drink again and, true to form, I fled for the safety of my room, feeling just as stupid and unworthy as I had all those years ago.

I rang the buzzer and waited. Except for the dim light within, the bakery was dark . . . as usual. Then, a bulky silhouette blotted out a portion of light.

Sophie ambled forward and unlocked the heavy plate glass door, her face creased with worry. "You don't look happy."

"I'm not."

She ushered me inside, closed and locked the door. "So come in and tell all."

I shuffled along behind her. "Nothing much to tell."

We sat down at the wobbly card table. Tonight, oblivious of the outside temperature, she had hot chocolate steaming in mugs with hairline cracks crazing them.

"It's this murder, isn't it?" she asked. I nodded. "Things aren't going fast enough for you, eh?"

I took a sip of my cocoa and shrugged. "The police arrested

the wrong man."

"What else?"

Again I shrugged. "You ever connect with someone who knew what you were thinking, feeling?"

"Your Maggie?"

"She's not exactly mine. But she says she can feel what I feel. I guess she's never done that with anyone else."

"Mmm."

"That a yes or a no?"

Sophie tilted her head to one side, considering. "I wish I could say yes. Sometimes these gifts we have isolate us from others. We both know how frightening it can be to know things we'd rather not know. Is Maggie afraid?"

"She's freaked. So am I."

Sophie leaned back in her chair, folded her hands over her ample stomach. "This murder—Maggie—that's not really why you came here tonight."

I met her gaze. "I guess not."

"Tell me."

She was right. I had come there to talk about something else, only now I wasn't sure I could.

She reached across the little table and patted my hand. "Guilt is a terrible thing to live with. I know about it firsthand."

I stared down at the circle of tiny bubbles rimming my cocoa.

"When Richard got shot, I actually prayed to God, 'Don't let him die.' I thought that would be enough. I thought everything would be all right if he made it and was okay. But I can't get away from the fact it's my fault he almost died, and makes me one helluva shit as a brother."

Sophie frowned. "That's not true. You love him and you need each other. And who's filling your head with this nonsense, anyway?"

Maggie. Myself. "Nobody important."

"Then why do you listen?" she scolded. "Does your brother blame you?"

"No. He worries about me like, like—" I laughed. "An old yenta."

Sophie reared back as though offended. "I'm not a yenta, but I do worry about you. I worry about all my," she hesitated, "friends."

I couldn't help but smile. "And you're not old, either."

"Oh, you lie so well." She grinned and reached across to pat my hand again. Then her smile faded and it was her turn to inspect the depths of her mug. "Your brother has reason to worry. Like what happened to you yesterday."

My head jerked up. Sophie's expression was reproachful.

"You think that was deliberate?" I didn't have to clarify what I meant. She already knew what had happened to me in the ramp garage.

"You need to be careful. More careful than you've been."

"That only proves me right. Getting Richard involved would only endanger him."

"You *need* him. And maybe somebody else will need him, too."

"What do you mean?"

"Drink your cocoa," she ordered, and took a sip of her own.

"What is it you aren't telling me?"

"I don't know the whys of everything, either. I just know." She leaned closer. "There's a reason you two were brought back together after so many years. It's best not to tempt fate by staying apart."

I sipped my hot chocolate, its warmth spreading through me, making me sweat. Sophie's logic didn't make a whole helluva lot of sense to me, but in only the short time I'd known her I'd learned to trust her advice. Still . . . "What if something happens to Rich again and it's my fault?"

"Didn't you tell me he pushed you out of the way of that bullet?"

My hands tightened around my mug. "Yes, but—"

"Then how was it your fault?"

"Because the killer came after me."

"Would you rather be dead?"

Sometimes—like right then—I wasn't sure about the answer to that question.

"I don't want anyone's death—particularly Richard's—on my conscience."

Sophie scowled, sat back in her chair and exhaled through her nose. "Didn't you hear what I told you just now?"

"Yeah —and didn't you hear what I told you?"

Sophie grabbed her mug of cocoa, chugged it, and smacked it down on the table. She pushed back her chair and stood. "Time for you to go."

I stayed put.

"Come on, I need my beauty sleep," she said and grasped my arm, pulling me up.

Her abrupt dismissal annoyed me, but I wasn't going to be obstinate about it. Then again, she probably thought I *was* being obstinate.

I followed her to the front of the shop. "Am I going to be welcome next time I come?"

Sophie stopped abruptly and I nearly fell over her. She stared up at me, looking at once puzzled and distressed. "Why wouldn't you be welcome?"

"Oh, I dunno—the fact you're kicking me out right now."

"I told you. I need my beauty sleep." She grasped my shoulders, pulled me down and gave my cheek a wet kiss. "Next time I'll make *placek*. You'll feel better about things by then."

"Okay."

She patted my back before leading me to the door. I passed

through it and she locked it behind me. I crossed the parking lot and paused, turned back to wave but Sophie had already retreated.

You won't solve this without him, she'd said.

I could take that two ways, I thought as I made my way to the corner to cross at the light. Either I just gave up and let the visions of a red stiletto high heel torture me for the rest of my life, or I caved in and put my brother's life at risk by letting him help me solve Walt Kaplan's murder.

I wasn't sure which was the worse form of purgatory.

Sleep didn't want to come to me. Tired as I was, there were too many thoughts, too many scenarios swirling around in my brain. In the early days of my marriage to Shelley, I'd often lie awake in the middle of the night. Sometimes during the torment of sleeplessness Shelley would wake and we'd make love. Those way-too-early couplings were the sweetest memories of our time together. We were in sync back then. Somehow she always seemed to sense when I needed her most, and she'd be there for me. That was, of course, before cocaine became her lover of choice.

I rolled over onto my side and tried to blank out my thoughts, but an image of Maggie flashed across my mind's eye. She seemed to want me, and God knows I'd wanted her from the first time I'd met her. And yet . . . I didn't want our first time together to be cheap or tawdry.

I closed my eyes and once again saw her sitting at Richard's kitchen table days before, her lashes long and the hunger in her eyes reaching out for me. I couldn't handle it then, but right about now . . .

A myriad of sensations swept through me and I allowed myself to enjoy them, letting it build inside me until—

My eyes snapped open, every muscle in my body tensing as I

made a grab for the bedside phone. "Maggie?"

"Jeff?" She sounded startled. "It didn't even ring."

I exhaled and rolled onto my back. "I didn't want it to wake Richard and Brenda."

"You knew it was me?"

"Yeah."

She was quiet for a few moments. "I was lying awake and had this irresistible urge to call you. I didn't even think that I might wake Brenda and Richard. Oh, God, what if you hadn't picked up? I would've looked like such an idiot."

"But I did pick up."

"Yes." Her voice relaxed, and I could envision her smile. "You did."

"I meant to thank you for the flowers. They were very pretty."

"I hope they didn't make you feel uncomfortable. Brenda said you liked flowers. She showed me your garden. You've done a beautiful job."

"Thanks."

I closed my eyes, concentrated until I could hear Maggie's soft breaths against the receiver. I was content to lie there and just listen, but eventually she broke the quiet.

"How long are we going to wait?"

I wanted to laugh. In my own mind, we'd already—"Are you in a hurry?"

"I . . . might be. It's been a long time since I even wanted— Since I . . ." Her words trailed off.

I remembered what she'd told me months before. A husband who'd preferred men to Maggie, and had been too chickenshit to admit it to her until they'd been married eight years. She knew my tale of marital woe, too. I thought we'd get together back then, but the timing hadn't been right.

"What are you doing tomorrow?" I asked.

"Working."

"All day?"

"What did you have in mind?"

A stupid grin creased my lips. "You ever hear of afternoon delight?"

She hesitated. "Your place or mine?"

"I haven't got a place . . . yet."

"Then mine it is."

"I get out of work at four."

"I could get out a bit early. Do you know where I live?"

"No, but I bet I could find you."

"I bet you could." Still, she gave me the address. I didn't bother to write it down. I wasn't likely to forget it.

"Then I guess I'll see you tomorrow."

"Tomorrow it is."

Long seconds turned into a minute, then two before Maggie finally hung up the phone.

Minutes later I drifted off to sleep, and dreamed of Maggie Brennan.

13

My second Friday at the bar was pretty much a repeat of the week before, except this time the customers had accepted Walt's departure from this world and the talk was back to sports.

I'm not the world's biggest sports nut. I can hold my own in conversations about basketball and football, but baseball and golf leave me yawning. I didn't want to dwell on my upcoming evening with Maggie, either, so I had a lot of time to think about Walt's death and what I did and didn't know about it.

If I hadn't been working, I might've accomplished more with my half-assed investigation. Like taking a look at Cyn Lennox's home, not that it would tell me anything more about her. I realized I knew virtually nothing about little workaholic Eugene Higgins other than he was Cyn's nephew. And how was I going to find out anything about him? I could tail him after we both got out of work, but I wasn't sure I had the stamina that a stakeout would require.

It bugged me that Walt hadn't fought against his attacker. Could he have been unconscious at the time? The newspaper reports hadn't mentioned any kind of head injury. Had he been drugged or even drunk? How long would it take for the crime lab to come back with a blood and tissue workup? They'd already closed the books on Walt's murder and weren't likely to prosecute Buchanan for months, so what was the hurry anyway—at least from the cops' or prosecutor's perspective?

Walt had been re-dressed and dumped behind the mill. If

Cyn had been involved in his death, it would be pure stupidity to dump the body behind her place of work, and Cyn didn't strike me as brainless. And yet, the flash of insight I'd had of Walt in her office was really the only evidence I had against her—pretty insubstantial at best. The two pairs of shoes were somehow connected . . . but how? It couldn't have been a coincidence that Cyn owned the shoes Walt had copied. For one thing, I didn't believe in coincidences despite the fact Cyn's vacation home's address and the storage locker number had been the same.

I could go back to Walt's apartment and soak myself in whatever was left of him, but I didn't think that would yield any results, either.

A dull pounding in my skull told me I needed to take a break from this train of thought—especially if I wanted to be in any shape to socialize later in the day. But suddenly something else occurred to me. That flash of insight I'd experienced in Cyn's office hadn't been from Walt's perspective. Someone had been looking at him, had experienced seeing Walt's smile of pleasure. I tried to refocus on the image but it wouldn't come. I'd been so obnoxious that there was no way Cyn was ever going to let me back in to soak up any leftover vibes, and I could kick myself for not thinking of it when I'd gone back to the mill to talk to Dana Watkins.

Had I been picking up on Cyn? Would she be attracted to an introverted loner who could no longer perform sexually? Or had she and Walt been casual acquaintances who shared a love of women's footwear?

Maybe if I could touch Cyn, I'd know, but that wasn't going to happen, either.

"Give it up!"

Startled by this piece of advice, I glanced up to see one of the customers shaking his fist at the TV.

"God, what a bunch of losers," he groused.

Give it up. Yeah, I ought to, at least for the day. The prospect of an evening with Maggie was far more appealing than beating myself over the head with circuitous arguments and half-baked theories.

I wanted to do something nice for Maggie, something she wouldn't expect. Flowers or candy seemed too clichéd. Something unexpected—but something that showed her a facet of my personality she might not have considered. A glance around the bar didn't fill me with creative ideas. Then again . . .

At four fifty-three, I pulled into the driveway of Maggie's rather average looking duplex in Clarence. She stood behind the screen door in a white tank top, pink shorts, and flip-flops, waiting for me. No sexy dress, no heels—looking the antithesis of tawdry.

"You're here," she said with pleasure.

"I am."

"Come in." Maggie opened the screen door and immediately a dog planted its nose in my crotch. "Holly!" Maggie admonished and pulled her golden retriever back by its collar. "I'm sorry. Dogs like to—"

"I know," I cut her off, and offered the dog my hand as an alternative. She sniffed my fingers and I must've passed muster for she licked them enthusiastically.

Maggie eyed the brown grocery bag in my other hand. "You didn't have to bring anything."

"It's not much. Just an icebreaker. That is, if you've got ice. I need to borrow your fridge, or maybe freezer, too."

"Sure. Come on into the kitchen."

I followed her up the stairs to the second floor apartment. If I was unimpressed with the outside of her home, the inside changed my mind. Contemporary leather furniture stressed comfort. Signed lithographs lined the walls—the ambiance peaceful and laid-back with a southwestern flair. For an absurd moment I wondered if I should introduce her to Cyn.

Maggie led me into the cozy kitchen with its butter yellow walls and frosted-glass-fronted cabinets. She leaned against the white Formica counter. "It's all yours," she said with a sweep of her hand.

I set the grocery sack on the counter. "So, what do you like to drink?"

"I'm strictly a gin-and-tonic kind of girl. At least when it's hot out. Winters, I revert to whiskey sours."

I thought as much. "It's the taste of juniper that attracts you in summer."

She shrugged. "I guess."

"Then let me make you a surprise. But first I've got to wash my hands. Dog saliva and a good drink don't go together." Maggie laughed and pointed toward the sink.

She watched as I withdrew a bottle of Beefeaters gin, a pint of Perry's French Vanilla ice cream, and a liter of club soda from the grocery bag. "I need ice, a tall glass, a shot glass and an ice cream scoop."

Maggie gave me what I needed before hauling out the remains of what was once a five-pound bag of ice. She radiated pure delight as I added ice, measured the gin, plopped in a scoop of ice cream, and topped it with club soda. I gave it a quick stir before pushing the fizzing glass toward her.

Maggie's expression was enigmatic as she picked up the glass and took a tentative sip. Then her eyes widened and a smile lit up her face. "Wow, you are a good bartender."

I wish I could've taken credit for the drink. "It's called a silver stallion."

"Tastes like magic." She took another sip. "Is this your way of lowering my inhibitions?"

"Do I really need to?"

She looked away, blushing. "I guess not. Are you having one?"

"I'll take a beer, if you've got one."

She crossed to the fridge and came up with a bottle of Labatt Blue. "Want a glass?"

"It's not necessary." I cracked the cap and held it out for a toast. *"Na Zdrowie!"*

Maggie's glass touched the bottle. "Cheers."

We watched each other drink, then Maggie said, "Let's go sit down."

She put the ice cream and ice in the freezer before leading me back to the living room. Her second-floor apartment was as hot as Hades, but a fan pointed at the couch recirculated the air. We sank into the sofa's depths, and Holly stood before Maggie, looking expectant.

"You had your dinner," Maggie said, but Holly didn't seem interested in our drinks. She maneuvered herself between the coffee table and us, sitting down so that her warm body pressed against my right leg. I petted her head and she turned her dark brown eyes on me. I didn't know dogs could smile.

Maggie set her drink down. "Holly, it's too hot for that. Go lie down." The dog obediently got up, trotted across the room to a plaid cushion and settled herself on it, perching her head on her crossed front legs, letting out a loud, doggy sigh.

I wiped my sweating beer bottle against my equally damp forehead. "Hot in here."

"You, or the air?" Maggie asked, her eyes glinting.

"Both."

She picked up her drink again, sipped it, not meeting my gaze. "My bedroom is air-conditioned."

I raised an eyebrow. "Do tell."

She flashed a glance my way. "I'm not usually this forward. It's just—"

I set my beer down, clasped her moist palm. A current passed between us. Her gasp was more surprise than pleasure—that came a few seconds later.

"Oh wow," she muttered, her breaths coming fast and shallow. Mine had picked up, too. We looked at one another for a moment, then I pulled her to me, kissed her. She returned it with equal vigor, the hunger I'd sensed days before building inside her.

"First kiss," she whispered, eyes wide with growing anticipation.

Despite the heat, a delightful shiver of longing ran through her—through me. Dizziness and desire whirled through me—a rush like I'd never known. She leaned in to kiss me again. "It's more comfortable in the bedroom," she breathed.

"I'm all for comfort."

She pulled me up from the couch, led me toward the back of the apartment. As she reached for the door handle, I stopped. She looked up at me, puzzled. I drew her close, nuzzled my nose against her ear. "Don't tell Brenda everything," I whispered. "Let's save this for just us."

She kissed me again and opened the door.

I didn't go home that night.

14

I sat at Maggie's kitchen table, the newspaper spread before me, nursing my second cup of coffee when her phone rang the next morning. "You wanna get that?" she called from the other room.

I pushed away from the table, grabbed the kitchen extension. "Maggie's house."

"Jeff?" It was Sam.

"How the hell did you find me this time?"

"I asked—"

"Yeah, yeah, my brother."

"Maggie's house, huh? Sounds like you got lucky. How'd you like to bat a thousand?"

"How so?"

"I'm going to interview a contact this morning. Thought you might want to tag along."

"What's in it for you if I do?"

"I dunno. Maybe you could play human lie detector for me. Tell me if this guy's hosing me."

"You don't trust your own instincts?"

"Of course I do, but I figure it can't hurt for you to tag along. You might get something he doesn't want to share with me—if you know what I mean."

"Just who are we going to talk to?" I asked.

"A cop wannabe. Jailer in the county lockup. He called and asked if someone wanted the inside scoop on Craig Buchanan. I told him I'd meet him since I can't get to Buchanan. You know they won't let a reporter talk to a suspect until after a trial. Think we might sway the pool of jurors."

"I did know that. But shouldn't Buchanan have been transferred to the county psych unit by now?"

"Apparently he talked to this guy before they shipped him out."

"Any reason why he waited so long to contact you?"

"No one else bit. He's got a bit of a reputation. You'll see what I mean when you meet him."

"Did you tell your contact you were bringing a psychic along?"

"You're a fellow reporter. A stringer."

"Gee, suddenly I feel empowered. When?"

"An hour. Meet you at your brother's house?"

"You got it."

Maggie had made other plans for later in the morning, so we said a quick good-bye, sealed it with a kiss and a vague agreement to meet again sometime soon.

She'd radiated happiness when I left her.

So did I.

I lay low when I returned home. Snuck in the back—went straight to my own room, showered, shaved, changed and was standing in the driveway when Sam's SUV pulled in. Never saw Richard, never saw Brenda, and I heaved a sigh of relief at not having to explain why I hadn't called to let them know I wouldn't be home the night before.

"Where are we going?" I asked Sam when I jumped into his car and buckled my seatbelt.

"To Starbucks. I hope you like coffee."

As Sam backed the car down the drive, a big black motorcycle blasted down the street, heading south. "Hey, catch up with that guy, will you?"

"What for?"

"Just do it."

Sam tromped on it, tires spinning, his Lincoln Navigator earning its reputation as a kick-ass vehicle. "What's going on?" he asked again as we roared down the quiet street.

"I got a hunch about that bike."

By the time we reached the Y where LeBrun Road runs into Saratoga, there was no sign of the biker. "Now what?" Sam asked.

I shook my head, exasperated. "We head out for Starbucks."

Sam took the right fork; that would take us back to Main Street. "What was that all about?"

"Somebody on a big black bike tried to run me down the other day. I guess I'm just paranoid."

"Or smart to be careful."

We turned right on Main and I explained what had happened, making light of it. I was glad when Sam went into his grand inquisitor act, asking me about Maggie in as many ways as he could possibly phrase one question. I resisted his attempts to wheedle information from me until we ended up on Transit Road and ordered our preferences. Sam paid—no doubt on an expense account—and we sat down at one of the tables. Some kind of new age music played in the background. Nice. Mellow. Very Saturday morningish.

"How are we supposed to know this guy?" I asked.

"He said he'd be wearing a Bills cap."

I looked around the joint. Two of the other four male patrons were Buffalo Bills fans. "Should we raise a flag or something?"

Sam scowled. "Shut up and drink your coffee."

I sipped my coffee.

"Oh, and when he gets here, make sure you shake his hand."

Sam hadn't been kidding when he said he'd wanted a human

lie detector. He'd be damned disappointed if I couldn't sense a thing about the guy.

I drank my coffee. In fact, I'd drained my cup and was about to start twiddling my thumbs when an acne-scarred bozo in a Bills cap, T-shirt, and team red-and-blue striped sweatpants entered the front door. I swear Sam actually cringed.

"My crap-o-meter just flew into the red zone," I muttered to Sam.

"Don't rub it in." He stood, braved a smile and waved the guy over. "His name's Mike," Sam said under his breath.

Mike swaggered over with the confidence of a high school jock who'd just made the big game's winning touchdown. But high school had been at least two decades ago, as evidenced by the beer gut expanding his sweats. Mike's confidence wavered as he saw me at the table. "Who's this guy?" he demanded. "I can't afford to lose my job because of this, you know."

"You won't lose your job," Sam assured him. "I keep my sources confidential. This is my colleague, Ernie Pyle."

I rose from my seat, offered my hand. Mike shook it and I was immediately toasted with a blast of what I can only describe as nonexistent hot air. At least fifty percent of what he was about to say was sure to be pure horseshit—just what I was sure Sam already suspected.

We all sat down.

"So what've you got to tell me?" Sam asked.

"You wanted to know about Craig Buchanan, the guy they got for murder in Williamsville."

Sam nodded.

Mike crossed his arms over his puffed out chest. "He's certifiable. Gonna plead insanity."

Sam gave me the fish eye, struggled for composure and asked, "How does Buchanan feel about that?"

Mike shrugged. "Aren't you gonna buy me coffee or something? I at least deserve a coffee for what I'm about to reveal."

Who did this guy think he was, David Copperfield?

"How do you take it?" Sam asked, sounding bored.

Mike ordered the most expensive brew on the menu board, taking great delight in his first sip. Then he settled back in his chair, ready to regale us with his tale. He didn't seem to notice our lack of real interest.

"Buchanan," Sam prompted.

"They dragged him in on a Saturday night. Poor creep stank to high heaven. We hosed him off and threw him in a cell 'til they could get a psychiatric evaluation."

"And after that?"

"The shrinks were gonna put him on meds to calm him down."

This could take all day. "What did Buchanan say about the murder?" I asked.

"He don't know if he did it or not. Says he found the knife in a Dumpster. Pretty thing. Silver sparkles in the handle."

I took in a sharp breath as an image flashed in my mind. *A smooth, manicured hand—firecracker red nail-polished fingers— holding the stiletto knife. Gently waving it in front of a sparkling silver high-heeled foot. Lightly tracing the blade along the ankle and up the shapely calf.*

Was this the same person who'd worn the red stiletto heels or someone else?

I wasn't sure.

Tuning back to the present, I found two pairs of eyes staring at me.

"Go on," Sam said, diverting attention back to Mike.

"Buchanan said he used the knife to kill rats. He'd build a fire in the parking lot behind the Burger King and roast 'em then eat 'em."

The horseshit had now begun. I tuned out and pondered the

significance of the new vision. I'd seen the murder weapon. Big deal. It didn't bring me any clearer understanding of what had happened to Walt. My certainty about a number of things wavered; was I seeing the knife and the shoes from perhaps the killer's perspective, not Walt's, Cyn's or somebody else's?

I needed to thin out my list of possible suspects. To do that, I needed to touch Cyn, or if not her, something of hers, something personal, to see if I could home in on the same aura—perspective—whatever. The only handy thing that came to mind was her car. She left it parked outside the mill seven days a week, so I would have access to the body, but I wasn't sure that would be good enough. I'd need to touch the seats or the steering wheel.

Damn, I should've checked out her house. If she parked outside, I'd have a better shot of breaking into the car under cover of darkness than in broad daylight in a commercial area where people came and went all day.

"Hey, Ernie. Ern," Sam called.

My head jerked up. I'd forgotten my pseudonym. "Yeah?"

"You got any more questions for Mike?"

"No."

Sam stood and offered Mike his hand. "Give me a call when you have another hot tip."

"You bet. And thanks for the coffee."

Mike swaggered away from the table and Sam reclaimed his seat. "Well that wasn't worth the price of admission."

"Tell me about it."

"But you got something. You always zone out like that when it happens?"

I ignored the question. "I saw the knife. Whether it was used to kill rats, I can't say." I wasn't ready to tell him about the other visions. "I need to break into a car without destroying anything. You know where I can lay my hands on one of those plastic things cops and tow truck guys use to open locked doors?"

"Breaking and entering. What do you hope to gain?"

"Knowledge."

Sam looked thoughtful. "I might be able to get my hands on one. But they don't work in every car, you know. If it doesn't, are you willing to smash a window and commit a misdemeanor?"

"I don't know. I'm not that desperate yet."

"Okay. I'll look into it. What's your next move?"

I didn't want to tell him, and that was unfair because he'd included me on what was for him a waste-of-time interview. "You want to come with me when I look into that car?"

"Not if you're going be destroying private property. But I'll bail you out if you get caught. That is, if you're willing to share what you learn."

"I'm willing—but on my terms."

He leaned closer, lowered his voice. "I'm giving you a lot more rope than I'd give any other source."

"Why's that?"

"You have your hunches, I have mine. And one day we're going to break a big story. Much bigger than this Kaplan murder. I'm willing to be patient."

For someone used to getting weird vibes and insight out of nowhere, his words sent an unexpected and frightening chill through me.

"Meanwhile," Sam continued. "I'm working on getting Kaplan's autopsy photos. You want a look?"

I shook my head. "I saw him dead, and I'll probably see him dead again—in a lot more detail than I'll want. That's enough for me."

Sam looked intrigued, but luckily didn't push it. He grabbed our empty cups. "Let's get outta here. I've got other things to do today that have nothing to do with murder."

Fifteen minutes later, Sam dropped me off at the base of Richard's driveway. I gave him a quick wave before I turned to head up the drive. I didn't see any cars except my own, but then Richard and Brenda usually parked in the garage. I hoped they were off playing golf, as I didn't want to run into them. Okay, I didn't want to run into Richard.

I headed straight for my car, had the keys in my hand when I heard my name called: Richard, coming at me from the backyard.

Slowly I turned, tried not to look annoyed. I couldn't say the same for him.

"Where are you off to now?" he demanded.

I couldn't tell him the mill, he'd already warned me not to go near the place. "Out."

"You just came back."

"And now I'm going out again."

"Where?"

"To the drugstore," I lied. "I'm running out of shaving cream. You need anything?"

"You didn't call last night. We were worried."

"You knew where I was. Otherwise you wouldn't have told Sam where to find me."

"Yeah, but—"

"Rich, you didn't keep tabs on me this close when I was a teenager. Why the sudden interest?"

"It's not me," he lied. "It's Brenda. You know how she is—how she worries."

"Uh-huh." I opened the driver's door, a burst of hot air assaulting me. "You didn't answer my question. You want anything from the drugstore?"

He shook his head. "You gonna be home for supper?"

"Probably. If not, I'll let you know."

"Good."

I got in my car, unrolled the window and buckled up before starting the engine. "See ya."

Richard moved aside as I backed down the driveway. He walked to the center of the drive and watched me take off down the road.

I hated this crap. I hated the tension between us. Maybe moving into the apartment over the garage was a big mistake. Maybe I needed to cut ties. But I couldn't. My job paid shit and in less than a week Richard had had to bail my ass out of trouble—twice, as he had already pointed out.

Sophie was right. I needed him. And not just for what he did for me monetarily. He'd helped me solve the banker's murder. Without him, I couldn't have done it. And, if I was honest with myself, I needed him because he was my brother and we'd wasted a lot of years—years we'd never get back.

I'd been so lost in thought I didn't realize I'd driven to the mill on autopilot. The lunchtime crowd hadn't yet piqued, but there were enough cars parked outside to hide mine further up the street. I grabbed a baseball cap from the back seat of my car and found my sunglasses in the glove box. Not much of a disguise, but all I had.

I felt conspicuous as I walked along the sidewalk and over to Cyn's car. As expected, it was locked with all the windows rolled up. I clasped the driver's door handle and closed my eyes. The sensations that traveled through me were vague, meaningless shadows of emotions I couldn't quite grasp. Was Cyn the same person who'd worn the sparkling silver high heels, played with the silver-sparkled knife that had taken Walt Kaplan's life? Dammit, I just wasn't sure.

The mill's door opened and a young couple stepped out onto the small front porch. I did an about-face and started back for my car. It would take a baseball bat to smash Cyn's driver's side window. My skull had been fractured by a baseball bat. I didn't want to sink to wielding one to get what I wanted. But I needed to get into that car, and if the lock opener wouldn't work, I'd have to seriously consider visiting the closest sporting goods store and buying a bat.

Unless . . .

Richard and Cyn had been friends. What kind of influence could he still have over her?

No, that wasn't an option. And convincing him Cyn might be capable of murder would probably be impossible. I'd have to continue on my own and hope that later I could make it up to Richard.

And what about the next time I got insight on a murder, because I had a feeling this wouldn't be the last time it would happen.

I got in my car, slammed the door and clasped the steering wheel until my knuckles went white. Giving in to this psychic shit felt like embracing the dark side, and I sometimes wondered if surrendering to it would condemn my soul to eternal damnation. I wasn't a churchgoer, wasn't even sure I believed in a higher power, but going after the scum of the Earth that committed murder had to be a one-way ticket to salvation. Didn't it?

The more experienced I became at it, the less sure I was.

15

Dinner that night proved awkward. Richard spoke in clipped sentences and seemed to have a stick up his ass. Brenda made innocuous small talk while I pushed peas around my plate until I felt I could gracefully escape their company. That still gave me way too long to wait until the midnight hour. I took a nap, first setting my alarm for ten fifty-nine p.m.

I wasn't used to staying up 'til all hours of the night anymore. Richard and Brenda weren't early-to-bedders, but they rarely stayed up past the eleven o'clock news, either. As a temporary member of their household, I'd adopted the same routine—in fact, often pooping out long before they did. So just the thought of waiting until after 11 p.m. to head out for an evening had me yawning.

Sneaking out without them seeing me was another matter. Then again, in the evenings the two of them tended to live in Richard's study before heading up to bed. The driveway was on the other side of the house. I just had to hope they didn't look out the window when I took off. To make sure, I didn't turn on my headlights until I was at least three houses down the well-lit block.

I had to wait eons for the light at Main Street to go green. The heat had backed off and I rolled down my window, hoping for a cool breeze. The light changed and I turned left, heading for the city.

Buffalo may be the second-largest city in the state, but the travel time was far shorter than traversing the same territory in Manhattan. Yet like the Big Apple, you could also count on every damn traffic light going red as you approached.

An old Stones tune came on and I cranked up the radio, glancing in my rearview mirror. Some damn fool behind me had his lights off.

Maybe I should've asked Maggie to come with me, then perhaps afterward she might've invited me back to her place for another night of pleasure. But then I really didn't want to involve her in any of this for the same reason I hadn't shared any of what I knew about Walt's death with Richard.

You need him.

The idiot without headlights was still behind me. The main drag from Amherst to downtown was nearly ten miles long, and it wasn't unusual for cars to travel in a pack.

The Stones gave way to Stevie Nicks and I felt like I was listening to the radio of my youth. Sometimes music had been the only high point of those shitty days. I pushed the thought away and noticed the jerk was still behind me. He or she was probably the same kind of driver who left their turn signal on for endless miles on a straightaway.

I paused for a red light and took note of the business addresses. Club Monticello couldn't be too much farther ahead and I wondered how far afield I'd have to go to find a parking space. Too far, it turned out. I had to walk two blocks before I stood in front of the nightclub.

Club Monticello looked to be the hottest spot in the neighborhood, with ribbons of DayGlo neon and colorful posters of the featured acts decorating the front facade. Smokers of both genders—and those in between—loitered the sidewalk out front, polluting the air while the thumping bass of canned music vibrated through us all. My internal batteries seemed to be recharging as I read the Coming Attractions poster. Then suddenly Richard strode up and was at my side.

My temper flared as I turned on him. "What the hell are you doing here?"

His eyes were blazing. "What do you think?"

"You followed me?"

"Of course. And I almost lost you at least a dozen times."

Understanding dawned. "You were the jerk on Main Street without headlights."

"I didn't want you to recognize my car."

"Brenda's car."

"Yeah," he admitted. He wasn't about to drive the Lincoln into unknown territory on a whim. "Now what the hell are you doing here?"

"Trying to find a lead in Walt Kaplan's death."

Richard glanced at the flashing neon sign. "At a drag show?"

"Hey, it was his preference—not mine." Sophie's words came back to me. *You won't solve this without him.* My apprehension soared even as my anger at seeing him dissolved.

I cleared my throat. "Now that you're here, you may as well come in with me."

"You just want people to think I'm your date so they won't hit on you."

I hadn't thought of that, but now that he mentioned it, it sounded like a good idea. "Come on."

We paid the cover and entered the dark nightclub which, as expected, was crowded and hopping. A part of me had been reluctant to dive into a place with so many people—fearful the mix of emotional pandemonium might overload my circuits— but instead of chaos, the overlapping emotions seemed to cancel themselves out. I felt like I was protected in a bubble of nothingness, and was determined to revel in it. We'd just missed the first show, and it would be another twenty minutes before the second.

"Let's get a drink," I told Richard. We threaded our way away from the theater and to the bar through the crowd of dancers. Club Monticello was not only a gay bar, but billed as the best dance club in Buffalo, welcoming gays, lesbians, and straights. We saw men with men, women with women and, true to their advertisement, a smattering of hetero couples. We also got bumped and jostled more than either of us would've liked. I ordered a couple of beers and Richard paid, receiving a wink from the heavily mascaraed male bartender. I had to laugh as he left a tip on the bar and quickly turned away.

I let myself move with the rhythm of the music and happily soaked in everything that was happening around me, eavesdropping on conversations. The drag queens—the amateurs and pros—seemed to be referred to as "girls," no matter what their chromosome structure. And damned if the happy gyrating people around me didn't all look just fine.

Meanwhile, Richard looked like he'd be more comfortable in a straitjacket. "Now what?" he yelled over the din of music and other people shouting to be heard.

"Don't get pissed, but I'm here to show Cyn's picture around. Ask the club personnel if they've seen her before."

"What makes you think she'd come to a place like this?"

"She had the same pair of shoes Walt had made."

"What shoes?"

I realized he was in the dark about everything I'd been investigating. "I'll fill you in later."

I turned back to the bar, and elbowed my way in, waiting until the bartender took a breather between customers. I pulled out Cyn's picture, shoving it under his nose. "You ever see this woman?"

He took the photo, squinting at it between the flashing lights overhead. "Yow—that's one ugly bitch. Never seen her here. But then she's kind of on the old side."

"You're positive? She wears sparkly red stiletto heels. Maybe a red dress and boa?"

"Come on, man, you're describing half the queens in here—not to mention the straights playing dress-up."

I thanked him and sucked on my beer until it was gone. Then I went into automaton mode, flashing Cyn's picture at anyone who had two seconds to focus on it.

"Oy, God, he oughta get a closer shave," said what I guessed to be a woman at the bar.

"Not my type," said a guy in a red velvet Bolero vest, his hairy chest heaving from exuberant dancing.

"Just another wannabe," said a guy in a bad blonde wig and a baggy blue dress.

"Wanna dance?" a voice beside me asked.

I turned to find next to me a sweating, shirtless male of indeterminate age bouncing to the music. Linking arms with Richard, I answered, "Sorry, I'm already spoken for."

Richard yanked his arm away and looked ready to commit murder.

I spent another twenty minutes flashing Cyn's picture to the patrons, but no one claimed to know her. Richard followed me to the closest exit. "That was a complete waste of time," he said.

"I'm not ready to give up yet. There're other, smaller clubs. And come to think of it, I probably should've started at one of those. Walt was a loner. He'd probably go for less flash and less notoriety."

Richard glanced at his watch, his mouth drooping. "The clubs are open until four. You intend to hang around until then?"

I didn't think I could. "Most of them have Sunday shows. Maybe I'll come back tomorrow." I met his gaze. "You game?"

He shrugged. "Maybe."

Liar. I had a feeling if I let him, Richard would have himself surgically attached to me, at least until Walt's murder was solved—and/or his vacation plane took off.

We walked out of the club into the clear, dark night. The thumping music faded as we walked farther away. Six motorcycles were parked on the street near the club, none of them looking flashy, hard to make out any distinguishing characteristics in the dim light.

You're being paranoid, something in me taunted. And no doubt would be every time I saw a motorcycle until Walt Kaplan's killer was found.

I put it out of my head. The evening hadn't been a total loss. Richard and I were back on an even keel. It felt good. It felt right.

Until something bad happened. But I wasn't prepared to think about it just then.

I got up early the next morning, went out for bagels and Danish, then made an extra big pot of coffee. If we were going to have a serious talk, caffeine would be a necessity.

When they finally showed up, I dragged Richard and Brenda out to the deck for breakfast alfresco. The cool morning air and bright sunshine were such a contrast to Club Monticello's gaudy interior that our adventure the night before almost seemed like a surreal dream.

Richard plastered his bagel with cream cheese as I told him about the visions of the sparkling shoes—both red and silver— the knife, and Walt. He didn't react when I told him my suspicions about Cyn, either. I'd already decided not to mention what happened at the ramp garage. It had no bearing on anything I was investigating. At least I wanted to believe that.

"There is something else." It must've been the tone of my voice that caused both Richard and Brenda to look up from their plates.

"This is the bad part," Brenda muttered.

"It could be. I see these . . . hands. They're covered in blood."

Richard leaned forward. "Whose blood?"

"That's what I don't know. And as far as I know, that blood is still circulating inside somebody. Only I don't know for how much longer. I got the vision the day we went to the mill and met Cyn, then again later when I touched something I found in Walt's closet: a little pillow that says 'Veronica.' "

"So find Veronica."

"Easier said than done."

"How much detail do you see with these hands?" Richard asked.

"Not much."

He nodded, leaned back in his chair. "So right now it's a dead end."

"Yeah, but it won't be for long." I poured a coffee warm-up from the insulated carafe.

"Let's get back to Buchanan," Richard said. "I can see why you don't think he makes a viable suspect. But your evidence against Cyn is pretty damned flimsy."

"That's why I need to keep showing her photo around. I know she's got something to do with this whole mess, I just don't know what. That's where you can help."

That stirred a response. "You can't ask me to implicate an old friend."

"I'm not. I'm asking you to distract her while I touch something that belongs to her. I was thinking her car's steering wheel. If I don't get anything from it, I'll know she's not the source of these visions. It would clear her."

"In your mind, at least."

"Yeah."

Brenda had been silent during all this. "What do you think?" I asked her.

She sighed. "Except when it comes to your own health, I trust your judgment."

"Thank you. I think."

She pushed back her chair, picked up her dish and silverware and put them back on the serving tray. "But how do you expect Richard to get her away from her car, and then to leave it unlocked?"

"Well, he could invite her here."

Brenda flopped back into her chair and for a second I thought she might lose her balance and fall off. "What makes you think I want to meet one of his old girlfriends?"

"Basic curiosity. Besides, she's at least thirteen years older than you—and she looks it."

That appeased her—a bit. "Be that as it may, what's his excuse for inviting her?"

"I don't know. Drinks. Show her your old yearbooks. Bore her with a talk on skin diseases of the Ecuadorian rain forest."

"Ecuador has no rain forest," Richard piped up.

"Then choose another country. Or you can use me as an excuse. You want to apologize for my oafish behavior—"

"Yeah, while you jump in her car and soak up her residual aura. Then I'm no better than you."

"Thanks."

"You know what I mean." Richard shook his head. "I don't know. I still don't like the idea. It's like entrapment."

"How? I can't prove anything without solid evidence, but at least I'll know for sure if I should continue to annoy her."

"Yeah, you're like a pit bull. Once you get your teeth into something, you don't let go."

I couldn't argue with that.

"But," he continued, "you're trying to get her thrown in jail."

"Only if she's guilty. If she's not . . . I've eliminated her from suspicion and I try something else."

"Couldn't you try something else first?"

"I have no other starting point."

"Then what happens if you eliminate her?"

"I don't know. Maybe I'll get some other insight from touching her car that will direct me somewhere else."

Richard drained his cup. "I still don't like it, but I'll go along with you, because I happen to think you *will* have to look elsewhere for Kaplan's murderer."

"All well and fine," Brenda said. "That is, if you can lure her here and she doesn't lock her car."

"Yeah."

Richard stared at his empty cup. "Why the change of heart?"

"What?"

His gaze shifted to meet mine. "Why did you decide to let me help? Just because you want to get to Cyn?"

I wasn't ready for this question, but I guess I knew he'd eventually ask it. "It's against my better judgment. But . . ." He didn't know about Sophie. I'd tried to tell him about her, even taken him to her bakery once, but the owner said she didn't live there. I couldn't tell Richard that a figment of my imagination had told me I needed him to help me solve Walt's death. It was all too complicated.

Then again, maybe it was time for truth.

"I need you, Rich."

For a second he looked puzzled, then the barest hint of a pleased smile appeared beneath his mustache. "Oh. Okay."

16

Richard was blessed with something I'll never have: charm. I don't know what he said, but Cyn Lennox agreed to come by after the mill closed later that afternoon. Richard had to promise her that I wouldn't be around, and we'd jockeyed Brenda's car out of the garage and put mine in to reinforce the deception.

The plan was for them to lure Cyn to the other side of the house so she wouldn't see me when I violated the sanctity of her Mercedes.

At 5:47, Cyn pulled up Richard's driveway. The loft apartment's living room window was the perfect vantage point. I stood to the right side, peeking around the drape as she stepped out of her car. I couldn't see the driver's side door, didn't know if she'd left the window down or the car unlocked. All this could be for nothing. I watched as she stepped out of the car, once again dressed in western garb. A cowgirl, Dana Watkins had called her. Well, not quite; her denim jumper was embroidered with multicolored flowers, and again she wore the silver-and-turquoise squash-blossom necklace, reminding me of what Monticello's bartender had said about straights playing dress-up.

Cyn glanced around the drive, craned her neck to see into the backyard—probably looking for me. I moved back a step. No way did I want to scare her off.

The phone rang.

I looked back toward it, imploring it to silence, but it rang again and again.

Another peek out the window and I saw Cyn was at Richard's back door, knocking.

Ring! Ring!

Thank God she couldn't hear it.

The back door opened. Cyn stepped inside.

Ring! Ring!

I charged across the room, snatched the receiver. "What?"

"Jeff?" Maggie.

"Oh, hi."

"Everything okay?" she asked, sounding uncertain.

"Sorry about the greeting. It's just—I'm kind of in the middle of something. Can I call you back?"

"Well, not really. I'm supposed to be at my parents' for dinner in ten minutes, and they live all the way out in Lackawanna, and I don't like to use my cell phone when I'm driving."

Good old letter-of-the-law Maggie.

"When I didn't hear from you yesterday or today, I wondered . . . I mean, I just thought—"

The clock ticked overhead. "I had a wonderful time Friday night. When can we see each other again?" Talk about pushing.

"Oh. Well, when are you free?"

"Every night this week." Speed it up, I need to get outside, I wanted to bellow.

"Well, maybe we could talk about it later tonight. Make some plans."

"I may be going out tonight. With Richard."

"You're not getting him involved in this murder thing again are you?" The disapproval in her voice came through loud and clear.

"Richard's a big boy. He can take care of himself."

Dead silence. This was not the way I wanted the conversation to go.

"What time do you think you'll be home later? I could call you—"

"That's okay," Maggie said. "Maybe we'll talk some other time."

"Maggie, wait—"

Clunk!

The receiver felt sweaty in my hand as I jammed it back into its cradle. For a moment, all I could do was stand there, seething. If we were destined to be together, and I honestly felt we were, then why the hell was it so fucking hard?

The window beckoned. I crossed the room and looked down on the empty car, then at my watch. Cyn had been inside less than five minutes. Surely Richard would have enticed her into the living room by now. Something inside me said Cyn wasn't going to stay long and I needed to get out there and in her car.

I trotted down the stairs and opened the door, not letting it bang shut. This felt weird—sneaking around our own driveway. Why couldn't Cyn have backed up so I wouldn't be seen from the kitchen window? Yeah, didn't everybody back into driveways when coming for casual visits?

The driver's window was rolled up tight, like the others, but the handle lifted under my fingers. The door opened and I slipped inside, pulled the door closed but not quite shut, and sank into German leather-clad comfort. The air inside was still cool from the air conditioning, but uneasiness threaded through me. I was getting something, but it wasn't the same connection I had with the red shoe.

I leaned back in the leather seat, my hands poised at four and eight o'clock, closed my eyes, and clutched Cyn's steering wheel.

An absurd thought flashed through my mind: Jacob Marley. Yeah, Marley's ghost, forever encumbered in death by fathoms of chains and cash boxes. Cyn's life revolved around her spreadsheets and the numbers on them. Cash flow, income, expenses. Money, money, money. And when she'd last held that steering wheel she'd been worried sick. But that didn't make sense. Ted Hanson said her café was already in the black.

I shook those thoughts away. That wasn't what I'd wanted to get. I wanted to tap into what Dana had called Cyn's theatrical side. I tried another position on the steering wheel. The image of the red shoes blasted my mind. Plural. I'd never seen more than the one when I homed into what I perceived as Walt's psyche. And though they were the same style, these shoes weren't perfect—they'd seen some wear: scuffed, with sparkles missing. These were the shoes made for Andrea Foxworth, the ones Cyn had bought at auction. She'd danced with joy in them and joy had not been abundant since the death of her beloved Dennis. She'd danced slow, and fast, with multiple partners. In those shoes she'd felt sexy, beautiful. She'd had *fun.*

I moved my hands up to ten and two o'clock on the steering wheel. Shards of music—too brief to comprehend . . . disco mostly—wound through my gray matter like a dozen radios playing simultaneously, much too much to assimilate. My fingers tightened and the sensation of joy swooped over me like a sirocco; wind, speed and the thrill of danger.

I repositioned my fingers to nine and three on the wheel. A horrible weight pressed against my soul. Something so terribly wrong—horribly bloody—could never be righted.

Walt's death?

I clasped harder, hoping for clarity, but I wasn't sure Cyn had actually seen Walt in death—seen his blood splashed on tiled walls—in a bathtub?

True? Real? Nothing was set in concrete. Nothing I could grab onto—truly understand.

One and seven on the wheel brought something different: Gene. A powerful pull to protect him. She loved him like nothing else in her life. But that, too, had been tainted. Her love for him was black and blue and the startling crimson of fresh-spilled blood.

Sorting through the plethora of thoughts and feelings that bombarded me, one thing was certain; Cyn had not killed Walt. Just the thought of his death had horrified her. I couldn't quite grasp what she knew or how she was involved, but instinct still told me that she knew or suspected something terrible about Walt's death and it had done much more than unsettle her. She was in deep denial about something. I couldn't comprehend what, but whatever it was had shaken apart this sometime party girl's world.

Nausea pulled at my insides as I tried to sort through the building maelstrom, but I couldn't seem to pick up any one emotion and stay with it. Like slogging through Jell-O, I kept getting bogged down and losing track of what it was I was tuning into. My hands fell limp to my lap, lay there for eons—lead weights too heavy to ever lift.

The dashboard's dark displays eventually drew my attention. How long had I been sitting there staring at nothing? A glance at my watch told me at least twenty minutes.

Had I suffered a seizure? One of the quacks I'd consulted during the past few months had warned I might have one—more—at some time in the future. Head injuries weren't predictable. There was so much medical science didn't know about the brain . . . probably never would.

I managed to pull open the latch, slunk out of the car, shoved the door with my hip to make it catch. I shuffled away from the Mercedes, ducked into the side door to shamble up the apartment stairs. Less than thirty seconds later, I was back behind the drape, panting, and counting. Ten, twenty, thirty—

At forty-seven seconds, Cyn stepped out of Richard's back entrance. She paused on the steps, speaking to my brother.

Afternoon shadows were already starting to lengthen.

Ten, twenty, thirty—

Cyn turned, took the last step and headed for her car. Richard came out on his step.

Cyn opened the driver's door, ducked to enter, paused.

Could she smell the stench of the fear I'd experienced—relived—in the cockpit of her Mercedes?

She straightened, staring down at her pretty little car, her brow furrowed. Then she tilted her head to look up to the apartment, her face pale, eyes shadowed. I jumped back, pressed myself against the wall, my heart thumping, my breaths coming so fast I was in danger of hyperventilating.

I closed my eyes and started counting again until I heard the car door slam, and seconds later the sound of an engine. I waited until I couldn't hear it anymore before peeking out the window. Richard stood in the driveway. He waved me down.

By then I had my breathing almost under control and trotted down the stairs. Richard's back was to me as I rounded the corner of the garage, his arms crossed over his chest, looking down the empty driveway.

"Well?" I asked.

He turned, his eyes troubled, and I wasn't sure if I was in for a scolding or a lecture—or both. "That's one unhappy lady."

"Go on," I urged.

Richard closed his eyes briefly and shook his head. "I need a scotch." He turned and headed into the house, with me at his heels.

The screen door slammed behind me and I followed him through the pantry and into the kitchen.

"You could've moved a little faster," Brenda scolded me from her seat at the table. We both watched as Richard opened the cabinet where they kept their kitchen liquor. "That woman wouldn't leave the room. You have no idea how nerve wracking it was to try to keep her attention from straying to the window while you were out in her car."

"I thought you were going to entertain her in the living room."

"What took you so long?" Richard asked, getting out a glass. "You sat there for the longest time."

I swallowed, afraid to tell him what I experienced—what might have happened. "I kinda got mesmerized."

"And?" Richard demanded.

Looking him in the eye wasn't easy. "She didn't kill Walt."

He let out a ragged breath, his shoulders slumping. "I told you so. But knowing that still doesn't make me feel any better about luring her over here. You want something, Brenda?"

"Wine. Pour it into one of the really big glasses."

Richard had a right to his feelings. And that he'd believed in me enough to risk what he thought of as betraying a friend said even more.

"Well, what went on?" I asked. "Cyn looked upset when she left."

Richard reached for one of the balloon stem glasses. "I don't know. Something to do with her business. She had an argument with one of her employees."

"Since she only has two, and one of them works mornings, that leaves her nephew, Gene." I had to swallow, didn't want to betray what I already knew—suspected—really had no clue about. "Did she say what the problem was?"

"No." Richard opened the fridge, retrieved the previously opened bottle of wine, yanked out the cork, and poured it for Brenda, then handed her the glass.

I tried another tack. "You looked upset when you came out of the house. Why?"

"You try keeping someone captive for half an hour when they'd rather be elsewhere. I had visions of her yanking out her cell phone and calling the cops on you. And you sat there and sat there and sat there." He poured his scotch. Didn't even bother with ice. "She asked about you, too."

"Yeah?"

"She wanted to know why you were so damned nosy. She inferred that your harassment was behind her rift with Gene."

"How?"

"She didn't say. *I* didn't know what to say." Richard downed another healthy swig.

"Sorry."

I watched him take another swallow. He hadn't offered me a drink. But then, I wasn't sure I wanted one. I needed a clear head to figure out my next move. And then there was Maggie—a sweet diversion from what we'd all just gone through.

"I got a call from Maggie just as Cyn arrived. She's pissed at me again."

"Why?"

"If I could figure out how women think, I'd sell the secret and be rich."

"Oh, I'm sure I'll hear all about it," Brenda said and swirled the wine in her glass.

Of that I had no doubt.

"So what's your next move?" Richard asked.

"I also got the feeling Cyn was upset about something and she was in denial about it. Someone was talking to Walt in her office. If it wasn't her—"

"You think it was her nephew?"

"It makes more sense, really, especially as she seems paranoid I'm going to find out what went on with her and Walt and Gene. Maybe Gene's a drag queen, and maybe he befriended Walt. I don't have a picture of him to flash around, and what good would it do if the people at the clubs only knew him in his female persona?"

"You think you'd recognize him dressed as a woman?"

"I don't know, what with makeup, a wig, and jewelry. If you see some of these before and after pictures, sometimes it's hard to tell. I've been in Gene's presence twice, and he didn't give off strong vibes, so it's not like I could just tune into him like I can with someone like . . ." *Maggie.* "Like I can others."

They'd both noticed my hesitation. Neither of them commented.

Don't think about her, I urged myself. My mind raced to grasp onto something—anything else. "I need a picture of Walt to flash around," I murmured, wondering if Tom had one back at the bar. Then again, I hadn't noticed one—not even a grab shot tacked behind the bar with a bunch of other photographs. "I think I'll go back to Walt's apartment. Wanna come?"

Richard looked up. "I'll sit this one out." He took another swallow of his drink. "Brenda, how about a steak dinner? You up for going out?"

"Any time I don't have to cook is cause for celebration. But I'll drive," she said, putting down her untouched wine and getting up from the table. "Think I'll go drag a comb through my hair first. Be right back."

I watched her head down the hall for the stairs, and waited until she was out of earshot before speaking again. "You'll hear all about it later tonight. Maggie's pissed because she thinks helping me look into Walt's murder will get you killed."

Richard poured himself a bit more scotch. "She's got it wrong. It's only me that's keeping you alive."

It felt like he'd punched me in the gut. Was that what Sophie meant when she said he had cause to worry about me—and that I needed him?

I wasn't sure I wanted to know.

17

The last time I'd been to Walt's apartment, I hadn't noticed if the air conditioning was on—or even if the place had air conditioning. Entering the dark apartment gave me a chill that had nothing to do with the ambient temperature. I turned on the light, paused in the doorway. Nothing looked different, but it felt like someone had been there. Not Tom. Someone else—and that person had gotten in with a key.

I did an abrupt about-face and looked around the dimly lit landing. Two sconces, with what could only have been twenty watt bulbs, faced one another, giving only enough light for the tenants to find a keyhole. I ran my hand across the lintel and found dust, as well as a dull brass key. Okay, so who knew Walt kept an extra? Had he locked himself out one time too many and used it himself, or did his friends know about it?

I pressed the key into my palm. Bam! The bloodied hands were back. But damn it, whose hands were they?

Replacing the key, I reentered the apartment, again picking up the feeling that someone had been there in the last day or so. I stood for a long time, studying the apartment. Maybe I'd found it so tidy on my previous visit because there really wasn't much in it. The walls and flat surfaces were devoid of homey touches. It was a place to eat a nondescript meal, watch a little TV, and hit the rack. The focal point of the apartment was the desk.

Made of cheap pine, the student's desk had been painted

glossy black and lacked the nicks and dings usually associated with such a piece of furniture. I pulled out the chair and sat down, turned on the goose-necked lamp. A blotter of faux leather covered most of the surface, and on it were a stapler, a mug filled with pens and pencil stubs, and a cork-bottomed coaster. Had Walt sat here with a beer or a cup of coffee to write out his bills?

It had been a tactical error for me to let Richard go through Walt's papers instead of doing it myself. Not that he probably missed much—but he wouldn't feel a psychic vibe during an earthquake.

Pulling open the center drawer revealed more pencils, pens, a legal pad, rubber bands, and Scotch tape. Just the usual junk. The contents of the other drawers were more interesting. Bold block letters labeled files as tax receipts, insurance papers, and one marked "Will." I ran a hand over the files and papers. Someone had rifled through them after Richard. Looking for . . . something they hadn't found. What that was, I had no clue.

The will wasn't that interesting. Walt had left everything to Tom. He probably thought he'd outlive his widowed, elderly mother.

I folded the document and laid it on the desk. I'd give it to Tom tomorrow. Yet I wondered why Tom hadn't gone looking for it himself, especially as he'd already been through the apartment, presumably right after the cops. Then again, he hadn't been back to clear out Walt's apartment, either.

My gaze focused on the blank wall in front of me. Something didn't add up. Tom flat out told me he didn't want to know what else I'd find, and made it clear he was revolted by his cousin's lifestyle. Yet he wanted Walt's memory kept intact. Or was it just a matter of family pride? As far as I knew, Tom had never married, either. Was he worried his customers might think he and Walt were lovers? It was only when I'd shamed him that he'd told me to go ahead and keep looking into Walt's death.

The will bothered me, too. Why cut the old lady out? Did she know about, or at least suspect what Walt's sexual preference was? Tom said it would kill her if the truth came out, so yeah, she probably did. Were she and Walt estranged because of it? I wasn't sure Tom would answer me if I asked.

I pawed through the rest of the documents. As Richard had said, the receipts were grouped by year in envelopes. I did a perfunctory check, but nothing looked to be of interest. It still bothered me that he appeared to have no real assets. Could he have had a safety deposit box somewhere that even Tom didn't know about?

The next drawer contained more file folders of uninteresting receipts and held six or seven envelopes of photos. The first couple were old family shots. Birthdays, dinners, other social occasions. A much younger Tom wore a green, cone-shaped, sparking Happy New Year hat, and toasted the camera. Happier times.

Two newer envelopes had recently been disturbed. I fished through them, all the same subject matter: Walt, usually dressed in dark slacks and sports shirts, looking shy, posing with a cadre of drag queens. Single shots, group shots, and none of these pseudo-women were the same caliber as I'd seen at Club Monticello the night before. From cheesy wigs and gaudy blouses, to holes in their fishnet stockings, Walt's "fancy women" were losers, pathetic souls who hadn't been able to cut it in the straight world, and didn't look like they were doing much better in their chosen haven. The background décor was just as seedy. I'd have to hit the less popular bars tonight to see if I recognized any of them.

Shuffling through the pictures also gave me a sense that Walt's alliances with his so-called fancy women were short lived. Tom had said that Walt wasn't gay, but was that something Walt was likely to reveal to his straight-laced cousin? I pressed a photo of Walt and one of his fancy ladies against my forehead and a stab of pain lanced through my skull, revulsion flooding through me. Walt's accident had left him impotent, but that hadn't been the end of his sex life.

Shoving the pictures back in the envelope, I pushed it away from me, wishing I could get that image—and the accompanying sensations—out of my thoughts.

Anxiety forced me to my feet to pace the room, to walk off the tension and work up the courage to pick up the last envelope. I hadn't thought of myself as a homophobe before this. Then again, accepting someone's lifestyle on an intellectual level and inadvertently experiencing it were two different things. I thought of Maggie and the way our bodies had melded together a couple of days before—how right it felt—and welcomed the returning calm.

I felt okay by the time I'd shuffled through the next set of photos. Same kind of stuff—the background decorations changed from New Year's to Valentine's to St. Paddy's day. I turned the photos over. By the date imprinted on the back, they must've been processed just days before Walt's death. I hadn't seen a camera when poking around before and wondered if Walt had used a disposable one. I counted the prints: twenty-four. Next I withdrew the negatives. The strips were in four- or five-frame segments. One of them had been lopped off, its slanted edge different from the uniform cuts on the others.

So that was at least one thing Walt's visitor had come to retrieve.

Or did I have that wrong? First the cops had gone through the apartment, then Tom. They had to have seen whatever foot-fetish stuff he had on hand. Tom had later eradicated it. But if the cops had seen these photos they would've done more investigating into Walt's background and wouldn't have been so eager to pin the murder on Buchanan.

So why would someone come in and plant the photos? Being dead, Walt had no use for them. His family wouldn't want them. Why not just trash them?

The rest of the desk's contents were of no consequence and I eased the drawer shut. But I took the planted envelope of photographs, along with Walt's will, and locked up behind me. I wouldn't be returning.

At ten p.m., Lambrusco's, a gay bar two blocks from Main Street, wasn't half as crowded or as flashy as Club Monticello. The cover charge was half the price and even the smokers on the sidewalk had a tired, used-up look to them.

Richard's steak dinner had revived his spirits and I was glad to have him along. We surveyed the poorly lit barroom and the sparsely populated tables. The patrons were also older than at their biggest competitor's. The canned disco music wasn't cranked up as loud as at Club Monticello, so we didn't have to shout at one another either.

"Think they wash the glasses here?" Richard muttered in my ear.

"Ask for a bottled beer."

The bartender was not overworked and stood watching an overweight couple jiggling out on the dance floor. I ordered a couple of bottles of Canadian to placate Richard, and we commandeered two stools at the bar.

"First time here?" the bartender asked. His name tag read "Kevin."

I nodded.

"Slumming?" he asked.

Richard eyed me, then tipped back his beer.

"Is it that obvious?" I asked.

Kevin shrugged. "We don't often get newcomers. And tonight

probably isn't a good night to be here."

I wrapped my right hand around my beer bottle and soaked up feelings of unease the bartender had imparted. My gaze went back to Kevin, but he wouldn't look me in the eye. I leaned closer to Richard. "Uh . . . I don't want to alarm you, but something's going to go down. And pretty soon."

"What do you want me to do?"

"Drink up."

He raised his bottle and took a swallow.

I turned my attention back to Kevin. "You pretty familiar with the regulars?"

He nodded. "Know most of them on a first-name basis. At least, the names they give me."

I took out Cyn's picture and one of Walt with one of his fancy women, placed them on the bar. "Ever see any of these people?"

Kevin squinted at the photos in the bad light. He tapped one. "That's Walt and Veronica. She was one of our featured acts back in the winter. 'Fraid she's moved on to bigger and better venues." He tapped Cyn's picture. "This one came in a few times with some queen I don't know. Drinks Cosmopolitans."

"Do you usually get straight women her age come in here looking for a place to hang and not have to worry about assholes trying to jump their bones?"

He shook his head. "This ain't Club Monticello where they encourage that kind of thing. She didn't fit in and—" he paused, sizing up Richard and me. "You don't, either."

I swallowed some more beer. "What do you know about Walt?"

"Nice guy. Shy. Made friends with lots of the girls."

"By girls you mean drag queens?"

Kevin shrugged, glanced at his watch.

"You see Walt lately?"

He shook his head. "Not for a couple of weeks."

"He leave with anyone special the last time you saw him?"

"I wasn't his babysitter." Kevin looked at his watch again. "You ought to drink up."

Richard, who had only been half-listening, tipped back his beer.

The uneasiness in my gut intensified. "We gotta get outta here," I said, pushing off my stool.

"What's the hurry?" Richard asked, proffering his half-drunk beer.

A commotion at the entrance made us look up. Kevin ducked behind the bar. I grabbed Richard's elbow, hauling him off his stool. "Let's get the hell out of here!"

Six or seven menacing biker-wannabes blocked the main entrance, pounding their studded, leather-gloved fists. Bikers— like the one who'd tried to run me down in the ramp garage. As one they charged forward, overturning tables, sending pitchers and glasses flying, and delivering what sounded like Indian war cries.

For a moment, the shocked patrons stood stock still, unbelieving as the Bee Gees wailed "Stayin' Alive." Then, like frightened birds, they scattered, heading for the sides of the room and the emergency exits. I tried to hustle Richard out, but his feet seemed glued to the floor.

One of the customers tripped and the bullyboys converged, their booted feet finding a target.

"Hey!" Richard was off.

I stumbled after him. "Rich, no!"

Richard charged into the melee. He was at least as tall if not taller than the bullies, but didn't have their bulk.

Fists flew, catching Richard off guard as he stooped to help the guy on the floor.

Someone grabbed the back of my shirt, hauled me off balance, tossed me against the bar. The ribs that had barely stopped hurting screamed in protest and I sank to the floor, winded.

Richard was in the middle of the fight now, arms pumping as he took out one, then another of the bullies, looking like something out of a cartoon.

Long seconds passed and still I couldn't breathe—couldn't join in the fray.

Richard ducked one punch, but caught another that sent him reeling.

The main lights flashed on and suddenly the place was swarming with cops.

The bikers evaporated in the chaos.

My diaphragm finally relaxed enough for me to take in short, painful breaths.

One of the cops grabbed Richard, hauling him to his feet. "Hey!"

The cop shoved him against the bar and handcuffed him.

Using a barstool, I hauled myself up, realized none of the bikers had singled me out.

"You in on this?" The cop snarled at me.

Kevin was back. "No, he and this guy," he pointed at Richard, "tried to help out."

The cop glowered at Richard. "What were you doing fighting?"

"I was trying to save some guy from being kicked. Then they went after me."

"Oh." Still, the cop didn't hurry to release Richard's bracelets.

"It's a hate crime," Kevin said. "Bikers picking on innocent gay people."

My insides seethed. "Bullshit. Officer, this guy," I jerked a thumb at Kevin, "warned us we'd better leave. He kept looking at his watch. He knew these bikers were coming to disrupt the bar."

The cop's sharp gaze was riveted on the bartender. "Go on," he told me.

"Could be a scam—break up the place and insurance pays for a quick facelift. Or maybe it's been just a little too quiet lately. A little notoriety might bring in curiosity seekers who'd spend money. And by the way, are there any motorcycles outside?" The cop didn't answer, but I'd bet a week's tips there weren't.

Still wrapped over the bar, Richard craned his neck to speak to the officer. "You guys got here awful fast. When did the call come through?"

Kevin kept quiet, his expression defiant.

The officer's glower could've blistered paint. He stormed off to confer with the other cops. Kevin glared daggers at me and slunk down the bar.

"You okay?" Richard asked.

I hitched in a breath and pressed a hand to my side. "I'm back to square one with the ribs. How 'bout you?"

"I'm fine." He struggled to straighten and I gave him a hand. There was something different about him. Something that had been missing from his eyes since the shooting three months before.

"My God, you enjoyed it."

Richard didn't bother to try and hide his delight. "Great, wasn't it?"

I noted the growing red puffiness under his left eye. "Brenda's gonna kill us."

18

The phone rang way too early. I blinked awake, grabbed it, hoping it hadn't already awakened Richard and Brenda. "What?"

"Jeff?"

Long, aching seconds passed before the voice registered. "Sam?"

"What's this about you and your brother being involved in a brawl at a gay bar last night?"

I closed my eyes and cringed.

"Hello?" Sam tried.

Squinting at my clock made me wince: 6:59 a.m. "How the hell did you hear about that?"

"Hey, I'm on top of everything that happens in this city."

"It was a setup, and don't you goddamn quote me. In fact, bury our names, willya?"

"My, we're a bit testy this morning. You get that setup angle from one of your . . . uh, pieces of insight?"

"It didn't take a genius to figure it out." I gave him the Cliffs Notes version of our adventures the night before.

"I got Kaplan's autopsy report, as well as photos. Pretty gruesome."

"What about those electrical burns?"

"Poor guy was tortured before he was stabbed. Had a couple of fingernails ripped off, as well."

"Nasty."

"Looks like he was sodomized, but there was also scarring, so it wasn't like this was the first time. You did know that, right?"

"Yeah, yeah." Okay, I hadn't until the night before, but he didn't have to know that. "And the cops still think it was Buchanan?"

"Not necessarily. The detective in charge wants to make further inquiries, but his superiors figure they've got an arrest and aren't pushing. It'll depend on what the DA says. They've scheduled a meeting for next week."

"Next week?" This whole situation would come to a head well before that.

"Where you going next with this?" Sam asked.

"My original suspect fizzled. But I might have a line on someone else. I'll keep you posted."

"You do that."

The mouse under Richard's eye was puffy and purple. Add a beard to his mustache, give him a bandana and a gold earring, and he would've looked like a pirate. Brenda hadn't exactly forgiven me for Richard's new look—muttering something about ruined wedding pictures—but she made me a hard-boiled egg and toast for breakfast and served it without dumping it in my lap.

"So what're we doing today?" Richard asked, setting aside the sports section.

I swallowed a mouthful of toast. "I'm working. Then later . . . I don't know. All I've got is a flash of insight from Cyn's office. I know she didn't kill Walt, and it wasn't Dana Watkins, the baker, or Ted Hanson, the miller, either. That only leaves Gene Higgins. I don't have a starting place for him. He comes up clean on a Google search. No address. He's not in the phone book—probably only has a cell. I was thinking of tailing him for a couple of days."

"That's *all* you have," Brenda interrupted, shoving her

engagement-ringed finger under Richard's nose. "A couple of days. We're getting married on Friday. No ifs, ands, or buts."

Richard saluted her. "Yes, ma'am, but we'll have a much better time in Paris if we aren't worrying about Jeff." He turned back to me, sounding like an excited kid. "We can use Brenda's car. They already know yours."

"Cyn saw Brenda's car on Saturday. It's your car or nothing."

That didn't please him, but he didn't protest either. "Why don't you see if you can get off work early?" he said.

"Because Gene doesn't leave the mill until at least five-thirty. And, besides, if I'm ever going to pay you back the gazillion dollars you've spent taking care of me these past few months, I need all the hours I can get."

Richard opened his mouth to speak, but I cut him off.

"You're welcome to come play with me later if you really want." I got up to leave. "I'll be back home about four-thirty."

Tom was vacuuming as I entered the empty bar, which meant he hadn't gotten to it the night before. I'd probably get to mop the floor—oh, the thrill of steady employment.

Tom saw me, waved a hello and continued his work. I tied an apron around my waist and grabbed a stool to wait for him to finish. Eventually he hit the off-switch, unplugged the cord and started reeling it in.

"You must like it here. You come in early most days," he said.

"I gotta be somewhere. You got a few minutes?"

"A few." I handed him the envelope with Walt's will.

Tom took a seat at the nearest table, pulled reading glasses out of his shirt's breast pocket and quickly scanned the paper, then let out a breath. "He left me everything?"

"That surprises you?"

He frowned, his gaze dipping back to the document. "I guess not. Besides his mother, I was his only other close relative. Not that we were ever really close. And what's he left me, a pile of bills?"

"Why didn't he mention his mother in the will?"

Tom sighed. "They didn't exactly get along. That branch of the family has a lot of money and although he was an only child, Walt was definitely a black sheep. He could've gone into the family business, but he opted not to. You've heard of Ben Kaplan Jewelers, haven't you?"

"Whoa—only their commercials every five minutes on the radio and TV. They've got to be the biggest jewelry retailer in the city. So why'd Walt go into construction?"

He shrugged. "He probably thought it would make him look . . . I dunno, more manly. He couldn't have been any good at it. He hated to get dirty. I think he was relieved when he got to quit after his accident."

"Your aunt still own the business?"

"Yeah, but Walt's cousin Rachel runs it these days. She's good at it, too. I wouldn't doubt my aunt leaves the whole thing to her."

I tapped the document still in his hand. "You're also listed as Walt's executor. That means you've got to settle his estate. By law you're supposed to get things started within ten days of a death."

"Man, I don't have the time for that. And after what you've told me, I don't want to know what Walt had in that apartment or storage unit."

"The apartment is already pretty clean, as you know." He didn't deny he'd already been through it, and I went on. "I found some pictures you wouldn't want to see, but I'll wait to dispose of them. Eventually the police might want them. In the meantime, you could call in an estate liquidator to get rid of everything else. If you leave the stuff at the storage place, eventually they'll either sell or dump it, although as executor of Walt's estate they might haul you into small claims court for back rent." I handed him Walt's keys. "You really should go through the storage unit, just in case there's something of value."

Tom nodded. "Walt was a pain in the ass in life, and is proving to be an even bigger one in death."

"I know you said you didn't want to know what else I've found out, but—"

He exhaled a long breath. "It was one of his fancy women killed him, right?"

"I think so."

"It's gonna come out," he groused, shaking his head. "It's all gonna be made public and . . ." He didn't finish the sentence. I wasn't quite sure if he was angry at me or just the situation. His gaze met mine. "You know who?"

"Maybe. But I don't know as we'll ever be able to prove it."

Tom was silent for a long moment, staring at the floor—or maybe he didn't see it at all. Finally he looked up at me. "Back off, Jeff. I don't want you to get hurt."

"You sound like my brother."

"I'm glad someone looks out for you. I should've looked out more for Walt. If I had—"

"From what I've learned about Walt, he didn't want a lot of people in his life. That he found something of value in his transient friendships with his ladies . . . well, maybe that's all he needed."

Tom didn't look convinced. He folded the will and stood, walked back to his office without looking back.

I'd finished swabbing the floor and was about to dump the bucket of dirty water when Tom finally emerged. "I'm thinking about adding happy hour food on the weekends. What do you think?"

"More important, what does the health department think?" I asked, accepting his change of subject.

"Yeah, I'd have to look into that. There's debate as to whether it encourages customers or just invites freeloaders. You have any experience with that?"

We talked about my former bartending job, then we moved onto sports when the first customers came in. No more talk of Walt. Until I could prove who'd killed him, I decided to keep it that way.

The two o'clock doldrums had hit and there were only a couple of Tom's cronies nursing beers in front of the tube when Brenda strode into The Whole Nine Yards. "Can I help you?" Tom asked, in his most surprised and subdued voice. It wasn't often a woman walked into the bar. It was almost unheard of for a black woman to do so.

"Sure," Brenda said, sliding onto a barstool. "I'll have a Coke."

"I'll take care of the lady," I told Tom. "She's a friend of mine."

Tom raised an eyebrow, gave Brenda a nod, and headed back down the bar to chat with his friends. Their eyes had been on Brenda, too, but Tom distracted them.

"Looks like I gave them something to talk about for the rest of the day," Brenda said.

I half-filled a glass with ice, and squirted the soda from the well trigger. "Here you are, ma'am." Brenda reached for her purse, but I stopped her. "It's on the house. What brings you to this part of town?"

"I didn't come to spy, if that's what you think." She took in the bar's décor: artfully suspended hockey sticks, baseball bats and other sports equipment. "Not a bad little place. But it was actually that little candy store where you got the chocolates that drew me out here. They were just the best, and I kind of ran out."

"Kind of ran out?"

"Okay, I pigged out on them and they're gone and I craved some more. Is that a crime?"

"No, I'm glad you liked them."

"Yes, well, I haven't made it there yet. On my way, I thought I'd take a look at Cyn Lennox's little café at the mill. You and Richard have spoken so much about it, and *her.* Not that I was going to go inside and actually check it out. I mean, the time we spent with her yesterday was just too awkward. But when I got there, there was a big hand-written closed sign on the door."

All my nerves went on red alert. "What?"

Brenda lifted her glass. "I thought you'd be interested, since you and Richard were planning to play Starsky and Hutch tonight—not that you bear the least resemblance to Ben Stiller. And you can't follow Cyn's nephew around if he isn't there."

"Did the sign say anything like, closed for repairs—or sickness, anything like that?"

She shook her head and took a sip of her drink. "No emergency telephone number, no nothing."

My mind was racing. Cyn had been upset when she'd come to Richard's house the afternoon before. She'd had an argument with Gene, and now her café was closed—just the vibe I'd gotten while talking to Dana Watkins.

"What do you think it means?" Brenda asked.

"Nothing good."

She nodded. "Where will you start now?"

"With the telephone book." I looked up. "Tom, a phone book?"

"In my office."

A minute later, I'd retrieved the telephone book. I'd already checked for Gene with no results. This time I looked for Dana Watkins. More than a column of numbers were listed under Watkins, and as luck would have it, one of them simply said D.

Watkins. I grabbed the wall phone and dialed. Unfortunately, D. Watkins stood for David Watkins, not Dana. I'd have to try them all, and there was always the chance her number was unlisted—or that she only had a cell phone.

I slammed the phone back on the receiver.

"No luck, huh?" Brenda asked.

I shook my head.

Brenda took another sip of her Coke, her gaze wandering to the still-open phone book. "I'm not doing anything this afternoon. If you want, I could call all those numbers and see if I can find your Dana. Would that help?"

"Oh, Brenda, that would be worth a million bucks to me."

"On the contrary, it's very selfish of me. Richard and I are not going to leave on this honeymoon if you're still looking into that man's murder. The quicker you nail the sucker, the easier we'll all sleep."

I could've kissed her.

She rose from her seat. "But before I do that, I really have to go to that candy store. See you at home." With a wave of her hand, she was out the door.

Before I put the phone book away, I looked up Cyn Lennox. Nothing listed in Amherst—just like nothing for Eugene Higgins. Then again, why would there be? She'd returned to Buffalo after it had been printed. Directory assistance was no help either; the number was unlisted.

I spent the next two hours doing any busy work I could think of while I pondered my next move. To find Gene, I'd have to find Cyn. I had a feeling she'd gone to ground, but I'd have to check out her house anyway. The actual mill wasn't part of the café. If Ted Hanson was on the premises, he might have an idea of where Cyn had gone. But even if he did, he might not tell me.

Tracking Cyn would be difficult, but not impossible. The

problem was, according to Sophie's timetable I was running out of time. Brenda and Richard's plane tickets were for Friday. And then there was the vision of the bloody hands. Time may have already run out for someone. Cyn? Gene? Veronica?

I caught up with Tom before I left, pulled him aside so the customers wouldn't hear. "I might need some time off in the next couple of days. The stuff I'm looking into has taken a turn I hadn't expected, and—"

Tom raised a hand, cut me off. "We've already been over this; I don't want to know about it." He exhaled a ragged breath, exasperated. "It's my fault. I should've never talked to you about Walt. I only thought . . . maybe, him being a nobody, the cops wouldn't care about finding his killer. And then they made the arrest . . ."

I remained silent, felt my fingernails dig into my palms as I waited for him to fire me.

He nodded toward the door. "Go on. Just call if you're not coming in."

I swallowed, my mouth dry. Cutting me this kind of slack would cost Tom; he'd either lose money if he had to open later, or he'd exhaust himself doing both our jobs.

"Thanks."

19

Brenda hadn't yet found Dana Watkins, having another ten or twelve numbers left to call. But she had packed a picnic dinner for Richard and me to eat should we need to go on stakeout duty. "I'm going on my damn honeymoon, and nothing is going to stop me," she'd said as she pushed us out the door with our life-sustaining supplies. Richard wasn't as thrilled. The value some people place on their car's leather upholstery is simply unnatural.

We hadn't even made it to Main Street when I'd investigated the large paper grocery sack and assured him Brenda had packed plenty of napkins, and a half-used tin of saddle soap—just in case.

Our first stop was The Old Red Mill. A metallic purple motorcycle was parked in front. The bike in the ramp garage had definitely been black. Still . . .

As Brenda described, a hand-written sign was tacked to the café's front door. The lights were off; already the place looked abandoned.

Richard and I circled the building, found a door on the far side and rang the buzzer until Ted appeared at the door. "You again," he muttered in greeting, his expression sour.

"I'm looking for Cyn Lennox."

"She isn't here, and I doubt she'll be back. She told me you were bad news."

"How am I responsible for her troubles?"

Hanson dragged a hand through his graying hair. "Sorry. It's just . . . since I found that guy dead on the hill, I had a feeling my life was going to change—that I'd be looking for a new tenant for the café."

"What was Cyn's excuse for closing?" Richard asked.

"She was so upset she was babbling when she called me last night. All I got was that she'd fired her nephew, and she had orders for restaurants that needed filling. I asked her about hiring someone else, but she said she couldn't talk anymore and hung up. The sign was up when I got here this morning."

"Did Dana come in today?"

Hanson shook his head. "I went in and had a look around the café. The office is a disaster. Cyn must've come in and cleared out what she could. Baking supplies and equipment were also missing."

"Did Cyn tell you why she fired Gene?"

"No, she isn't talking to me at all. I don't understand it. She thought the world of him. What could he have done to make her so angry?"

I had a suspicion. And I had another suspicion: that Ted and Cyn were—or had been—lovers.

I offered Hanson my hand and we shook.

The floodgates opened and I was bombarded with images and sensations. One in particular he enjoyed, though might never happen again: Cyn, on the back of his motorcycle, her arms wrapped around him.

Ted took back his hand.

"Thanks," I managed.

He nodded, went back inside and closed the door.

We started back for the car. "Well?" Richard asked.

"Cyn and Ted have been more than just landlord and tenant."

Richard raised an eyebrow, said nothing.

"He's worried about her—and probably with cause."

Richard's cell phone rang. He answered it, handed it to me.

"Get a pencil," Brenda said, her voice sounding tinny on the little phone. "I've got Dana's address. Wouldn't you know it was the next to last name on the list?"

I had a pen and jotted it down.

It was a toss-up if we went north to Cyn's house or south to locate Dana. I was pretty sure we wouldn't find Cyn home, but I had to check it out. So north we went, battling the last of the commuter traffic.

As anticipated, the drive was empty and no one answered when I knocked on the condo's door.

"She's not home," came a quavering voice. Sitting on a white plastic chair on the front porch of the next condo was an elderly woman in a green-plaid cotton housedress, with worn, what had once been pink, fluffy slippers on her feet.

I descended the steps and joined the old woman. "Do you know when she'll be back?"

She shook her head, her tight white curls never moving. "Not soon. She had suitcases."

"Last night?"

"About ten o'clock. She didn't even turn on the porch light when she loaded the car. And when she drove away, her headlights were off. I thought to myself, 'that is strange.' "

"Yes, it is," I agreed. "Has anyone else been around asking for her?"

"Just a nice young man in a silver car."

"Kind of thin, short and balding?"

"Yes. Reminded me of my husband Charles when we were first married, oh, sixty years ago now."

"When did the young man stop by?"

"Oh, several times today. You just missed him about ten minutes ago."

Damn. But at least Gene didn't know where Cyn was, either. That meant she was probably safe.

"Thanks for your help," I told the old woman and went back to Richard's car.

"So?" he asked as I slammed the door shut. I gave him a recap. "You want to hang around in case Gene comes back?"

"There's no guarantee he will. We'd better go see Dana. That is, if she'll give me an audience."

Richard started the car.

Dana Watkins lived in a typical, older middle-class housing tract in Cheektowaga. Rows of purple petunias bordered the sidewalk up to the front door of the neat little brick bungalow. Richard and I got out of the car and headed up the path. Dana's car was parked in the driveway, and there were lights on inside the house, but no one answered our knock.

Richard followed me around the side of the house to the back, where a central air conditioner hummed. I stretched to peer through a kitchen window. Dana was hard at work, kneading dough on a 1950s chrome-and-Formica table. I tapped on the window. She looked up, annoyed.

"Can we talk?" I yelled, probably loud enough for her neighbors to hear.

"Go away," she mouthed. "I'm busy," and went back to her kneading.

I tapped on the window again. No reaction. I kept tapping. Thirty seconds. One minute. Finally she stomped to the back door, yanked it open. "Will you stop bothering me!"

"I need to talk to you. We're pals, remember?"

"You are not my pal."

"I was last Wednesday."

Impatience shadowed her eyes. "I have a lot of work to do. And you're keeping me from it."

"Then tell me where to find Cyn or, better yet, Gene."

Anxiety tightened her lips into a thin line. She breathed through her nose, her breaths coming in short snorts. "I suppose if I asked you to leave you'd ignore me and just keep bugging me."

"A man has died and the police have arrested the wrong person for the crime. I'm working on behalf of the murdered man's family to find out the truth."

She scowled. "Well, you might've put it that way earlier. Oh . . . come in."

I climbed the three concrete steps with Richard right behind me. The aroma of breads, cakes and cookies filled Dana's kitchen, which was overrun with flour sacks, spices, and cans and jars of other ingredients. The oven timer counted down thirteen minutes and six seconds. The table and sideboard in the dining room beyond were stacked with boxes and racks of baked goods. Dana was already back to work at her kitchen table.

And there was something else in the room. An aura I recognized and it didn't belong to Dana.

"You're filling Cyn's orders?" I asked.

"It's a great opportunity for me."

"Why did Cyn close the café?" Richard asked.

Dana looked up, for the first time noticing Richard. "This is my brother. He's also a friend of Cyn's," I said.

She didn't believe me. "Look, all I know is she said she was shutting down. I don't know any more."

"This doesn't look like a licensed kitchen," Richard said conversationally.

Dana's head snapped up, her eyes blazing.

"I'm a physician. I've got friends who work for the health department. I wonder what they'd say if they knew about your little operation."

Dana's grip on her pile of dough tightened. "I've got a line on a commercial kitchen. I just need to find the financing." The words were fine, it was the quaver in her voice that belied her conviction.

"That won't help if you're shut down," Richard added.

Dana bit her lip, turned back to the dough on the table. "I don't know why Cyn closed the café. The two of us could've handled the business for a couple of days or weeks. She was in such a snit—"

"Why'd she fire Gene?"

Dana paused in her work, but didn't look up. "I don't know." She was a terrible liar.

"Cyn called me about seven o'clock last night, told me she was shutting down the business. By the time I got there, she'd already cleaned out most of her office. I asked her about the orders, but she said she didn't care. She told me if I wanted to take them on, I could. She even gave me the supplies to do it, too."

"That seems overly generous of her."

Dana merely shrugged.

"Cyn's neighbor said she saw Cyn leave with suitcases last night. Did she tell you where she was going?"

Dana shook her head. "Just away."

"You said she cleaned out her office. Does that mean her financial records?" I asked.

"I guess."

"Could Gene have been embezzling from her?"

"Gene and I weren't really friends, but we did work well together. I won't believe he could do that to Cyn."

"I don't suppose you know where Gene lives?" Richard asked.

She shook her head. "Just that he had an apartment on Hertel Avenue or just off it."

"That's a lot of territory," I said. "What's he drive?"

"A silver Alero."

"New York plates?"

She nodded.

I reached back and took out my wallet, withdrew one of my old calling cards with Richard's phone number written on the back and handed it to her. "I don't know where your loyalties lie, but I honestly want to help Cyn. If you hear from her, please consider calling me."

She scrutinized the card, said nothing.

"I'd like to talk to Gene, too. If he's threatening Cyn, she really should go to the police. This isn't something she should try to handle on her own."

Dana stood in the doorway and watched us until we turned the corner for the front yard.

"Well?" Richard asked.

"That was a nice piece of blackmail you pulled back there."

"I like to feel useful. Did you believe anything she said?"

"Most of it. She may or may not be there now, but Cyn's been in that house. I can't blame Dana for not saying more. She's scared."

We got back in Richard's car. "So what's next? We pull stakeout duty here and wait for Cyn?"

I shook my head. "Dana would only warn her away. Our best bet is to find Walt's fancy lady, Veronica. She might know Gene, or might be able to point us in the right direction."

"And how do we find her? More gay bars?"

"The bartender at Lambrusco's said she'd moved up. We might have to try all of them."

"Didn't you say most of the bars only have drag shows on weekends?"

"That doesn't mean we can't flash her picture around."

The dashboard clock said 7:12 p.m. "Most bars don't even start to fill up until at least ten," Richard said.

"Most popular bars," I clarified. To my knowledge, The Whole

Nine Yards had never filled up.

"May as well go home to wait," he said, and turned the key in the ignition.

Three hours.

"Some of those drag queens had their own Web sites. You think maybe this Veronica does?" Richard asked.

"It wouldn't hurt to do a search."

Three long hours.

Bloodied hands. A rivulet of scarlet cascading down a wrist . . .

Whose hands? Whose damn blood? And was it already too late to save him or her?

Thunderclouds threatened the sky to the west. Nightfall looked imminent instead of two hours away. Richard pulled his car up the driveway, parked the car in his garage. The humidity had almost doubled since we'd left Dana's house some twenty minutes before. A storm hadn't been predicted, but the weather along Lake Erie changes fast.

Richard hit the button on the remote above the visor and the garage door obligingly closed. "We don't have to take my car tonight, do we?"

"No, it can rain on mine or Brenda's."

We got out of the Lincoln, went out through the side door and headed for the house. Brenda was waiting for us in the kitchen. "Got a message for you."

"Me?" Richard asked.

"No, Jeffy. Dana Watkins called."

"That was fast," Richard muttered.

"She said Gene Higgins lives on Norwalk Avenue, off Hertel. Here." She handed me a slip of paper with the full address.

"Why didn't she just tell us when we were there?" Richard asked.

"My guess is she had to wait until Cyn wasn't listening."

"Cyn was there?"

"I had a feeling she was close by. I'll bet her car was in Dana's garage. I should've looked."

"Why wouldn't Dana want Cyn to know she gave us the address?"

"The bigger question is why doesn't Cyn want us talking to Gene? Especially if she's so angry with him—angry enough to close her business?"

Richard looked thoughtful.

"I guess this means you're going out again." Brenda said.

"I guess."

"What about looking up Veronica on the Internet?" Richard asked.

"Yeah, let's do that first." So off we went to the study.

Brenda accompanied us, plunking down on the leather couch and picking up her novel. We spent at least an hour jumping back and forth between the Buffalo gay bar Web sites looking for Veronica. If she had moved on to bigger and better things, she hadn't shown up on anyone's radar.

The sky outside had darkened. Brenda got up to turn on another lamp. Thunder rumbled, and the phone rang. She picked up the extension. Richard clicked back to Google, typed in another keyword.

"Who is this?" Brenda asked, annoyed.

Richard and I looked up.

Brenda held out the phone, covering the mouthpiece. "It's for you, Jeffy. Sounds like a nutcase. Got one of those voice disguisers working."

I got up from my chair. More thunder reverberated overhead as I took the phone. "Jeff Resnick here."

"You will cease poking your nose into other people's business," said the slow, electronically altered voice.

"And if I don't?"

"I could've killed you in that ramp garage."

My spine stiffened, my hand growing tight around the receiver.

"I won't be so generous next time."

The connection broke.

Lightning flashed out the window.

I hit the phone's rest buttons, then punched *69.

"That number is out of range," came the prerecorded voice. Whoever it was had probably called from a cell phone.

Thunder boomed and I replaced the receiver.

"What was that all about?" Richard asked.

I exhaled through my nose. "A nutcase," I said, echoing Brenda's assessment.

"Did that person threaten you?" she asked.

"Sort of. Just that—" The image of Richard lying on the cold stone floor, shot, blood soaking his London Fog raincoat, came back to me. "That I'd be sorry if I didn't mind my business." Lightning flashed again. "You'd better log off before the storm fries your hard drive." As though to reinforce my words, thunder crashed overhead.

Richard turned back to his monitor, logged off and shut down the computer. "You worried?" he asked, swiveling his chair to face me.

"I'd be a fool not to be concerned, all things considered. But worried?" You bet. "No."

"Where does someone get one of those voice-altering devices?" Brenda asked.

"At the mall. Radio Shack sells them. Or the Internet. Anybody can buy one."

Neither of them looked too worried and I was glad I hadn't mentioned the incident at the parking garage. "You about ready?" I asked Richard.

"Yeah." He got up, kissed Brenda good-bye, and we headed

for the back door.

We crossed the drive and made it to the garage just seconds before the rain hit, coming down in drenching sheets of liquid silver. For a long minute or two Richard and I stood under the eaves looking out at the house with the curtain of rain before us. I can't read Richard at all, but a weird kind of electricity crackled between us. He kept looking out at the rain pouring down and his smile grew wider and wider.

"What's with you?" I asked. "You're happy."

"It's my last couple of days of freedom and I want to enjoy it."

"Freedom? For years you've nagged Brenda to marry you. You having second thoughts?"

"Not at all. But getting married means commitment and responsibilities, and—"

"Being a real grown up?"

His smile dimmed. "Yeah, but it's also the first time in months that I've felt good."

I envied him that. I didn't like to dwell on it, but the fact I might never fully recover from the mugging, might even develop new symptoms, like seizures, was a constant shadow hanging over me. And now the threat from that phone call loomed over me as well.

"You've got to get over it, Jeff. What happened, happened. It's over. Move on."

I stared at the rain dancing on the driveway. Was he talking about the shooting that nearly killed him, or me being mugged? It didn't matter. And I didn't want him to know how much that weird electronic voice had freaked me.

"I'm working on it."

"Good." His smile returned. Then he hauled off and punched me, hard, on the arm.

For a long second I stood there, stunned, then I punched

him back with equal force.

He rubbed his bicep, grinning. "Come on," he said. "Let's go!"

A torrent of rain did nothing to improve the gray, peeling exterior of the house where Gene Higgins lived. As luck would have it, a parking space was open right out front—just like always on a TV drama. Richard did a superb job of parallel parking and we sat there gazing at the drab building.

"Ugly, isn't it?" Richard said.

"Butt ugly." Most of the houses were either duplexes or had been divided into apartments, which meant off-street parking was at a premium. I scanned the road for a silver Alero, but didn't see one.

"Think it's worth knocking on the door?" Richard asked.

"Nah. But as long as we're here."

Richard glanced over his shoulder to the back seat. "I think Brenda's got an umbrella back there."

"You won't melt."

"I've already got a black eye. Do I need to catch cold four days before I leave on my honeymoon?"

"Wuss."

"Idiot."

He might be right. "Come on."

Leafy maple trees sheltered the car and sidewalk, so we weren't actually soaked as we made a run for the cover of the duplex's porch. At the sound of our footsteps, the muffled sound of a dog barking came from within the house. A plastic strip labeled "Higgins" was attached to the second-floor apartment's mailbox. I pressed the doorbell. Some part of me was hoping to tap into the vision I'd seen with the red sparkling shoe, the polished nails, and the stiletto. I didn't. Then again, how many people actually push their own doorbell?

The dog continued to bark.

"He here?" Richard asked.

I clasped the door handle, closed my eyes and concentrated. I expected the vision of the red shoe to burst upon my mind, but nothing happened. I opened my eyes, stared at the door's chipped white paint.

I jiggled the handle; locked. "I figured I'd get something, feel something familiar, and I'm not getting anything."

Richard shifted from foot to foot.

The door to the other apartment opened, and the wild yapping got louder. A short, white-haired woman in dark slacks and pink polyester tunic stood behind the screen door. "What do you want?" she snapped.

Richard faced her, had to shout to be heard. "We're looking for Gene Higgins."

The old lady homed in on his black eye, scowled. "He's not home."

"He's usually here weeknights, though, isn't he?" I asked.

"That any of your business?"

We'd get nowhere with her. I took out my wallet, another calling card, and my pen. I jotted a note on the back and wedged it between the doorframe and screen. Gene might miss it if I just shoved it under the door.

"I'd appreciate it if you wouldn't remove the card. Mr. Higgins needs to talk to me."

A brown-and-white terrier mix jumped up and down at her side. "You some kind of repo guy?"

"I'm a friend of his aunt's. She's gone missing. He'll want to talk to me about it."

She looked skeptical, but my mostly true explanation would probably keep her from ripping the card to shreds the minute we took off.

I took the steps two at a time. Richard murmured a "good

evening" and was right on my heels.

Once back inside the car, Richard grasped the steering wheel and looked out through the foggy windshield. "We forgot the bag with the food in it."

"Damn. It's still in your car."

"Where to now?"

"You want to get something to eat, right?"

"It'll help kill time until we can hit the gay bars."

"You say that with such enthusiasm."

He ignored the comment. "If you didn't get anything on Gene just now, whose vibes have you been tuning into? Veronica's?"

"It's a possibility. But Gene is definitely involved. What if Veronica killed Walt? Dumping his body by the mill could have been done to implicate Gene."

"Only the cops didn't bite?"

"Exactly."

"What if Veronica has skipped town?"

"I don't think so."

"Gut instinct?"

"I trust it."

Richard started the car, switched on the front and rear defrosters to take care of the windshields. "You got a motive?"

"Not yet." The old lady continued to watch us from her door, her yappy dog still bobbing up and down like a yo-yo. She'd probably wait up for Gene just to tell him about us, which was okay with me—if it made him call. I had a feeling that right now he was sweating. Cyn must've pieced things together and wanted to distance herself from her nephew—even if it meant closing her café. But what was it that Gene feared if Veronica was Walt's killer?

And what if we found Veronica? I wasn't sure what I'd do.

Richard pulled away from the curb and headed for Hertel

Avenue. He was enjoying the chase. I wish I could say the same. The closer we got to resolution, the more my insides squirmed. It wasn't going to be a happy conclusion—of that I was sure. Something inside me—and the damned vision of the bloody hands—told me it would be awful and messy and . . . somebody was going to die.

I just hoped to God it wasn't going to be Richard.

20

BoysTown was probably the next-to-best gay hotspot in Buffalo after Club Monticello. Loud disco music boiled from within and gyrating, shirtless men in tight jeans hopped around the dance floor in—what else—gay abandon.

"God, they look happy," Richard shouted in my ear.

"Of course they're happy. They're—"

"Gay!" he finished. "I need a beer." He headed straight for the bar and ordered for us. I fished out Walt's and Veronica's, as well as Cyn's, pictures. We sucked back our brewskies and I asked everyone within listening distance if they'd ever seen any of the people in the pictures.

No. No. And—no!

I asked the bartender which was the next club below them.

Fifteen minutes later, Richard and I had moved the car two blocks and headed for Club QBN—Queer Boys Network—and had ordered another round of beers. More disco music, more sweating, shirtless guys boogying down.

I shoved the pictures under every available nose. No, no one had ever seen Walt. Veronica looked familiar, but nobody would stake his or her life on it. Sparkly red stiletto heels? Why darling, every girl in here has at least one pair!

Next down the line was Daddy's Place. A little less noisy, a little less boisterous, and still no one knew Walt. Veronica, however, was a known entity, although no one had seen her in at least a week—maybe two.

Closer, but no cigar.

Richard wasn't looking quite so cocky. "What the hell do we do if we find her?"

Good question. Confrontation was out—especially in such a crowded venue. She could deny she even knew Walt—except for all the picture evidence, and even then she could say Walt had been a patron and it was just good PR to pose with the clients. Then again, the bartender at Lambrusco's could verify she and Walt had at least been acquainted. That is, if he could be trusted to swear by it.

That Veronica was familiar was one thing. Where she lived, no one knew. No one knew the name on her/his driver's license. Wigs and makeup and fancy dress were great concealers of the truth. In a feel-good place like a bar, who knew or who cared what people did in their regular lives—what their day jobs entailed and/or how they made their daily bread?

I hefted my third bottle of beer and found I couldn't take another sip, setting it back down. Richard, however, sat facing the dance floor, elbows on the bar, enjoying the spectacle. "I haven't been bar hopping since my college days," he said, his head nodding in time with yet another Bee Gees favorite.

"Why don't you get out there and dance?" I suggested.

"If Brenda was here, I might. Then again, this isn't my kind of dancing. I'm better cheek-to-cheek."

"Any time, sailor," said a skinny guy with a black tank top and painted-on white pants.

I snagged the guy's shirt strap. "You ever see this queen?" I shoved Veronica's picture under his nose.

God knows how he focused in such bad light, but his eyes lit up. "Veronica! Oh, she's a sweetheart. Yeah, I've seen her. Every weekend over at Big Brother's. She's moving up in the world. Another year or so, and she'll be the toast of the town."

"And where do we find Big Brother's?" Richard asked.

"Over on Pearl. But not until the Wednesday night show. She does a mean Brittany Spears. Doesn't quite have the nose for it—but hey, you can't have everything." He danced by us and dissolved into the crowd.

"Two days?" Richard almost whined.

I glanced at my watch. "Technically, it's one day and twenty-two hours. And I thought you were enjoying yourself?"

"Sure, as a change of pace. But I wouldn't want to do this on a regular basis."

"We ought to go over there and ask, just to make sure. But I won't go flashing Veronica's picture again. That could scare her off. As it is, if someone I've already shown it to mentions it to her, she'll probably leave town in a hurry."

So off we went to our fourth bar that night.

Big Brother's was smaller than I anticipated; intimate was how it was advertised out front. Sure enough, a poster-sized color photograph of Miss Veronica Lakes in a white, baby-doll dress, blond wig, and pouting lips greeted us. Her co-stars, Margarita Ville and Sandy Waters, only rated eight-by-ten black-and-white photos.

"I don't think she looks like Brittany," I told Richard.

"I couldn't pick Brittany out of a lineup," he admitted.

"God, you're an old fart." He followed me inside, where we made sure that yes, Miss Lakes would be appearing on Wednesday. Did we want to make reservations?

We headed out the door. A glance at my watch told me it was after one. The sidewalk was still wet, but the storm and the lingering rain had passed, breaking the hot spell. Richard yawned as we walked toward the car. "I'll drive," I said, and unlocked the passenger side door for him, then moved to the driver's side.

Richard fastened his seat belt, crossed his arms over his chest, and settled back in his seat. "Home, James, and don't spare the horses."

I pulled away from the curb and headed back for Main Street. Richard was asleep before we got there.

I braked for a red light, one of those crazy ones with the strobing bar of white in the middle. Bloodied hands flashed before my eyes. I tightened my grip on the steering wheel. Not now, not when I'm driving.

Bloodied hands. Rivulets of scarlet cascading down the wrists, soaking into a forest of dark hair past the wrists. No jewelry, no nail polish.

Slowly the hands turned, palms out to face me. Strong, masculine hands.

So much blood!

Honk!

The vision winked out. I jammed my foot on the accelerator and the car lurched forward. Richard didn't stir.

I was glad to have the wheel to hang on to—it kept my hands from shaking. I wouldn't have to worry about some crazy coming after Richard if I crashed the car and killed us both. But the vision didn't replay. I drove like an old lady, made it home and parked the car in the garage before giving up my death grip. I sat there, listening to the engine make tinking noises for at least a minute before I could move. The garage door opener's light would go off in another minute. I gave Richard a poke to wake him.

"We're home."

He took in a deep breath and straightened. "I wasn't asleep."

"Sure," I said and opened my door. Richard did likewise.

We got out of there and I closed and locked the garage's side door before the light winked out. Brenda had left the outside lights on and I sorted through my keys to open the back door. Richard bumped into me. "God, I'm tired."

I opened the door. "Go to bed."

He saluted me and stepped over the threshold. "Yes, sir."

Stepping up behind him, I pushed him in the direction of the kitchen. "Good night."

Eyes closed, I stood in the silent pantry, listened until his footsteps faded, realized I was too wired to sleep. What I needed was a walk. A nice long walk to calm my nerves.

I headed back out the door, paused to lock up, and started down the driveway.

"You're late tonight," Sophie told me as she ushered me inside the bakery, then locked the door behind me.

"I was out."

"Investigating?"

"Sort of."

She scuffed ahead of me in her worn slippers. Tonight it was tea. The cups were set out with a little white pitcher of milk and a plate of fresh-sliced *placek*—just as she'd promised days before.

"Sit, sit," she urged, taking her own seat.

I sat.

She poured milk into my cup, then added the strong, dark tea from an old brown pottery pot. "See, no need for a spoon," she told me, proud of her cleverness. She pushed the plate closer and I took a slice, setting it on the napkin she'd provided. It was still warm.

"How do you always know when to have things ready for me? I didn't even know I was coming here until I started walking."

She shrugged, then leaned forward, her eyes worried. "You have a lot on your mind."

"Yeah," I admitted, and broke a crumbly corner off my cake. "I got one of those flashes of insight when I was behind the wheel of the car. I don't know if it was that or the vision that freaked me more." I stuffed the morsel in my mouth, savoring its sweet, buttery—comforting—taste.

"The bloody hands," she said.

"Yeah."

Sophie nibbled on her own piece of *placek*. "I don't know what to tell you. Only that . . . you have to do what you feel is right. That's not always easy."

"Tell me about it." I wasn't sure how to tell her—how to phrase—what I was feeling. "The vision was much stronger tonight, telling me that whatever happens will come pretty damn quick. And when it does—I'm worried I won't react in time to do what's right, what'll save lives, or time, or—anything! Dammit, I'm scared to death whatever I do is going to cost someone's life."

"Your brother?" She shook her head. "Now you're being paranoid."

"Can you guarantee it won't happen?"

"Nobody can. But, to ease your mind—I see things ahead for your brother."

"Good things?" I asked, thinking about Brenda, their wedding, and the future.

She shrugged. "Uh . . . things."

Things?

Like living as a veg in a nursing home?

Crippled?

Maimed?

Okay, so maybe I *was* being paranoid. And then there was the incident in the parking garage. Should I ask her if I had a future? She hadn't volunteered the information.

Sophie sipped her tea, avoided looking at me. I sipped mine, did the same.

Finally, Sophie pushed back her empty mug. "You have someplace else to go."

"Yeah."

"If you can, come and see me on Saturday," she said, rising from her chair, her expression solemn.

Saturday. That meant whatever happened, this whole convoluted mess would be over with by then. Then again: *If you can.* Maybe I wouldn't be able to. Her words had given me no peace.

But she was right; I did have somewhere else to go.

I did a sweep around Norwalk Avenue, didn't find Gene Higgins's silver Alero, and so cruised the surrounding dark streets. Sure enough, two blocks over the little car sat parked under a dripping maple. Thanks to alternate street parking, Gene was going to have to move the car by eight o'clock or risk a ticket. So I had a decision. Stick with the car, or stake out his apartment until he emerged. If he emerged.

I circled back to Norwalk and found a space with a clear view of the house. By parking so far away, Gene had obviously tried to make me—or someone else—think he wasn't home.

Talk radio bored me, and I could find nothing but loser love songs, hip-hop or gangsta rap on every other station. I snapped off the radio and hunkered down in my seat, gaze fixed on the homely gray house. Green numerals on the digital clock gave me the bad news. I'd been awake twenty hours, and fatigue had settled in with a vengeance. Now I not only had to hope I wouldn't fall asleep, but that some cop wouldn't find me and roust me.

I had to be out of my friggin' mind. Gene was probably nestled in his warm, comfortable bed and here I was cold, cramped, sleep-deprived and verging on misery. I didn't have a clue what I was going to say to him if I caught up with him. Tell him about the sparkling red shoe? Ask him about Veronica?

A car rolled past, its red taillights glowing. Already the sky to the east was beginning to brighten.

An hour after that, I was sure my mind teetered on the verge of imminent brain death from lack of sleep and absolute boredom.

I'd been staring at the house so long, it took a good ten seconds for me to realize someone had come out of the door to the upstairs apartment and had descended the steps to the street. A shot of adrenaline rushed through me as I stumbled out of the car—slamming the door and running across the street.

"Gene! Gene Higgins!"

Gene stopped dead, his head hanging. He didn't move as I jogged to catch up with him.

"What do you want?"

"Tell me about Walt Kaplan. How you knew him. Why his body was found on the hill by the mill."

He took a step away and I grabbed him by the shoulder. The image of the bloody hands burst upon my mind and I let go as though scalded.

Gene whirled on me, caught me with a fist to the gut. I fell flat on my ass on the still-damp sidewalk, doubled over onto my side, gasping for air.

Gene crouched beside me. "Jeez, man, I'm sorry!"

I looked up into his panicked face.

"I never hit anybody before."

Anybody in a position to hit back, I'd bet.

Crawling onto my knees, I struggled to catch my breath as I inched toward the curb and a parked car to haul myself up. Gene hovered over me, babbling apologies, but I couldn't focus on the words.

Once upright, I found I couldn't stand straight, and hunched over, hands clutching my knees, my ass plastered to the water-beaded Sebring's fender to keep from falling over.

"You're not going to sue me, are you?" Gene asked anxiously.

I looked up at him, my breaths finally coming easier. "You

answer my questions and I might not call my attorney the minute I get home."

"I don't know anything. Ted found the guy dead by the building. End of story. Besides, the cops already arrested someone. Case closed."

"Their case against the homeless guy will fall apart as soon as the DNA evidence comes back from the lab. Walt had back-door sex before he died. They'll have a new angle to investigate and how long to you think it'll be before they start asking you questions?"

Gene said nothing.

Time to bluff. "How did you end up with Walt's pictures, and why did you take them back to his apartment? Uh, all but one. The last negative on the roll had been snipped—your picture. Did Walt tell you about the key over the door?"

"You've got no proof."

"When the cops go back to Walt's apartment, they'll find your fingerprints. Walt was a bit of a pack rat. Did you know he kept shoeboxes filled with stuff to remind him of his past liaisons? And who knows what other keepsakes he kept from his time with you at the house in Holiday Valley."

"Holy Christ," Gene wailed and smashed his fist against the roof of the car, leaving a noticeable dimple.

I stayed rock still, hoping like hell he wouldn't hit me again.

"Where are they? Do you have them?"

"I gave them to a reporter at the *Buffalo News,*" I lied. "I disappear from his radar and he goes straight to the cops with it and my suspicions." Well, it sounded good.

"Shit!" This time Gene punched his right thigh.

"Pipe down," I warned. "You want your neighbors calling the cops? Then again, it would make it easy for me to file a police report for assault."

Gene squeezed his eyes shut, about to cry.

"Look, why don't we go get some coffee and talk?"

"I can't—If it gets out—My parents—Cyn will kill me."

"It's only a question of time before everything comes out. Either you cooperate and spill what you know or the cops are going to try to nail you for everything, and life without parole can be pretty damned boring."

Arms hanging limply at his sides, Gene stood in the middle of the sidewalk, his lower lip trembling, looking at least ten years younger.

With some effort, I managed to straighten, my insides taking their time to settle back into their rightful places. "Coffee," I repeated. Gene nodded. I gestured toward my car. "Come on."

He followed me like a docile lamb, got into the passenger side.

The drive to Dunkin' Donuts was silent. I stopped at the drive-up menu, gave our order and proceeded to the window. A perky blonde teenager held out her hand for the money, made change, and handed me the cups in less than thirty seconds. I handed Gene his before pulling over to an empty parking space on the far side of the building.

As though on autopilot, Gene removed the cap from his cup and blew on it to cool it. I took a sip, burned my mouth and thought of Dana Watkins and her asbestos esophagus.

"You want to start at the beginning?" I prompted.

Gene's gaze seemed to be focused on the door handle. "It started off as fun. Cyn wanted to cut loose. Dennis was a great guy, but he had no soul for adventure. When he died, Cyn mourned him but was ready for new hobbies, new friends, an escapade or two. I took her to one of the gay bars on drag night and we had a ball. We kept going back, but we liked the smaller clubs best. Less people. More fun."

"She accepted that you were gay?"

He nodded miserably. "Cyn has always been there for me.

She's more like a sister than an aunt. If my father finds out, he'll disown me."

"How long have you been—" God, this sounded stupid. "—dressing up?"

"Since I moved out of my parents' house. But I never went out in drag. Never had the nerve until Cyn dared me. She bought some costumes at a charity auction a few months ago. She gave me the dress as a joke."

"But you didn't take it as a joke?" I guessed.

He wouldn't look at me, but nodded. "She helped me build an outfit."

"But she kept the shoes."

His head bobbed again. "They didn't fit me."

"And then you met Walt." It was all falling together in my head. "He admired Cyn's shoes, then later, once the two of you got better acquainted, he surprised you with a pair to go with your red dress."

Gene said nothing.

"How does Veronica fit into this?"

"She and Walt broke up before I came along. See, Walt used to brag about money. He dressed nice and always flashed a big wad of cash at the clubs—paid for lots of drinks. Veronica insinuated herself into his life. She kept hounding him for money so he dumped her."

"But she wouldn't let go. She was angry he took up with you."

His head sank to his chest. "Yeah."

"Did she know Walt's family owns the Kaplan Jewelry stores?"

"Everybody did. Course, Walt didn't let on that he had virtually nothing to do with them anymore."

"Then how did you know?"

"I told you; we were friends. We spent a lot of time talking."

"At the clubs?"

"Sometimes. Sometimes we just went out for dinner. Walt and I weren't . . . I mean, I like older guys, but we only did it a couple of times. It wasn't like we were—"

"But you were with him hours before he died."

"We had dinner at Eckl's in Orchard Park that night."

"I know the place. And afterward?"

Gene was silent, wouldn't look at me.

"After the sex, what happened?" I tried again.

"Walt dropped me off at my apartment, said he was going home. Veronica must've tracked him down and killed him. I figure she dumped him by the mill to implicate me."

That wasn't all. "Did you find him?"

"Veronica called me." Gene closed his eyes, let out a shaky breath. "I don't even know how she got my cell number. She said they'd argued—about me. She said she'd dumped Walt by the mill. She made it sound like he was hurt—but alive."

It had been Gene's revulsion I'd experienced when I'd first visited the mill. "Why didn't you call 911?"

"Walt was my friend. He'd never come out to his family. I wasn't going to do it for him. So I rushed right over there and—"

"Found him dead."

Gene nodded miserably. "She'd dumped him all right— naked. I wasn't about to let him be found that way. But he was a lot bigger than me. I knew I'd never get him up the hill on my own so I put his clothes back on him. I hated to leave him there, but what else could I do?"

"Why didn't you call the cops?" I pressed.

"I was scared. I still am. Of her."

"Have you heard from Veronica since?"

Again he nodded. "She's left threatening messages on my voice mail. Someone broke a window in my apartment. I think Veronica tried to get in. My landlady heard a noise and let her dog out. Since then, I've had a new lock installed and have tried to watch my back."

"What about Cyn?"

"She was furious when Walt turned up dead. Like it was a stain on *her* character." He turned anguished eyes toward me. "I told her about Veronica's call, how she blamed me for her and Walt breaking up. How she wanted the ring."

That grabbed my attention. "You've got Walt's ring?"

Gene dug into his collar, pulled out a chain from around his neck. A sparkling, man's diamond ring flashed. The stone was easily three or more carats. "How—when—did you get it?"

"Walt didn't want Veronica to get her hands on it. He said he didn't have a safety deposit box and asked me to take it for safekeeping. It was only supposed to be for a couple of days. She killed him that night."

Had Walt finally told Veronica he was broke? I could imagine someone with an obsessive personality being angry and determined enough to try to seize Walt's only real asset. She must've tortured him until he told her what happened to the ring.

"Anyway," Gene continued, "Cyn and I talked about it and decided to keep quiet. Cyn was ecstatic when that homeless guy was arrested. But you kept poking around and she got paranoid. We argued on Sunday afternoon. She went berserk after she visited your brother. She was afraid she'd be accused of being an accessory to the crime. She wouldn't listen to me—to reason. She left town. At first I thought she'd gone to Holiday Valley, but I went out there and she hasn't been around. I don't know where she is."

And I wasn't going to tell him. Yet, I believed him. He wasn't a killer, and he wasn't a drag queen. He was just a boy in a dress on Saturday nights.

Gene held his coffee under his chin, but didn't seem willing or able to drink it. The hands holding onto the cup were small, soft, the nails short. They weren't the bloodied, masculine hands I'd been seeing for almost two weeks. Yet, when I'd touched him, the vision had exploded across my mind.

A chill ran through me. It was Gene's blood on those glistening hands.

Like a slaughterhouse, Sophie had said.

"Why did Veronica think Walt had money?"

"He drove that big Caddy. She never saw where he lived—how he lived. See, at first Walt was a sucker for her, wanted to impress her. He told her that after his accident he received a million-dollar settlement."

"But he didn't."

"Nah, more like a hundred grand."

"He must've eventually told her the truth."

"He did. She didn't believe him. She's . . . one scary person."

"How did you and Walt become friends?"

He laughed. "Golf. He told me one day we'd play a round. Never happened." His mouth sagged. "Never will now."

Walt hadn't had many people in his life that cared about him. Hell, I'm not even sure Tom really gave a damn about him. But wimpy little Gene did. And now he was just as vulnerable as Walt had been.

"I'm sorry you lost your friend."

Gene looked over at me, his eyes bright. "Thanks."

"You're not safe here in Buffalo."

His gaze intensified, fear tightening his lips. He'd seen firsthand Veronica's handiwork.

"Does Veronica know about the Holiday Valley house?"

He shook his head.

"It might be a good idea for you to go stay there for a few days. Do you have clothes there?"

"Yeah."

"Good. Because I don't think you should go back to your

apartment. I won't say I'm great at reconnaissance, but I can usually pick up a tail. I'll drop you off at your car and follow you out to the Thruway to make sure Veronica isn't staking you out. You stay put out there until at least Saturday. After that—"

After that he'd either be dead or alive, but the truth would be out.

"What do you say?"

He sighed, recapped his coffee. "Okay."

21

It was almost nine-thirty when, feeling punch drunk, I staggered into Richard's kitchen. He and Brenda were at the table, finishing breakfast, and neither of them looked happy.

"Where the hell have you been?" Richard demanded. "Didn't you think we'd be worried sick? Your car's gone, your bed hasn't been slept in."

"That'll teach me to make the damn thing every morning," I said and collapsed into a chair.

"Did you sleep at all?" Brenda asked.

"Not since yesterday."

"You want something to eat?"

"Toast, please."

She got up to make me some.

"Well?" Richard asked. His eye wasn't so black this morning; it had turned a bit green with yellow edges—healing.

Resting my elbow on the table, I leaned my cheek into my palm and tried to keep my eyes open. "I went back to Norwalk Street, found Gene Higgins."

"And?"

"He says Veronica admitted to him that she killed Walt and dumped him behind the mill. Poor kid's scared shitless."

"With cause, I'd say."

"He's going to hide out at Cyn's house in Holiday Valley for a few days, but I don't for a minute think he's safe."

"Why not?" Brenda asked.

I sat up straighter, cleared my throat. "That vision of bloody hands I keep getting—it's Gene's blood I see."

The toast popped up, and Brenda put it on a plate, handed it to me. "I don't see how you can eat it dry like that."

"I like it that way."

"Want some milk with that?"

I nodded.

"What makes you think it's Gene's blood?" Richard asked.

"I touched him and bang! There was the vision. What I don't get are the hands themselves. They're very definitely strong, masculine hands. And so far nobody involved in this murder has hands like that."

Brenda placed a short glass of milk in front of me. "I could warm it up," she offered.

"No, thanks."

"What'll you do next?" Richard asked.

I chewed and swallowed some toast. "Crash for a few hours."

"Oh, good," Brenda said, "because the zipper broke on one of the suitcases and I want to see if we can get another one."

"You don't need me for that." Richard said.

"It's your suitcase," she deadpanned.

End of that discussion.

I gulped down the milk, grabbed my second piece of toast and pushed myself up from the table. "If I'm not up by one, give me a yell, willya?"

"Will do," Richard said, resigned.

I threaded my way through the pantry to my room off the back hall. I needed to call Tom, tell him I wouldn't be in before I could allow myself the luxury of sleep. And later in the day, I'd have to turn my efforts to figuring out how to protect Gene and corner Veronica.

And I didn't have a clue how to accomplish either.

★ ★ ★ ★ ★

Instead of Richard, it was the telephone that woke me. It rang four times and I grabbed it before voice mail picked up. "What?"

"Do you always answer the phone that way?" Maggie asked.

My grip on the receiver slackened. "When I'm yanked from a deep sleep, yeah."

"It's almost one o'clock. What are you doing in bed at this time of day? Are you sick?"

Eyes closed, I asked myself the same question. Maybe. Subtle rumblings behind my eyes told me I'd better take my meds when I got up, in hopes of staving off one of my all-too-frequent skull pounders.

"I don't know where Brenda is. You want to leave a message?"

"Well . . . actually, I wanted to talk to you."

That statement warranted the opening of one eye. "Oh?"

"I . . . kind of wanted to apologize to you."

The other eye opened. "What for?"

"Apparently it's none of my business if you risk your brother's life."

"Who told you that?"

"Richard."

I blinked.

"He called me earlier this morning and very politely told me to mind my own business."

"And what did you say?"

"I apologized."

I rolled onto my back, stared at the ceiling. "Does this mean the two of us can move forward?"

"I'm not sure what it means."

"Neither do I, but it might be fun to find out. What are you doing on Friday?"

She laughed. "I'm the maid of honor at a wedding."

"What a coincidence. I'm the best man. I meant after that."

"I took the whole day off from work."

"Me, too."

"Then maybe we could spend the rest of the day together."

"How about the evening, too?" I suggested.

"Maybe."

"That sounds nice."

"Yeah, it sounds nice to me, too." Did I detect the hint of a smile in her voice? "Okay," she said at last. "I guess I'll see you Friday."

"For sure."

The phone clicked in my ear and I hung up the receiver. My grin of anticipation waned. Now if we all lived until Friday, we might just have a happily ever after.

The first time my bony ass had ever settled in an Adirondack chair had been on a trip to Vermont with Shelley. We'd stayed at a quaint country inn, sucked in clean mountain air and decided that rural vistas could entice us away from the city. That is, until Shelley realized that cell towers and kosher delis weren't available on demand.

The sun had already maneuvered around ninety percent of the deck when I'd gone to sit outside to soak in its rays on Brenda's new lawn furniture. She'd won that battle, but still hadn't convinced Richard that a hot tub was a necessity.

Sitting back, my face tilted toward the sky, legs outstretched before me, arms limp on the long flat rests, I lazed, inviting sleep to come. And maybe I even dozed for a few minutes before something cold thwacked beside my hand.

"Don't spill it," Richard chided.

My eyes jerked open, my fingers closing around a frosted glass. A lemon wedge floated amongst a cluster of ice cubes. I took a sip. Unsweetened iced tea—just the way I liked it.

Richard had taken one of the other rustic chairs and sipped his drink.

"Where's Brenda?" I asked.

"Ironing and packing for the trip. She's making it a ritual, taking pictures and everything. It's unnatural."

No, it was Brenda's way of coping with what Richard and I were doing. She was worried, with reason, after what had happened to Richard less than three months before. Yet she loved him enough not to be clingy.

I leaned back in my chair, the sun warming my face. "Shelley was the same way the first six months we were married," I said, lamely. It was later that everything soured. That the mere thought of her made me angry. That she lied and cheated on me and stole all our assets to feed her drug habit.

I put her out of my mind and wondered if Richard realized just how lucky he was to have Brenda.

"What's on your mind?" I asked, changing the subject.

"Airplane tickets for Friday night."

This wasn't a conversation I wanted to have. I took another sip of tea, waited for him to continue.

"We have to wrap up this investigation of yours. Fast."

"I don't know where to find Veronica until tomorrow night."

"It's time you told the police what you know."

All the muscles in my body tensed. "I haven't got a shred of tangible evidence."

"You've got pictures of Walt and Veronica together. You've got Gene Higgins's testimony." Richard had adopted his patient, comforting, reasonable physician's voice, which tended to piss me off.

"It's not enough."

Richard set down his glass, crossed his arms over his chest, his expression dour. "To use an old cliché, I'm caught between a rock and a hard place. You and Brenda."

"No you're not. Brenda's your future. I'm only a small part of your past, and damn lucky to still have a place in your life. You can't let whatever's going on with me influence the big decisions in your life."

"That's a crock, and you know it. If I needed a kidney tomorrow, you'd be there for me—just like I'd be there for you."

I shook my head. "It's a question of priorities. It's—" Useless to argue with him, my better judgment screamed.

There were alternatives. I could call Sam, tell him everything I knew and let him run with it. But that wouldn't stop the visions, the nagging feeling I'd picked up at Walt's apartment that told me to find the truth.

Sophie had more or less told me everything would be over by Saturday, but that was a day too late for Richard's timetable.

I picked up my glass but found I couldn't take another swallow. I set it beside me on the deck. "Look, give me two days. If I don't have everything wrapped up by Thursday night, I'll share what I know with someone. Either Sam Nielsen at the newspaper or the Amherst police. Will that satisfy you?"

He took a few moments to mull over what I'd said. "I don't like it. But I guess I understand where you're coming from, and I suppose I'll have to accept it. What do we do next?"

I let out a breath. "Hang out tonight at Big Brother's and see if Veronica shows up. She might socialize there as well as perform. But it could mean a long night."

"Hey, I'm up for it."

After pulling an all-nighter and with only three hours of sleep, I wasn't sure I was.

22

After supper I spent two hours pulling weeds, which proved to be a satisfactory way of working off aggression—tension—I wasn't sure exactly what emotion prickled through me. My bushel basket was full by the time I finished and the garden looked beautiful. If I didn't get around to mulching, I'd have to do it again in another week, but the thought didn't bother me. It gave me a goal—a reason to live. The garden also represented order, and that's exactly what I craved.

The sun had set by the time I wandered into Richard's study. Brenda sat under the glow of a genuine Tiffany lamp, a yellow pad on her lap, refining her final packing list while Richard pored over the latest issue of the *New England Journal of Medicine*—still boning up for the new job, I supposed.

"You about ready to head out?"

Richard set his reading aside. "Sure thing."

Brenda looked up. "If you come back early, bring some wings, will you?"

Richard paused to give her a kiss good-bye. She grabbed his hand—hung on for long seconds, didn't say anything. He gave her a reassuring smile, kissed her fingers and pulled away, and we headed for the door.

Richard drove and the ride across town was a silent one.

"You seem preoccupied," Richard said.

"I am. You want to wrap this up and I've got a feeling . . ." I had a feeling, all right. Only I wasn't sure what it was. Uneasy covered a lot of territory. I was almost afraid to close my eyes because I knew the vision of those damn bloody hands could swoop down over me at any time. I was going to see those hands in reality in the not-too-distant future and dreaded it. Blood in that volume meant death and I was probably going to be an unwilling witness to Gene Higgins's death.

My paranoia shifted into overdrive. "When we get there, you wouldn't want to just wait in the car, would you?"

"Why?" Richard asked.

He had no clue how . . . well, dead he'd looked lying on the floor with a bullet wound to the chest. How I never wanted that to happen again. How thinking about Gene's probable death was scaring me shitless.

I looked out the passenger side window. "Just wondered."

"Why don't you tell me everything you know about those bloody hands," he said.

"I've told you everything."

"I don't think so. You've seen hands. Can you focus in on what's around them? What else do you see?"

I wasn't sure I could conjure the vision on command. I closed my eyes—concentrated. I felt the car slow . . . for a red light? I heard the radio as background noise. Squeezing my eyes shut tighter still didn't bring up the vision. No, it would show up when I *didn't* want it to.

"I can't get it."

"Next time it hits, pay more attention to the periphery. It might give you a clue as to where you need to be."

Where I needed to be. He'd accepted the inevitable, too. Only he was banking on it happening before Friday.

So was I.

Big Brother's wasn't as kinetic as the other gay bars we'd visited. A glittering silver disco ball revolved overhead, but it was a ballad—Ella Fitzgerald?—playing in the background, while a few couples, males only, clung to one another on the small dance floor. The stage up front was unlit, the folds of its heavy curtains melting into the darkness. Flickering oil lamps glowed on each bistro table, illuminating the faces of the few patrons. Either we were too early or the place was dead on a Tuesday night.

I spotted Veronica right away, sitting at the far side of the horseshoe-shaped bar, a nearly full martini glass set before her as she swayed dreamily to the music.

"This is where we part company," I told Richard.

"Not on your life."

"Look, I don't want to argue about this."

"Then don't," he said, and stalked across the room, taking the empty stool on Veronica's right. He signaled the bartender, gave his order.

I couldn't let some other joker grab the seat on her left, so I hurried over to take it.

The bartender handed Richard a bottle of Labatt Blue and a glass. He paid for it and received his change, laying down a couple of bills and shoving them forward.

The bartender wandered up before me. "Get you anything?"

"Bottle of Molson."

He nodded, handed me my order in record time. "Three fifty."

I shoved a five toward him, waved him to keep the change. Veronica hadn't opened her eyes, hadn't noticed her new neighbors.

Richard leaned forward around her, gave me an imploring look.

I cleared my throat. "Miss Veronica?"

Veronica turned her head in my direction. "Yes?"

Her startling blue eyes surprised me—reminding me of my mother's, of Richard's. I offered my hand. "My name is Jeff

Resnick. I'm a friend of Tom Link's."

"Sorry, I don't know anyone by that name." Her voice was higher than I anticipated.

"No, but I believe you knew his cousin: Walt Kaplan."

Her spine stiffened and her gaze traveled from my offered hand to my face. "I'm afraid I don't. You must have me mixed up with someone else."

I pulled back my hand and withdrew a picture of her and Walt from my pocket, placed it on the bar, shoved it in front of her. "Did you know this man?"

Veronica feigned indifference. "I don't think so."

She'd missed that my question was asked in the past tense.

"This is you in the picture, isn't it?"

She smiled. "Sure. Although it couldn't have been one of my better days."

"So you knew him?"

"I have my picture taken with lots of the customers." She picked up her drink, took a small sip.

I studied her long fingers; the nails looked phony—removable, but there was strength in the hand that held the stemmed glass. Long sleeves covered her arms. No way to see if the hair on her forearms was thick and black. "Let me refresh your memory. His name was Walt Kaplan. He was found dead two weeks ago behind the Old Red Mill in Williamsville."

"The poor man. Heart attack?"

"Stabbed. Forty-six times."

Veronica simpered. "Oh dear."

"So you didn't know him?"

"Not that I remember."

"That's funny. I have quite a collection of pictures of the two of you together."

She pouted. "I find that hard to believe."

"Believe it."

"Just what are you getting at, mister?"

"I've been wondering who might find these photographs of particular interest."

"I can't imagine."

"Perhaps the police. Especially since Mr. Kaplan's death wasn't an accident."

"So you say." Veronica picked up her sequined clutch purse and slid off her barstool. "Excuse me, but I'm meeting someone." She took a step away from the bar, then turned back, snagged her drink and, hips swaying, sashayed off in her black high heels.

Richard eyed me. "That didn't do much except tip her off that you're interested in her. Is this where we start watching our backs twenty-four/seven?"

"I asked you to back off."

"Yeah, like that's an option." He downed a mouthful of beer.

"I wish she'd left her drink. Who knows what I might've gotten from touching that glass."

"Excuse me," said a low, soft voice from behind us. "But I couldn't help but overhear parts of your conversation with Miss Veronica."

I looked behind me to see what appeared to be quite a beautiful black woman in a form-fitting, chartreuse sequined gown with a plunging neckline, blonde wig and sparkling silver heels. "And you are?" I asked.

She offered her hand. "Margarita Ville." Her voice held just the hint of a Southern lilt.

I took her fingers in mine and gave a gentle squeeze. She simpered coyly, batting her false eyelashes. Under her serene veneer lurked a panther ready to spring. "Won't you join us?" I asked.

"Why, thank you." She settled herself on the stool next to Richard, smiled sweetly at him, smoothing down her hair, her gaze lingering on the remnants of his black eye, raising her eyebrow in approval before turning back to me.

I signaled the bartender, and gestured toward Margarita. "The usual?" he asked.

She nodded. A minute later, he presented her with what had to be her signature drink, a margarita. She took a dainty sip, setting the glass back down on the cocktail napkin. "Now I know this will sound utterly catty of me," she told me, confidentially, "but Miss Veronica Lakes' life is totally based on a lie—including most of what she just told you."

"Oh?" I asked.

"Well, it can be said that all the 'girls' here have based their lives on a lie. We are, after all, not women. But Lord don't we look and act more like ladies than half the gals you've ever met?"

"Uh . . . yes." I didn't know what else to say. "What can you tell me about Veronica?"

Margarita tossed her synthetic mane. "A person of good repute does not accept monies from gentlemen she beds."

"She turn regular tricks?"

Margarita shook her head. "Veronica doesn't go in for that. Like me, she's an artiste, not a prostitute. That said, she does hook her gentlemen friends for the long haul. She has a goal."

"Which is?" Richard asked.

Margarita dabbed a finger on her tongue and pressed it against the salt on the rim of her glass—then licked it. "Miss Veronica needs several hundred thousand dollars to pay for gender reassignment surgery. I believe she plans to go to one of those former eastern block countries."

"Why doesn't she have the surgery here?" Richard asked.

"One must pass a number of psychological examinations. The requirements aren't quite so strict elsewhere."

"She wouldn't pass?" Richard asked.

"I am definitely not an expert on the subject—but apparently I am not the only one who believes that Miss Veronica has more than just one screw loose."

"Doesn't sound like you approve of sex-change operations," I said.

"Look, dear, beneath all the sham, you're still who you were born. I may look like an enticing, beautiful woman—" She paused, gave me a pointed, expectant look.

"Oh, you are," I agreed.

"But the fact is, that under the makeup, wigs and beautiful clothes— " She smoothed her hands over her hourglass figure. "I'm still just a gay man in drag. And most days, that's pretty damn all right—despite what my father may have told me to the contrary."

Richard gripped his beer bottle, taking a healthy swallow before leaning back in his seat.

"And Miss Veronica?" I prompted.

"Amputating her penis and adding silicone breasts won't make her any more a woman than you are. I mean—let's face it, chromosomes don't lie, no matter what the outside package looks like."

I couldn't contradict her there.

"So Veronica wants a sugar daddy to pay for her surgery?"

She sipped her drink. "Daddies," Margarita emphasized. "She takes them for all they're worth. Eventually they get tired of her. I mean—she's not the brightest bulb on the Christmas tree."

I withdrew the photo of Walt and Veronica from my pocket. "Ever see this guy?"

Margarita scrutinized the photo. "That would be Mr. Walt. Ever such a nice man. Kept a select few of us entertained with tall tales of money and excess. It's a pity he was always attracted to trash."

235

"He had other 'friends' besides Veronica?" Richard asked.

Margarita nodded, tucking a blonde lock behind her multi-pierced ear. "Those friendships were rather transitory. But Miss Veronica—well, she has very sharp claws and an attraction to fat wallets. Once she hooks a Sugar Daddy, she squeezes the life out of him."

Squeezes, or stabs?

"Did you know Walt Kaplan was stabbed to death?" I asked.

Margarita blinked several times, her gaze riveted on mine. "I do believe I read that in the paper."

"Do you think Veronica was capable of—?" I let the sentence hang.

"I wouldn't want to accuse anybody of anything," Margarita said, watching herself in the mirror on the backbar, batting at the curls around her face. "But it's common knowledge that Miss Veronica is quite handy with a knife. She always carries one. One never knows how violent a gentleman caller may become. Some of the girls feel they need to be prepared with hardware. I do not happen to be one with that mindset."

"Let me guess. You're well acquainted with the martial arts?" The way she spoke was positively contagious.

Margarita smiled. "Just something I picked up along the way." She sipped her drink, her gaze straying once again to the mirror in front of her.

"Veronica thought Walt had a lot of money?"

"Mr. Walt was very generous to those he liked. He was part of the Kaplan Jewelry empire, you know. I always admired that diamond ring he wore on his right hand. A gift from his father, if I'm not mistaken." Margarita raised a heavily penciled eyebrow. "I wonder if it went missing. Miss Veronica seems to have come into some money of late."

Since Gene had the ring, it was more likely Veronica had sold Walt's car.

"If someone wanted to contact Miss Veronica at her home, where would they find her?" I asked.

"One would merely have to look in the phone book. The name would be M. Bessler." She spelled it for me, then gave a little shudder. "The M stands for Myron."

"Any idea how Myron makes a living?"

"By day he stands behind a counter and hands out keys for rent-a-cars—not much brain power required. By night Veronica has delusions of being a diva." She rolled her eyes. Richard's mustache twitched over a smile.

Margarita gathered her purse and carefully eased off her barstool. I stood as well. "It's been very nice speaking with you, gentlemen. I do hope you'll come back tomorrow to see my show." She offered me her hand.

I figured what the hell, and brushed my lips against her fingers. "Thank you."

Margarita took one more appraising glance at herself in the mirror and turned. "Until we meet again." She gave us a little wave and wandered off into the darkness.

"My weren't we gallant?" Richard commented.

I climbed back onto my stool. "There's something about the way she talks. It rubs off." My gaze flickered across the mirror behind the backbar, looking for Veronica. That I didn't see her didn't mean she hadn't been watching during our conversation with Margarita. She could've changed clothes, and personas, and I probably wouldn't recognize her—him.

Richard drained the last of his beer. "You get anything else out of her?"

"Margarita had an ulterior motive for ratting on Veronica. Until this week, *she* was the headliner. With Veronica out of the picture—"

Richard eyed our surroundings with disdain. "Talk about a big fish in a small pond. What's our next move?"

"Sleep on it. I don't know about you, but I'm tired. Maybe tomorrow I'll come up with an idea."

I pushed back my stool and stood again, taking in the bar and its patrons. Still no sign of Veronica.

I followed Richard out and we walked back to the car. I kept looking over my shoulder, but the darkness swallowed details. Anyone could've watched us leave, could've followed.

We got in the car and Richard started it, pulled away from the curb. I nearly broke my neck straining to see if anyone had pulled out behind us. If they did, I didn't see their headlights— didn't hear the roar of a motorcycle. All the way home I kept checking the side mirror, kept looking over my shoulder. Richard noticed, but didn't say anything. He parked the car in the garage, and we walked in silence into the house.

"See you in the morning," Richard said, and headed out of the kitchen and into the hall for the stairs.

I locked up and waited for his footfalls to disappear. Richard had been right. Now that Veronica knew I was onto her I'd have to watch my back, and Richard's, twenty-four/seven.

I slipped off my shoes and retraced his steps, diverting to the darkened living room. Peering through the leaded windows, I surveyed the quiet street in front of the house. No sign of a car or a motorcycle. No sign of movement. No sign of anything.

Veronica was out there somewhere, and within days she'd attempt, and probably succeed in killing Gene Higgins.

Find the truth.

I'd found it. Now to figure out how to use it.

23

It took hours for me to fall asleep. I woke up late the next morning feeling marginal again. I wasn't sure if it was because of an impending migraine or the growing uneasiness inside me. Time was running out and I had no idea how to nail Walt Kaplan's killer.

I let my new routine rule; I took my meds with a cup of coffee, ate a bowl of cereal, and headed off for work.

"We missed you," Tom called when I came in the back door. The bags under his eyes told me he'd probably had to man the bar alone the day before.

"Dave work last night?" I asked.

"Nope."

Major guilt. Especially since I'd spent the day either in bed or dozing.

"I'm assuming you've made some progress?" Tom asked. He didn't have to specify what he meant.

"I'm getting close."

He didn't ask any more questions.

I usually liked the daily tasks necessary to gear up for the day's customers, but not that day. The words *find the truth* kept eating into my brain, along with a new refrain: *cover your ass.* Covering my ass meant talking to someone about Walt's death. My first choice wasn't the Amherst Police.

The lunch crowd was just beginning to leave when Sam Nielsen strolled into the bar. Again, he sat down at the farthest

stool from the taps, setting a steno notepad down in front of
him as he waited for me to finish up with a customer. I grabbed
a beer from the cooler, cracked it open, and snagged a clean
glass before heading down to see him.

"You ought to serve sandwiches," he said as he focused on
our one remaining customer. "Might be a boon for business."

I handed him the beer. "It's on the back burner. Thanks for
stopping in."

"So who's your murderer?"

"A drag queen named Veronica Lakes."

Sam raised an eyebrow, then poured his beer. "Oh he, or she,
of the custom-made shoes?"

"Not exactly. But that's what got me started on her trail."

Sam sipped his beer and listened, occasionally making a note
but not interrupting, for the next ten minutes as I gave him an
abbreviated version of what I'd been pursuing for the previous
two weeks.

"And your plan now?" he asked at last.

"I don't know. Something's going to break soon. But until
Gene makes up his mind to tell the cops what he knows, he's in
real danger from Veronica. She's going to have to do something
to protect herself, and it's gonna happen before Saturday."

"Another one of your insights?"

I nodded.

"What do you want me to do?"

"One of the other drag queens said Veronica had squeezed
her other sugar daddies. Can you find out if any other gay men
have been stabbed to death?"

"The answer's no. There were two other homicides of gay
men in the past three years, but neither fit this MO, both solved.
One was a robbery gone wrong, the other was a domestic
dispute."

"Then the good news is our murderer isn't a serial killer. But where does that leave us?"

"I'll do some digging on your drag queen. Past history, arrests, the usual. I'll also dangle a carrot in front of my source at Amherst PD, see what kind of reception I get." He got up from his stool. "I'll give you a call this evening, let you know what I've found out. Maybe we should go together to see Veronica's debut tonight."

Excellent. Then I wouldn't have to involve Richard. He could stay home, nice and safe.

"Thanks." Again Sam reached for his wallet but I waved him off. "On the house."

Sam smiled. "You're never going to get your cell phone if you keep buying drinks for the general public."

"Get out of here and start your digging."

He gave me a salute as he exited through the bar's side entrance.

Time dragged for the rest of the afternoon, while the tension within me mounted. I poured beer, washed glasses, and tried not to think about Gene sitting alone up at the Holiday Valley house, and how easy it would be for Veronica to pick him off if she found out he was staying there.

It was almost three and I'd been polishing the taps with such vigor they glowed, when Tom called to me. "Phone."

Tossing aside the rag, I dipped into Tom's office and picked up the phone on his desk. "Jeff here."

"It's Richard. I just heard from a frantic Cyn. She said she got a call from a man saying Gene had been in an accident and was critical. She wanted me to meet her over at the ECMC Emergency Room. I tried to tell her Gene was in Holiday Valley, but she hung up on me. I called Dana Watkins, and she said Cyn had just flown out the door."

The vision of the bloody hands exploded across my mind.

He continued. "I asked how Cyn had found out about Gene's

so-called accident. Dana said the call came in on the café's voice mail, which Cyn had had forwarded to her cell phone."

"When did Cyn leave?"

"Less than five minutes ago. Dana said she tried to tell Cyn the call could be phony, but Cyn said she couldn't take the chance it wasn't."

This was happening much too fast.

"Look, I've got to go. I hope I can get to Cyn before Veronica does."

"I want to talk to Dana, then I'll meet you there."

"See ya." Richard hung up the phone.

I borrowed Tom's phone book once again, called Dana's number. "Cyn?" she answered, breathless.

"No, it's Jeff Resnick. Tell me what happened."

She did, in an amazingly calm voice, despite the evident worry within it. "And then she jumped on Black Beauty and was outta here," Dana finished.

"Black Beauty?" I asked.

"Her motorcycle."

It all made sense. Cyn hadn't wanted me to prove Craig Buchanan didn't kill Walt. That would mean the cops would start asking harder questions—questions she didn't want answered, about Walt's lifestyle, about his relationship with Gene. Maybe she hadn't believed Gene was innocent, but she didn't want to see him go to jail. She'd followed me to the Backstreet Playhouse, and maybe other places, and called me with the voice-altering device. She'd managed to crank up my paranoia, but not high enough to stop me.

"I thought Cyn was angry with Gene. That she wanted nothing more to do with him."

"You don't abandon your child when he's in trouble," Dana said.

"Child? I thought he was her nephew."

Dana sighed. "We've had a lot of time to talk in the past two days—we may have even become friends. Gene is Cyn's biological son. He doesn't even know it. But that's the reason she's always been so close to him. Cyn wasn't up to being a single parent. Her sister adopted him because she couldn't have children of her own."

My mind was racing. "I'm meeting Richard at the hospital. Will you be at this number later?"

"Yes, and please call. I'm afraid for both of them."

I said good-bye and hung up.

"Tom!"

Tom, who'd apparently been eavesdropping, poked his head around the office door as I was untying the apron at my waist. "Something's come up. I have to go."

"Does this have anything to do with Walt's killer?"

"Yes."

He didn't hesitate. "Go."

The light ahead turned red and I braked. Even in heavy traffic, Richard's house was only minutes from the hospital, much less at this time of day. He'd get there in plenty of time to intercept Cyn, who had at least a twenty-minute ride from Cheektowaga. Rich *would* make it there on time.

Oh yeah? If I believed that, then why did I feel so antsy?

The vision of the bloody hands assaulted me once again. I squeezed my eyes shut. When I opened them again, the light went green. I hit the gas.

The should-haves started circulating through my brain. I should have contacted Sam sooner, I should have insisted Gene go to the cops.

The light at Eggert turned red. Goddamn the timing on these things.

I hung a left at Bailey Avenue, nearly sheering off the bumper of a Volkswagen Jetta, and stepped on the gas. I ran the first couple of lights, but got caught in traffic and had to wait. At this rate, I'd get to ECMC after—

Bloody hands, glistening—rivulets of scarlet cascading—

Yeah, yeah, yeah. The same old scene was getting tedious.

I gunned it, weaving around cars, SUVs and minivans, their horns blasting me from every direction.

I didn't bother with the hospital's parking lot, pulling right up to the Emergency entrance. Richard was there, waiting for me, hopped right in the passenger side of my car. "She's gone. Head for the Thruway."

My wheels spun on the asphalt. "Tell me."

"I flashed my ID and told the receptionist Gene was my patient, that I'd been told he'd been taken to the ER. She said Cyn had been there only minutes before looking for him, but told her no one by that name had been admitted. A tall skinhead approached Cyn, spoke to her in low tones, and then they left together."

"What makes you think they're going to the Holiday Valley house?"

"Thank god for smokers. They had a brief conversation outside the door, one of the nurses heard Cyn say Holiday Valley. Then they walked to the parking lot, got in a car and drove away."

"Wow, you're getting good at this investigation stuff."

"Must be your influence. Can't you go any faster?"

I was already breaking the speed limit, but I pressed harder on the accelerator, giving myself another five mph and hoped like hell the Amherst cops were all on a donut break.

"So how much of a lead do you think they've got?" I asked.

"No more than five minutes."

"Did your smoker mention Cyn's emotional state?"

"She said Cyn seemed to go willingly."

"Sure, if I had a knife sticking in my ribs—and that's Veronica's, or Myron's favorite weapon—I might appear to cooperate, too. Did your smoker say who was driving?"

"I didn't think to ask."

"I'll bet it was Cyn. If she's smart, she'll crash the car, but who knows what cock-and-bull story Veronica told her. And by the way, Dana Watkins told me Gene is Cyn's biological son—*not* her nephew. She had the unfortunate timing to have her baby out of wedlock and her sister adopted the boy."

"That ups the ante," Richard said.

"She might've been angry with him on Sunday, but now she's on a quest to save him. Cyn probably doesn't even know that Myron is Veronica."

We hit the Thruway ramp, headed south.

"It'll take at least an hour to get there," Richard grumbled. "You got a map?"

"Glove box."

He hit the button, pulled out a New York state map, spent far too long unfolding and refolding it to the right section. "You know where this house is, right?"

"Yup."

Richard kept staring at the map. "How weird is this? I hadn't seen Cyn for thirty years, and now I'm rushing to try to save her life."

"That's pretty weird," I said. Then again, since I'd been smacked in the head with a baseball bat, a big portion of my life had gone majorly weird.

Richard set the map on his lap, looked at his watch. "What are we going to do when we get there? We can't just drive up the driveway and yell 'Surprise!' "

"No shit. I figure we'll park on the street and go in on foot."

"And do what? Threaten Veronica with a stick?"

"You got your cell phone?" I asked.

"No, dammit. That lets out calling the cops. Unless we find a pay phone."

"Cyn's house isn't in Ellicottville. It's up in the hills; there aren't any pay phones nearby, and cell coverage is probably spotty, too. And anyway, what would we say? We think someone *may* be plotting murder at this location—meet us there. And what if we find Cyn, Gene, and Veronica sitting around the pool drinking gin and tonics and chowing on nachos?"

"You're full of answers," Richard groused.

My fingers gripped harder on the steering wheel. "Gene did give me the phone number at the house, but he told me he had caller ID and unless he knew the number—"

"Surely he'd answer a call from Cyn."

"I doubt Veronica would let her tip him off."

Richard kept consulting his watch, while only the air conditioner's fan and road noise filled the car for the next ten minutes.

I took the cut off for Route 219 and the traffic around us petered out. The expressway ran for another ten or fifteen miles before narrowing to a two-lane highway. Forty minutes down, another twenty to thirty more to get to Cyn's vacation home. Despite the car's cool interior, my palms were sweating. Richard was still fiddling with his watch. "Damn. The band just broke."

"Well if you hadn't been playing with it for the last half hour."

Richard pocketed the watch.

The "Welcome to Ellicottville" sign flashed by on our right. With no bypass, we were forced to go through the middle of town, stopped by traffic lights and pedestrians. Richard's fists kept clenching and unclenching. "Come on," he murmured at the longest red light in western New York.

Green. Go!

The village grew smaller in my rearview mirror. I pulled off the main drag and onto one of the side roads, leading up into the hills.

"This is where a plan would be helpful," I said.

"I haven't come up with anything. You?"

I shook my head. "Then it's on foot to reconnoiter. And after that—we wing it."

"Winging it sounds like it could be dangerous. And I don't know about you, but I'm not wearing my Superman underwear."

And bullets hadn't bounced off his trench coat back in March, either.

I hit the brakes and the car skidded to a halt. "Get out."

"What?"

"You heard me, I said get out. You're not coming with me."

"Don't start that shit again." He crossed his arms over his chest. "You can't make me. I'm bigger than you."

Brenda was right. Sometimes we did act like a couple of overgrown kids.

"You're wasting time," Richard said. "And unless you want Cyn's and Gene's deaths on your conscience, I suggest you get your foot off the goddamn brake and move this car."

We glared at each other for maybe ten seconds before I looked away, hit the accelerator.

24

Only one car sat in the middle of Cyn's vacation home's driveway, and it wasn't Gene's. Richard and I peered at it through a thicket. No other sign of habitation. Nice and quiet. Idyllic.

Too damned isolated.

"Okay, now what?" Richard asked.

I certainly wasn't going to risk his life. "I go in."

"And do what?"

"See if I can diffuse the situation. Veronica can't stab all of us at once."

"And what if she has a gun? Let me tell you from personal experience, getting shot hurts. A lot."

"Thanks for the news flash. Look, you're my ace in the hole. Someone's got to go for help if the situation warrants it."

"And how am I supposed to know when and if to do that? I'm not the one who's psychic."

Okay. Thinking rationally was and wasn't going to do it. Sophie told me to come see her on Saturday night—*if I could.* That wasn't an automatic death sentence. If I trusted her—and I did—that meant there was a possibility I'd survive. She saw a future for Richard. Maybe not a great one, and I didn't want to think about what that meant, but she saw a future for him. The missing elements of the equation were Cyn and Gene. Her clairvoyance hadn't included them.

I turned to Richard. "My gut tells me at least one of us is going to come out of this alive, but I don't know about Cyn and Gene."

"One of us? And who might that be?"

I hesitated. If I said him, he'd probably make some stupid, grandstand move that would blow Sophie's predictions about his future straight to hell. "I don't know for sure," I lied. "If we walk away, we're okay. If we storm the joint—we might both live. Living isn't the same as thriving, or happily ever after. You almost met your maker already this year. What do you think?"

Richard let out a breath. "Jesus, you couldn't give me something easy to contemplate?" He wiped a hand across his mustache, his expression grave. "The way I see it, Veronica's got two hostages. She's killed at least one person. I trust your gut. If we can save only one of them—we've got to try." He nodded, reaffirming it. "Yeah. One is better than none."

"What if it isn't Cyn?"

"From what you've said, Veronica is angry at Gene for replacing him—her—in Walt's affection. She'll go after him before Cyn."

"I don't want either of them to get hurt—"

"You think I do? A physician's first responsibility is to do no harm."

"I thought that was the witches' credo."

"Hippocrates came before Wicca."

"Says you."

"We're wasting time."

I wanted to believe Sophie. I wanted to believe with all my heart. But what if she was wrong?

I didn't have time to worry about it.

I studied Richard's worried blue eyes. "Okay. I'll go to the door. Knock. If it's open, I'll go in."

"If it's not?"

"I'll smash the window. If nothing else, that'll get Veronica's attention."

Richard cast around, found a rock the size of an Idaho spud on the ground, handed it to me. "Here. Use this instead of your fist. If you get the chance, use it against Veronica, too."

I took it from him, hefted it. Smashed against a skull, it could do considerable damage. Yeah, like the baseball bat had done to me. I gulped, unsure if I could inflict that kind of damage on anyone else. Then again, if it meant my survival . . .

I met his gaze. "Whatever happened to do no harm?"

Richard shrugged, the barest hint of a smile on his lips. "You've got the rock. Not me."

I turned back to look at the house, took a couple of big gulps of air. Yeah—I could do this—and stood, pushing aside the branches.

I walked into the clearing that was the front yard, slowly making my way, as though a landmine might explode under my feet.

Nearer, nearer to the closed front door.

In less than two days Richard would marry Brenda. Maggie and I would stand up for them, then spend the rest of the day— and possibly the night—together.

I hoped.

I was within five feet of the door when it cracked open. My hand with the rock snaked around behind me as I backed up a few steps.

"What do you want?" asked a male voice I didn't recognize.

"Myron?"

The door opened wider. A swollen-eyed Cyn, her face streaked with tears, stood rigidly in front of the skinhead the hospital receptionist had described, the long barrel of a shotgun pressed against her jaw. "Help," she squeaked.

"Myron, you don't want to do this."

"Wanna bet? Seems to me I don't have a whole helluva lot to lose." He laughed, smug. The voice was and wasn't Veronica. Lower, rougher.

"You're looking at twenty-five years to life for Walt Kaplan's death."

"So what's a few more years on the sentence? I could probably have a whole lot of fun in jail. Think of all the fine, rough sex that could come my way? It might just be the answer to all my prayers."

"No operation. No more dresses. No more shoes, wigs, makeup—fun."

"Please help me," Cyn sobbed.

I gulped air. "Where's Gene?" I asked, sounding a lot braver than I felt.

"He's here. He's just—" Myron laughed. "A little tied up."

I stood only ten or twelve feet from the door. If he swung the shotgun down, he could very easily take me out. Had he ever used a gun before? Had he—?

Cyn slumped, catching Myron off guard. She rammed an elbow into his stomach.

Myron let out a painful oomph, fell back inside, landed on his backside.

Cyn stumbled down the steps. I dropped the rock and grabbed her hand, pulling her with me as I ran for the bushes.

No gunshot followed.

The front door slammed.

The yard was hauntingly silent.

Richard captured Cyn in a rough embrace and she started to cry in earnest.

"Where's Gene?" I demanded.

Cyn pulled away, wiped at her eyes. "He's . . . Veronica tied him up. He was kicking Gene, over and over again. I tried to stop him and he hit me."

Gently, Richard pulled the hair away from her face to reveal a bright red mark that would be a bruise before nightfall. "That was a pretty brave thing you just did."

"Cowardly you mean," she snapped. "I left Gene in there to die!"

Richard turned to me. "Why didn't he fire at you?"

"That might alert the neighbors, who might call the cops." I turned my attention back to Cyn. "Where's your cell phone?"

"In his car. But it's locked. He's got the keys."

"Damn!" Still, getting Cyn out of the house and away from Myron was one less life to worry about saving.

Richard's imploring stare cut through me.

"I've got to get in that house."

"*We've* got to," he corrected.

"No! You stay here with Cyn. In fact, get the hell out of here—both of you. Go to the neighbors. Call for help."

"Not until you promise to wait right here."

Placate him, placate him! "Okay. Yeah. I'll wait here. Go!"

"If you're lying to me—"

I pushed his shoulder. "Go!"

Richard grabbed Cyn's hand, pulled her through the trees, back toward my car.

I watched until they were out of sight, then turned my attention back to the silent house. Staying put was the smart thing to do. But knowing we were out here meant that Myron was going to have to do something. He knew we knew he'd killed Walt. He'd held Cyn hostage. That she got away didn't mean he couldn't be charged for it. If he made a break for the car—

The drapes in the leftmost front window moved. Still clutching the gun, Myron peered out, looking for us. He scanned the hedges, stared long and hard before the curtain fell again.

I waited, panic growing within me. My own or Gene's? My connection to him had never been strong, but I couldn't ignore the feeling. I stood, feeling like magnetic north had made a sudden shift south and I was being pulled toward the house.

Closer.

Closer.

My heart pounded so loud and hard as I approached the front steps that I thought cardiac arrest was imminent.

My trembling fingers clasped the aluminum door handle, pulled the screen door open. Relief flooded through me as I entered the empty entryway and wasn't blown to pieces.

"Myron?" I tried calling, but only a croak came out.

No answer.

I moved a few tentative steps forward, peering into what looked like the living room.

No one.

A grand, wide oak stairway in the center of the foyer led to the second floor. To my far left a set of opened French doors led into a tidy library-office filled with wall to ceiling bookshelves. A large rectangular, intricately woven Persian rug in hues of red and gold covered the floor.

My ears strained, but no sounds broke the stillness, save for the call of a crow somewhere outside.

I took another step forward. The hardwood floor creaked beneath my sneakered foot.

I froze.

Sweat trickled down the back of my neck.

Bypassing the library, I crept along a long hallway that opened into a dining room. A door at the end was propped open with a wedge. I tiptoed up, hesitated, before darting into what turned out to be an orderly kitchen. The components of a chef salad graced the dark granite counter, with a large clear glass bowl half filled with lettuce.

No sign of Gene or Myron.

I tiptoed across the linoleum, tried the back door, found it double locked. They hadn't escaped out the back. That meant they had to be upstairs.

Creeping back down the hall, my heart nearly stopped when I heard a noise in the foyer.

Back pressed against the wall, I edged closer to the source of the sound. The doorway was only two feet from me when I saw a figure standing in the open. Weak with relief, I had to lean against the doorframe for support.

Richard.

"How did you ever become a doctor when you can't god-damn follow directions?" I grated.

"Look who's talking."

I pressed a finger to my lips to silence him.

He pointed down the hall where I'd just come.

I shook my head.

He indicated the floor above us. I nodded.

Cyn? I mouthed.

At the next-door neighbors'. Now what?

I jerked my thumb toward the ceiling.

He shook his head emphatically. *Let's wait for the cops.*

The cops' arrival might push Myron to pull the trigger. And if it didn't, how long would it be before they could pull in a hostage negotiator and a SWAT team from Buffalo?

Richard's anxious gaze implored me to think this through rationally. He was right. Why *should* we give Myron another two hostages?

Okay, I mouthed.

Richard turned, reached for the screen door's handle when we heard scuffling overhead and the muffled sound of yelling.

Then a gunshot.

Without thinking, I dashed across the foyer for the stairs, with Richard right behind me. My heart raced as I hit the landing, saw Myron standing in a doorway, an arm around Gene's shoulder, the shotgun jammed under his chin. A hole had been blasted in the ceiling above them, and powdered plasterboard clouded the air.

"Back off!" Myron shouted.

I raised my empty hands in surrender, took a step down, ran into Richard.

Gene's legs were bound at the ankles, his hands tied behind his back; his wide eyes were nearly black with fear. A panty hose gag tied around his mouth kept him from screaming.

"You don't want to do this," I told Myron and heard Richard swallow behind me.

"Oh yeah?" He jerked the gun's barrel, shoving Gene's head back farther. Panicked, strangled whimpers escaped the gag.

Richard backed down two steps, with me following suit, hands still held out in submission.

"That's it. Nice and easy and nobody gets hurt," Myron said, and laughed.

Richard retreated another couple of steps.

Gene's cries weren't clear enough to understand, but the look in his eyes pleaded, *Don't leave me!*

Myron stepped back, pulling Gene along with him farther down the hall until we could no longer see them. A door slammed shut.

"Now what?" Richard breathed.

"Unless he intends to jump, there's nowhere he can go."

The sounds of a struggle broke the quiet. I closed my eyes, my stomach turning as the vision of the bloody hands flashed through my mind.

Then came the second gunshot.

I bounded up the four or five steps, thundered down the hallway and kicked open the door.

Two bodies lay on the floor. Blood and globs of flesh peppered the pale pink walls of what looked like a little girl's bedroom. I turned away, closed my eyes.

Dear Jesus, not again.

Shelley had been killed execution style, though she'd been cleaned up before I saw her that last time. I'd seen another body with a bullet through the brain that had taken off the top of the skull.

The shotgun blast had obliterated most of Myron's head.

Richard pushed past me, paused, taking in the scene—his breaths ragged.

I held a hand up to block my peripheral vision, could just make out Richard pulling a blood spattered chenille spread from the bed, tossing it over Myron's body before he knelt beside Gene.

My hand sank another inch. I could see Gene beyond Richard, took in what was left of his face—bloody, hanging flesh, the white of bone and a few shattered teeth.

"Holy Christ," Richard muttered and sank back on his heels. "He's still alive."

"Oh, God, no!" I turned away, quickly stepped into the hall.

"Jeff, get some towels from the bathroom. And call 911!"

I escaped and ran down the hall. The linen closet held neatly folded towels and washcloths. I yanked them all off the shelf and barreled back to the bedroom, tossing them at Richard. He balled up several washcloths and tried to staunch the bleeding.

My chest was heaving, the smell of blood was thick, sickening. I tried not to look, but like a rubbernecker at a car crash, my eyes were drawn to my brother.

To the glistening, scarlet blood that covered his hands.

The fear inside me twisted into downright horror.

"Holy Christ, Rich, you don't have gloves!"

Richard didn't bother to look up. "Did you call 911?"

"Rich, what if he's HIV positive?"

"Goddamn it! Call 911!" he shouted.

My feet foundered under me and I staggered away from the stench of death, found a phone in the next bedroom, punched in the numbers.

"I'm calling to report an attempted murder-suicide. He blew half his head off with a shotgun—the other guy's still alive."

Who was the person speaking so calmly? It couldn't have been me. Shock was catching up with me. My legs felt rubbery. I sank onto the edge of the bed. The phone grew heavy. I wasn't sure I could hold it up for long.

I'm pretty sure I gave the address, told them a doctor was attempting first aid. I don't remember much else about that conversation.

Over and over again, the vision of Richard's bloody hands kept replaying in my head.

Gene was gay—possibly HIV positive.

You don't know that! You don't know that! my mind screamed.

Exposure to HIV days before Richard was to marry was just not fucking fair. And once again it was All. My. Goddamn. Fault.

By dragging him into this, I'd risked Richard's life again. Contracting a fatal disease was not as quick a death, but surely was as lethal as a gunshot.

"Sir? Sir?" the voice on the telephone implored.

"Can you give me a hand back here," Richard hollered.

The tinny-sounding voice kept calling me, but I dropped the receiver as the sound of running footsteps came from the stairwell. I dipped into the hall in time to capture a breathless Cyn. "What happened? What happened?" she cried, frantic to escape me.

"Myron's dead—but Gene's been badly hurt."

Her struggles intensified.

"Believe me—you don't want to see him right now."

More footsteps pounded up the stairs. Cops, firemen, EMTs.

The house had suddenly exploded with people. I pulled Cyn into the bedroom, where the voice on the phone still bleated.

"Oh god," one of the cops wailed from down the hall.

Cyn sagged in my arms, her wrenching sobs robbing her of any strength she might've had left. I pulled her close, this woman who had directed her hatred at me for the past two weeks, had threatened me, and I let her cry, her tears soaking into my shirt.

She faced the death of a loved one.

I wondered if I was in the same position.

25

The water ran hot. Steam curled into the air, vapor clinging to the cabinet mirror overhead. I watched as the last of the rusty water went down the drain, unable to take my eyes off the soapy brush in Richard's right hand. He worked at his fingernails, scrubbing, scrubbing, adding more soap, scouring hands that were already lobster red.

A uniformed cop stood in the hall outside the bathroom, watching, listening to us. We hadn't yet given a statement. They didn't want us talking about what we'd seen, comparing notes — contaminating each other's potential testimony. I didn't give a shit about their procedures. I had more important matters on my mind.

I cleared my throat, afraid to voice the fear that had been torturing me for the past twenty-seven—and longest—minutes of my life. "They can test Gene's blood. You could probably know tomorrow if he's HIV positive. Right?"

Richard avoided my gaze. "It's not as clear-cut as you might think."

"What does that mean for you?"

"It means I'll have to get tested for the next six months to see if I develop antibodies."

"And then?"

"And then we'll know."

He sounded so goddamned calm.

"But . . . you're supposed to start a new job at the clinic in a few weeks."

"They'll restrict me to noninvasive procedures."

"You were going to get married day after tomorrow."

He looked up sharply at me. "If Brenda still wants me—I will get married."

"Yeah, but, now—"

"Brenda and I are medical professionals. Risk of infection is something we and every other doctor, nurse, and EMT deals with every day. Granted, this isn't something I would've wanted to happen, but I wasn't going to stand by and just let Gene die."

"Oh, come on. He hasn't got a chance."

"Yeah, and where did you get your medical degree?" He turned his attention back to the brush in his hands.

I settled my weight against the wall, grateful the bathroom wasn't closet-sized. Richard squirted on more soap, began working on his other hand again.

"What about your honeymoon?"

"What about it?"

"The whole idea of a honeymoon is to—"

"Brenda and I have been together seven years. Besides, there's more to intimacy than just intercourse." His words had an edge, but I guessed they were directed more at the situation than at me.

The din of voices continued down the hall. Thanks to Richard's actions, the EMTs had been able to stabilize Gene and he'd been whisked away in an ambulance that would meet a Mercy Flight helicopter once they got clear of the hills. He was on his way to a trauma facility in Buffalo where he'd either live or die. And if he lived, his disfigurement would probably make him wish he'd died.

Some future.

We might never know if Myron meant to take himself out or

if Gene's struggles to get away had caused Myron to pull the trigger. Myron . . . Veronica . . . was going to miss her opening night at Big Brother's. Margarita Ville would have to step back into the star's limelight. Somehow I didn't think she'd mind. Life at the drag club would go on, just as it had gone on at The Whole Nine Yards without Walt.

Some epitaph.

Richard set the nail brush aside and turned off the water. I straightened, handed him a clean towel from the chrome wall rack. "I'm sorry."

He wiped his hands. "What for?"

"They were your hands I kept seeing. I didn't know that. I could've warned you. I could've—"

Richard grimaced. "You're not going to start with that guilt crap again, are you?"

I winced at the rebuke. "Well, I kinda thought I might."

"Give it a rest." He tossed the towel into the sink. "One of these days you're going to learn that shit happens. Today it happened for Veronica and it happened for Gene. But guess what, of the three of us, I'm the only one walking out the door and I'm damned grateful for it. I'm going to celebrate. I'm going home, kiss my fiancée, and in two days I'm going to get married. Then I'm going to Paris, drink the best-damned champagne and have the time of my life. And when I get back home, I'll start my new job and a new phase in my life. Just like you did."

"Me?"

"Hey, you could've just given up after you lost your job, had your head smashed in, and lost almost everything you had. But you didn't. And you know why? Because despite all the garbage in our pasts, we survived. We're alike. We're brothers."

Yeah. We were.

ABOUT THE AUTHOR

A native of Rochester, N.Y., **L.L. Bartlett** was a finalist in the St. Martin's/Malice Domestic contest for best first traditional mystery and is the author of *Murder on the Mind*. L.L.'s short story sales include "Cold Case," featuring Jeff Resnick.

To learn more about Jeff's world, complete with maps and photos that chronicle his adventures, and to enter contests, visit L.L. Bartlett online at www.LLBartlett.com.